MUFFINS MASKS MURDER

MUFFINS MASKS MURDER

AUNTIE CLEM'S BAKERY #10

P.D. WORKMAN

ISBN: 9781989415580 (IS Hardcover)

ISBN: 9781989415573 (IS Paperback)

ISBN: 9781989415542 (KDP Paperback)

ISBN: 9781989415559 (Kindle)

ISBN: 9781989415566 (ePub)

pdworkman

Telepathy of Gardens

Delusions of the Past

Fairy Blade Unmade

Web of Nightmares

A Whisker's Breadth

Skunk Man Swamp (Coming Soon)

Magic Ain't A Game (Coming Soon)

Without Foresight (Coming Soon)

Zachary Goldman Mysteries

She Wore Mourning

His Hands Were Quiet

She Was Dying Anyway

He Was Walking Alone

They Thought He was Safe

He Was Not There

Her Work Was Everything

She Told a Lie

He Never Forgot

She Was At Risk

Kenzie Kirsch Medical Thrillers

Unlawful Harvest

Doctored Death (Coming soon)

Dosed to Death (Coming soon)

AND MORE AT PDWORKMAN.COM

To all those who are loyal, to a fault

"Ah, finally." Vic took a long breath of air as they stepped off of the plane. "I can get warm again!"

Erin laughed and shook her head at her young, blond assistant. Vic had not been able to get properly warm since crossing the border into Canada. Even though she had bundled up on their Alaskan cruise, she just had not been able to get comfortable.

It hadn't been so bad for Erin. Her body was more acclimatized to Maine weather than to Tennessee, so she had fared better. But she had to admit that she still preferred being warm to cold. And while the cruise had been intended to be a nice diversion from her life in Bald Eagle Falls, things had not exactly gone as planned. A relaxed, carefree vacation it had not been.

"There's no place like home," Erin declared.

"There shorely isn't," Vic agreed, drawing out the words in her longest southern drawl.

"We'll need a vacation from our vacation," Officer Terry Piper said, as the men followed the women off the plane and through the corridor to the terminal.

"You're not kidding about that," Vic agreed.

Erin glanced back at Willie, who was characteristically quiet, to see how he felt about it. His skin, darkly stained from the mining and metal processing he did, was disconcerting to someone just meeting him for the first time, but Erin was so used to it that she hardly even noticed it anymore. A far cry from when she had first arrived in Bald Eagle Falls and had taken him for a dirty homeless man and had been afraid to let him help her carry supplies into Erin's new gluten-free and specialty bakery, Auntie Clem's. Now, Erin wouldn't have given it a second thought. Willie was one of the family. He might be nontraditional, picking up whatever odd jobs he felt like between working his mineral claims, but she knew he was a hard worker, not the layabout that many people seemed to think. He had been in Bald Eagle Falls much longer than she had and the townspeople should have known better. There was still prejudice against people who didn't conform, and Willie was about as nonconforming as they came.

Willie smiled and nodded at Erin, acknowledging her look, but didn't have anything to contribute to the conversation. He moved forward to put his arm around Vic, who also faced prejudice for her gender identity. He bumped against the cast on her arm.

"Just about time to get these off, Miss Victoria." He indicated the cast on his leg as well. "It will feel good to be able to get the darn thing out of the way."

"And to scratch," Vic said fervently. "If there's one thing I want more than to be warm right now, it's to be able to scratch this arm like a dog at a flea circus." She scratched around the end of the cast, sliding her fingers under the edge as far as they could reach.

Terry didn't take Erin's arm, but was trying to keep K9 under control. K9 wasn't usually on a leash, but was well-trained to heel and, other than when he had first met the stray orange kitten who had wandered into Auntie Clem's Bakery, Erin had rarely seen him out of Terry's control. But he clearly knew that they were going home. He was sniffing the air and dragging Terry along, eager to get out of the airport terminal and back to familiar settings.

"Heel," Terry commanded in a low, firm tone. "Come on, buddy. Let's show some professionalism here."

It took a few tries before K9 was finally at his side, behaving as was expected from a veteran police dog. But his nose still quivered and his ears pointed forward.

"Do you think he's looking forward to getting back to work?" Erin asked.

"Animals like routines. He's not used to being cooped up on a ship. Even though I walked him plenty, it's not the same as patrolling all day, and I'm sure he felt it worse than I did. I'm going to have to work off a few extra pounds here…" He patted his sleek belly. Erin couldn't tell that he'd put on any weight, but she knew it was bothering him.

"Who knew you could gain weight eating vegan food?" She laughed. "I was sure we'd all be thin as rails by the time we got back. Unfortunately… no such luck." She was so short, every pound she put on looked like two. Her frame was not nearly as forgiving as Vic's tall, slender physique. "But I can't tell you've gained anything, and after you've been hitting the streets of Bald Eagle Falls again, it will just melt away."

"I hope so. I have no intention of turning into one of those cops with a big beer gut hanging over his belt."

"I don't think you need to worry about that."

Erin couldn't help admiring her "Officer Handsome." He had boyish good looks, cut a very dashing figure in his police uniform and, when she made him smile, had the cutest dimple in his cheek. He was intelligent and kind, and it was a wonder he hadn't been scooped up by some other woman long before Erin had shown up on the scene. But he was married to his work, and maybe no other woman had wanted to compete with that devotion and the long hours of days and nights that he was gone. In a little town like Bald Eagle Falls, with its minuscule police force, he was frequently the go-to man, even when he wasn't supposed to be on call.

It was another hour before they finally got all of their baggage off of the carousel and were on their way. They retrieved Willie's truck from long-term parking and piled everything into the back before climbing up into the seats.

"Are you glad to be home?" Vic asked Erin, looking back over the seat of the cab to where Erin and Terry sat in the second row of seating.

"I'll be glad when I am home," Erin agreed. She might be back in Tennessee, but she wasn't in her house yet, and that was what she wanted. Just to be home and away from all of the drama and excitement that had surrounded their cruise, back in her familiar environment with her lists of things to do and her baker's schedule and something to keep her busy. The idea of a cruise had been nice, and Terry had thought that it would help Erin to be away from the stressful day-to-day business of running a bakery, but it had been more difficult not to have something to keep her hands and her mind busy, so she didn't have to think about finding the body of Mr. Inglethorpe, or the other traumatic events that had preceded the cruise. Erin had to admit that she wasn't a "fun" person. She wasn't interested in going out to a restaurant or dancing or watching a lounge act or going on a tour. She was happier following her set routine.

"You'll be happy to get back to your house, the bakery, and your animals," Terry agreed.

Erin reached down and scratched K9's ears. K9, being a specially trained service dog, had been allowed to go with Terry on the cruise without too much hassle. Erin bringing her cat and rabbit would have been another story, besides which, they wouldn't have enjoyed it at all. Like Erin, cats preferred familiar surroundings and routine. She didn't know what rabbits thought about changes. Marshmallow was pretty chill and took everything in stride, but Orange Blossom, who had grown from that straggly little orange stray to a sleek, luxurious adult cat, would have been miserable.

"I'll be thrilled to see them again," she agreed. "I didn't know how much I was going to miss them. Do you think everything is okay with them?"

"Adele would have told you if there were any issues. They don't take a lot of care, and they're not old, so I don't think a short vacation away from them will have been a big deal."

"She would have told me if one of them got hurt, or lost, or wasn't eating." Erin needed to hear the words to reassure herself. Of course Adele would have let her know. Except that they had not had much contact with Bald Eagle Falls while they'd been on the cruise, telecommunications being pretty spotty. And Adele had known the trouble they had run into there, and maybe wouldn't have wanted to put any more stress on Erin if something *had* been wrong with one of the animals. She might have just kept quiet about it, figuring it would keep until Erin got back.

"I'm sure she would have," Terry agreed. He rubbed Erin's back, digging down into the tense muscles and trying to massage the stress away. "You're going to see them in just a little while."

*E*rin watched out the window, looking at the trees that surrounded Bald Eagle Falls. It was so lush compared to what they had seen in Alaska. She had gotten accustomed to the rocky cliffs and sparse trees that faced the ocean in Alaska, the gray water and clouds more reminiscent of what she had seen during Maine winters, and she had forgotten how full of life the Tennessee scenery was, even though it was fall and the weather was starting to get cooler. The trees were a brilliant canopy of oranges and reds, something tourists would be flocking from miles around to see.

When they pulled into Bald Eagle Falls, it looked just as Erin had remembered leaving it.

It wasn't like she'd been away for years. It had only been a couple of weeks. It just seemed like a lifetime ago. She finally felt like she had a home. A place where she belonged. She was no longer moving from job to job and from one sad, empty room or apartment to another. Instead, she had her own house, courtesy of Aunt Clementine who had left it to Erin in her will along with the bakery. She was the boss instead of someone who had to listen to everyone else and obey the whims of some old lady or frustrated high school dropout. It hadn't been easy, especially when she lost her first location to a fire, but things were running better than ever at Auntie Clem's Bakery 2.0, and Erin finally felt like she had some security.

Everything looked just right. A little more gold and yellow in the leaves. The traffic was the same, the people whose faces she saw as they drove in on Main Street were the same familiar faces. It was all exactly as it should be.

And then they pulled onto Erin's street. She let go of a big breath of air she hadn't realized she'd been holding, the muscles in her body finally relaxing. There it was. Nothing had happened to it while she was gone. It hadn't been burned down or burgled or anything else.

She was the first one out of the truck and was at the door while everyone else was still climbing out and then pulling the luggage out of the back of the truck. Erin unlocked the door and disarmed the burglar alarm.

"Hello?" she called. "Where are my furry beasties?"

There was silence. Orange Blossom was a very loud and vocal cat, so Erin was disconcerted that he didn't answer and rush to the door, complaining loudly about her having abandoned him for so long. She looked around.

"Blossom? Marshmallow? Come on, guys…"

Marshmallow hopped around the corner and slowly approached her, then nuzzled her leg and nibbled at her pant cuffs. Erin smiled and bent down to scratch the white and brown rabbit's ears.

"Hello, Marshmallow. Did you miss me? Was I gone for a really long time? You knew I would come back, didn't you? I hope you didn't worry too much."

He didn't seem to be the least bit concerned about her absence, though her shoes clearly smelled very interesting. Erin moved farther into the living room and nudged him out of the way so that the others would be able to get in the door without stepping on a curious rabbit. She stroked his velvety ears and looked around.

"Where's Orange Blossom? Has he shut himself in the bathroom?"

It wouldn't be the first time. Reg suspected that he did it on purpose just to get attention. She walked down the hall to the bathroom to check, but the door was still open. His litter box was in there, looking as spotless as if Adele had just been there and refilled it. Erin checked the spare room and then her bedroom.

Orange Blossom was curled up in the center of Erin's bed, having made a little nest for himself in the blankets. His nose was tucked into his tail and he didn't move when she entered the room.

"Blossom! Oh, Blossom…!"

She poked and prodded, and eventually he deigned to lift his head and look at her. Then he stretched and tucked it back in again, shutting her out.

"Orange Blossom! What are you doing giving me the cold shoulder? Aren't you happy Mommy's home? We can cuddle up to read, and I'll give you nice treats…"

He ignored her, even though she knew he understood the word "treat." Even just the mention of a treat would usually have him trotting to the kitchen, meowing at Erin to follow and get him the promised goody.

She could hear the thumps of the others putting down the luggage and their voices as they talked to each other. There were footsteps in the hall and Erin turned her head to look as Terry looked in the doorway.

"Everything okay then?" he prompted.

"Sure, fine. I guess he's just mad at me for leaving him alone."

"He'll get over it. Then he'll be bossing you around and demanding that you feed him."

"I suppose. I don't like it, though."

"You're not supposed to like it; that's why he's doing it. To train you not to do it again."

Erin chuckled. "I thought I was the one who was supposed to be training him."

"Hate to tell you this, but…"

K9 made a huffing noise and Orange Blossom's head popped up. He glared at K9 and scrambled to his feet, fur puffing out as he hissed and made his opinion of dogs in the house known to them all. Erin shook her head.

"You're going to have to get used to K9 being around. Any other cat would have accepted him by now. I don't know why you have to be so stubborn."

The cat ignored her, staring at K9 and hissing at him to go away. Erin threw up her hands in exasperation. "Okay. We will leave you alone, how about that?"

She left the room, all of them going back to the living room. Vic was bending down to pet Marshmallow.

"Where's Blossom? Is he okay?"

"Oh, he's in fine form. I think I'm going to have to put up with the cold shoulder for a while. He isn't happy with me."

"His loss." Vic stepped into the kitchen, raising her voice slightly to make sure that the cat could hear her clearly. "I'm going to get Marshmallow something out of the fridge."

Erin heard Orange Blossom thump to the floor. She looked at the bedroom doorway and waited for him to come out. A little orange head peeked around the doorframe. When Blossom saw Erin watching him, he withdrew and did not leave the bedroom to investigate the possibility of treats. Erin suspected he was washing, pointedly ignoring her and pretending that he didn't want any treat anyway.

Vic gave Marshmallow a carrot. She looked at Erin and raised an eyebrow. "He isn't going to come?"

"Nope. He's pretty mad. I guess he's mad at both of us, not just me."

"Too bad for him. Shall we all have a quick bite to eat before we go our different directions?" Vic looked at her watch. "It's later than I expected, and I'm beat after the plane trip and waiting around. I'm going to either have a nap or go to bed early."

"You could get out some rolls and jam," Erin suggested.

"That's really all we need. Well, it's all *I* need." She looked at Willie and Terry. "The menfolk may need something more substantial."

"A bit of bread and jam is good for now," Willie said. "I'm planning on hitting up Fatburger later on. I desperately need to top up my fat and cholesterol levels."

Erin laughed. "How about you?" she asked Terry. "I could see what else is in the freezer. Maybe you'd rather have a chicken sandwich? Something that will stick with you a little better?"

"Jam is fine. I need to start working this belly off."

It only took a few minutes to defrost some rolls from Auntie Clem's Bakery and to put out the various flavors of Jam Lady jams Erin had in stock. She wondered fleetingly whether Roger would ever be back with Mary Lou again to whip up some more batches of jam. If not, their Jam Lady supply was going to run out and they were going to have to go back to store brands or find another artisanal jam that was made locally. Other brands were sure to cost an arm and a leg. Jam Lady had always been very reasonably priced. Especially since Erin bought it wholesale to sell it out of the bakery.

Conversation lagged as they each spread butter and whatever jam they preferred on their rolls. Erin had given K9 a gluten-free doggie biscuit. He munched on it quietly while they ate. Orange Blossom still didn't show his face.

"Are you going to go back in to the bakery in the morning, or take a few days off to recover?" Terry asked Erin.

"I've just had a vacation. I don't need recovery time."

"Except that you didn't actually rest on your vacation. I'm worried you're going to try to do too much and your health will suffer."

"No, I need to get back to work. I need my job more than sleep."

"Okay… if you're sure."

Erin smiled. "You might make me feel guilty about jumping right back in if you weren't going directly onto shift tonight."

He looked sheepish. "Well… I do want to get back to normal police work. I know my town and what goes on here. I didn't like the uncertainty of living on a cruise ship. It will make me feel better to know what's going on in Bald Eagle Falls and to know that nothing has changed."

Erin took another bite of her sandwich. She understood exactly what Terry was talking about.

CHAPTER 3

hey were finishing up when there was a knock on the
front door and Erin heard a familiar young male voice
calling out, "Where's that sister of mine? A little bird said you
were back in town."

Vic hurried out of the kitchen. "Jeremy!"

"There she is!"

Erin looked through the doorway to see Vic and Jeremy
hugging and slapping one another on the back.

"So, how was the trip?" Jeremy demanded. "Doesn't look like
you wasted away to nothing or fell off the ship."

Vic threw an apologetic glance in Erin's direction. She drew
back from Jeremy, smiling. "No, there was way too much food
there to lose anything. In fact, I may have found a few."

Jeremy laughed. "Good. You put the rest of us to shame! It
wouldn't hurt you to find a few pounds."

Vic rolled her eyes, smiling at being able to see her brother
again. "And you survived while I was gone? Without your little
sister to take care of you?"

"Well, it was tough, but I had—" Jeremy stopped abruptly
and looked around for his girlfriend.

Beaver was standing just outside the door, looking back at the street. Jeremy and Vic waited for her to come in. Erin stepped into the living room, wondering what was going on.

"Hey, Ro?" Jeremy called tentatively.

Beaver didn't turn toward the house or enter. She stood there, just in front of the door, looking intently over her shoulder. They all stood there for a moment, frozen, wondering what was going on. Eventually, Beaver turned around and saw everyone looking at her.

Her body relaxed into a loose, casual pose. She smiled widely, chewing on her ever-present gum. "Everyone waiting for me? You don't have to do that."

"What's going on?" Jeremy asked. "I thought you were right there behind me, and then you…"

Beaver looked back over her shoulder one more time and shrugged as if it was nothing. Her eyes sought out Terry, back in the kitchen behind Erin. She didn't say anything to him, but it was apparent from her expression that she wanted a word.

"What's up?" Terry asked.

She shrugged lazily, maintaining a casual and relaxed body language. "Nothing important, Officer Piper. How was your vacation?"

"You probably know more about it than anyone else around here… maybe even more than me, since no one wanted to talk to me in any official capacity. Things didn't go… exactly as planned."

Beaver chewed her gum, chuckling. "I would say that was an understatement. Can't you people even stay out of trouble on a holiday cruise?"

"We didn't really have any control over the circumstances." Terry looked over at Erin, gauging her reaction to the conversation. He smiled at her reassuringly and didn't bring her involvement into it. "Things just fell into our laps and I was the only police officer aboard, so…"

"They did have their own security forces. I assume you could have left it to them."

"You wouldn't say that if you had been there."

"No, I probably wouldn't," Beaver agreed with a sage nod. "Why don't you tell me all about it while you take K9 out for a walk?"

Terry's eyes went to K9, who was completely relaxed, stretched out on the floor in his favorite spot where everyone would trip over him as they cleaned up. "I don't think K9—" he started. Then he stopped. He snapped his fingers for K9, who looked up alertly. At Terry's signal, he got to his feet and went to his side.

Beaver nodded.

"Won't be long, Erin," Terry said. "I'll take K9 for a short walk and then I need to be getting into work. You'll be heading to bed pretty soon."

"Early to bed and early to rise," Erin agreed. She watched Terry and Beaver, wondering what it was that Beaver really wanted to talk to Terry about. It was clear that she didn't want to talk about it in front of everyone else. And Rohilda Beaven, with her three-initial federal employer, had every reason to contact the local law enforcement if something were going on.

She and Terry and K9 headed out the door. Erin looked at Jeremy.

"Is something going on?"

"Uh… nothing that I'm aware of. She didn't say that she needed to talk to Terry about anything, and was looking forward to a little something to eat." He looked at the food that was still out in the kitchen. "She shouldn't be too long, so could we leave this out a bit longer? If she's not back by the time you want to head to bed, I'll get everything cleaned up."

"Yes, of course. Let me just put the rolls in a bag, so they don't dry out. Rice flour makes them dry out faster than wheat rolls."

Jeremy nodded distractedly. He looked in the direction that Terry and Beaver were walking, their heads bowed as they talked.

"Everything was quiet while we were gone?" Vic prodded.

"Sure. Everything has been perfectly normal. Ro hasn't said that anything was bothering her. And I've just been working… everything has been quiet at the farm."

"No more ginseng poachers?"

"No, and it's getting late in the season for them now. They won't have much need for security in the winter months."

"Can't poachers harvest it any time of the year?" Erin asked, frowning.

"Sure. But they can't find much of a market for it. The government only allows legal harvesting until the end of December. They won't be able to sell it as legitimately harvested after that and the margins on black market ginseng are pretty brutal."

"Oh." Erin shrugged her shoulders and shook her head. "You learn something new every day."

"At least you got your harvest in good time."

Erin nodded. The surprise wild ginseng harvest had been a windfall for her. She was still getting used to the idea that she had money. Real money. She'd always been on the edge of poverty before, and had been struggling with running Auntie Clem's Bakery after the fire and rebuilding.

She wouldn't want her friends to know just how near she had come to closing down.

Erin put the rolls into a bag and twisted it shut. She looked around the kitchen to see if anything else needed to be done.

"How about tea? Would anyone like a cup?"

Willie caught Vic's eye. "Maybe we could repair to the loft for some adult drinks."

"Oh." Vic looked uncertainly at Erin. "Well, I guess it would be nice to make sure everything is still where we left it. Uh, Jeremy, did you want to come up with us, or…?"

Jeremy rolled his eyes. "Oh, *please*. I don't need to be around while the two of you are making googly eyes at each other. I'll hang out here until Beaver gets back. I'll say goodnight to you now," he gave her a quick peck on the cheek, "and I'll stop by the bakery sometime tomorrow for my complimentary muffin."

"Complimentary? Sorry, you pay full price, just like everyone else."

"But I'm your brother," Jeremy pointed out, pouting.

"So I should charge you twice as much for all of the stuff you did to me when we were kids!"

"Twice?" Jeremy backtracked. "No, I'll pay full price. Full price is a good deal."

"Yeah, you'd better believe it," Vic agreed, giving him a little slap on the arm. "Now, goodnight. Come by tomorrow."

She and Willie said their goodnights and thank yous to Erin, and headed out the back door to Vic's loft over the garage. Vic paused to arm the back door burglar alarm, gave another little wave, and closed the door.

Jeremy smiled at Erin. "If you want to get ready for bed, go ahead. Just ignore me, I can entertain myself. I'll just find a bit of string and play with... where's the cat?" He looked around, eyebrows raised.

"He's upset with me."

"What for?"

"For being away for two weeks. Cats don't like changes in routine. So he's rebuffing my advances... at least until he gets hungry."

"Silly cat. Where is he? I'll talk some sense into him."

"My room, last I saw." Erin checked the front door to make sure it was shut tightly and that Orange Blossom couldn't sneak out. He didn't usually try to get away, but while he was in a snit, he might decide to try it. She yawned. "I'm going to take you up on that and have a warm bath before bed."

"Let me just get that reprobate out of your way."

Jeremy went down the hall to Erin's room and looked in. He grinned, and in a minute he was back with Orange Blossom turned upside-down in his arms and looking awkward and embarrassed. "This little baby? He's the one who's been giving you trouble? Look at him; he's so cute!"

Erin reached over to scratch the cat's stomach, and he kicked at her with his hind legs. Erin narrowly avoided being raked by his sharp back claws. She shook her head. "You'd better have a good talk with him. Tell him scratching isn't very nice and Mommy won't give him anything but kibble in the morning."

Jeremy nodded and took Orange Blossom with him back to the living room. Erin got her nightgown and robe and retired to the bathroom.

～

When Erin got out, Beaver was back and Terry had already headed to work. Erin snuggled into her robe and nodded at Beaver.

"Everything sorted out, then?"

Beaver nodded. Her expression was still casual and relaxed, but her eyes were hooded and she wasn't about to tell Erin what the conversation with Terry had been about. Erin didn't know whether Beaver had told anything to Jeremy, but she suspected not. Beaver kept her own counsel.

"I had some nosh," Beaver said, nodding toward the plate with breadcrumbs and a few splotches of jam sitting on the coffee table. "Very good, as always."

Erin nodded and reached for the plate.

"Don't you dare," Jeremy warned, swooping in to take it from her. "I told you I would clean up. You can sit down and visit with Ro or go to bed. Your choice. But no cleaning up after us."

Erin watched him take the plate into the kitchen and then heard him clearing away the jam jars and whatever else was still out.

"He's well-trained," Beaver said. "Don't you worry about him."

"I'm not worried." Erin stood there for a minute, then decided that it would be rude not to at least visit with Beaver for a few minutes. She had just been away for a couple of weeks, after all, and it was only right that she should catch up on anything that had happened while she was gone.

She sat down on one of the easy chairs. Orange Blossom was watching her from the back of the couch and made no move to approach her. He was usually very cuddly, and Erin found it disconcerting for him to be giving her the cold shoulder for more than a minute or two. It must have really upset him that she'd been gone for so long. She hadn't thought it would make that much difference to him. Cats were more concerned with people meeting their needs than they were with specific people. Or so Erin had thought.

Marshmallow hopped over to Erin and lay down on her feet. Erin bent over and picked him up. She settled him on her lap and scratched his ears and stroked his short, silky fur.

"It's so nice to be home after being away. Vacations are nice, but nothing compares to being back in your own space where you belong."

Beaver nodded. "Always good to get home after I've been away. Not that you had much of a vacation, from what I hear."

"It was okay. We still saw all of the sights, and I enjoyed cooking with Chef Kirschoff while we were there. That part was fun."

"Well, that's good. A few days to recover from your vacation, and you should be right as rain."

Erin wasn't so sure that she was going to be right as rain. She had not been quite right before she had gone on vacation, and the vacation certainly hadn't fixed anything in that regard. She still had nightmares and anxiety. She had an oppressive sense of doom even when there wasn't anything to be worried about. She didn't like it and wished that things would just go back to normal.

She would sleep on her usual schedule, and get up, and make muffins, and everything would be okay again.

She hoped.

She really hoped.

CHAPTER 4

*E*rin tossed and turned after heading to bed. She had thought that she would hit the sheets and fall immediately asleep, but she should have known it wouldn't work out that way, despite how tired she was. It always took her time to get to sleep and, with the trouble she had been suffering the last few weeks, it was that much worse. Sometimes it seemed like she was trying to fall asleep for longer than she was actually sleeping. And when she did sleep, it was restless and disrupted and she felt like she was monitoring everything going on around her even while she slept.

She waited for Orange Blossom to come in, but was convinced that he wouldn't. He would leave her to toss and turn all night and still be pouting in the morning and withholding his affections. But after a couple of hours, she felt him jump up onto the bed and start nosing at her.

"Hey, you," Erin whispered. "Come and cuddle and help me get to sleep."

She stroked him and he settled in beside her and started purring. Erin listened to his breaths and the deep, loud purr, and waited for it to lull her to sleep.

Erin awoke with a start in the morning, just about jumping right out of bed with a gasp. She flipped Orange Blossom over by accident, luckily catching him before she rolled him right out of bed. He put his ears back, glaring at her, and squirmed away to jump off the bed and stalk off. She imagined he probably didn't like being startled awake any more than she did. So much for making up with him; he would probably be pouting the rest of the day about her scaring him awake even if he hadn't already been in a mood.

It was going to take a while before he was back to being her friend.

Erin picked up her phone to look at the time and decided she might as well get up, even though it wasn't quite time yet. She would continue to have nightmares if she stayed in bed, and she'd end up being even more tired than if she got up. She wouldn't get any more restful sleep in, so she might as well not even try.

She rubbed her eyes and climbed out of bed.

Orange Blossom was already in the bathroom using the cat box, so she detoured to the kitchen to put on the teakettle and putter around until he was out. No need to make things worse by intruding on a private moment.

By the time Vic's light came on in the loft across the yard, Erin had nearly finished drinking her tea, had written a list of tasks to be completed at the bakery that day, and had fed the critters, only one of whom showed any appreciation.

She didn't have any messages from Terry and wondered how his shift had gone. He had seemed just as eager to get back to the routine as she felt—two workaholics who didn't know how to handle a vacation. Of course, stumbling across s criminal conspiracy hadn't exactly been in the plans.

There was a tap at the door, and Vic let herself in and checked the burglar alarm.

"Already up?" she questioned through a big yawn.

"Been up for a while."

"Are you that excited to get back to work?" Vic put the kettle back on to warm up the water.

"No. Well… I am happy to get back to work and to make sure everything is okay and to get back into the swing of things. But I couldn't sleep any longer, so I got up."

"Are you okay?"

Vic had some inkling of Erin's disrupted sleep patterns of late, but didn't know all of the details. Erin tried to keep that to herself. And to Terry, who of course knew from the nights that he slept over.

"I'm fine," Erin dismissed. She studied Vic's face. "How late did the two of *you* stay up last night?"

"Well… maybe a bit too late," Vic admitted. "Wanted to get in a bit more vacation time before we got started again today. You see we…" She interrupted herself with another wide yawn. "*We* know how to enjoy ourselves."

"You keep telling yourself that when the afternoon slump hits. You're going to be asleep on your feet."

Vic shrugged. "I'll be fine once I get the motor running here."

They were both quiet while Erin looked over her lists and Vic petted Marshmallow and then washed her hands before preparing her tea. Orange Blossom was in the corner washing, still in a snit and ignoring both of them.

"How long is he going to keep acting like we've committed an unpardonable offense?" Vic asked, eyeing him with amusement.

"You'll have to ask him. I thought he'd get over it after a few minutes, but he's still nursing a grudge. And I startled him awake this morning, so he's started his day in a bad mood."

Vic shook her head. "Well, he's not going to get any treats while he's acting this way."

Everything was in order at Auntie Clem's Bakery, and Erin was happy to lose herself in the routine. She hadn't realized how much she had missed her regular customers. She smiled and greeted them all and enjoyed catching up on all of the little things that had happened in Bald Eagle Falls during her absence. The Fosters came by before school and Peter happily chattered to her about what had happened at school while she was gone. Mrs. Foster usually liked to do her shopping while the older kids were in school, so Erin appreciated that they stopped in before the start of the school day to give her a chance to see them. She had missed their happy faces and even cleaning the finger smudges from the glass of the display case once they were gone. She felt buoyed up by the visits and catching up on all of the local gossip. Everyone was full of questions about what the cruise had been like, and Erin and Vic were careful to tell them only the things they had enjoyed, staying far away from any mentions of murder or kidnapping.

Mary Lou arrived, her ash blond and gray hair carefully coiffed and her pantsuit neat and without a wrinkle. She gave Erin a warm smile, not quite as reserved as she used to be. A lot had happened during the time that Erin had known Mary Lou, and she was more open to their friendship since Roger's incarceration had turned many of the townspeople against her.

Erin couldn't understand how they could think that Roger's mental health issues were Mary Lou's fault and why they held his failures against Mary Lou any more than they did his getting lost before he had been put into care. How was she supposed to be responsible for everything he did? She had done her best to keep an eye on him, but it was more than one person could do.

"How is everything?" Erin asked warmly as Mary Lou considered the goods on display.

"Well, the new normal, I suppose. I haven't heard much from Campbell, but he is still around and I hear from him or Rohilda Beaven from time to time. So it's just Josh and I, and we're managing."

"Is he still having problems with school?"

"It isn't the academics… I thought at first that it was getting too difficult for him or he wasn't spending the time that he needed studying… but I think he's just too distracted by everything that has happened in our family. It's hard for a boy his age to understand what happened to his father or why Campbell left." Mary Lou paused. "It's hard for a woman my age! It's hard when we're just expected to go on as if nothing has happened. But what else is there to do?"

She pointed out the pretzels and rosemary pizza shells, deciding what she was going to need for suppers that week.

"Has he had any counseling?" Vic asked. "Maybe a professional could help him to work through it."

"We'd have to go into the city, and I can barely get him out of his room and to school most days. He doesn't want to do anything. I worry about the amount of time he spends in bed and on his tablet. I know he's not working on homework, but he won't talk about it. Just acts all… teenagerish about his privacy and me not interfering with his life."

"Isn't there anyone in town? There must be someone at the school that could talk to him."

"There is… but he needs someone who hasn't already heard about everything that happened from other sources. Someone who is more… impartial and unbiased. It's easy to say that a therapist has to be impartial and just listen, but they are human; they do form their own opinions about events without all of the facts."

Vic nodded slowly as she wrapped up Mary Lou's purchases. "I suppose so. One of the problems living in a small town. Everybody knows everybody else's business."

It was one of the reasons that she had left her own hometown. She hadn't been an adult yet herself when she had shown up in Auntie Clem's Bakery that first time. She knew what it was like to have everyone consider her a pariah because of something that was beyond her control.

As they finished ringing up Mary Lou's order, Melissa hurried in through the door, setting the little bells jingling wildly. Her wild brown curls bounced around her face and her expression was eager. She was not, Erin surmised, just excited about a chocolate muffin. She was definitely there to tell them something. Everyone had said that things had been quiet while they were gone, so Erin wasn't sure what kind of news Melissa had that was so exciting. She couldn't be in a hurry to tell them that everything had been normal while they were gone.

"Did you hear?" she asked breathlessly, approaching the counter.

Erin looked at Vic and Mary Lou, but neither of them had any idea what Melissa's news was any more than anyone else. Erin gave her a quick, discerning look, trying to see if there was anything out of place, but Melissa looked just the same as she always did, her full mouth set in an eager smile, ready to tell them all of the latest police department gossip. Even though she was only a part-time admin for the local police, she always seemed to know everything that was going on.

"Hear what?" Erin asked. "What's happened?"

"Terry—Officer Piper—just arrested Bo Biggles."

Erin looked again at Vic, who looked just as shocked by this news as Erin felt. With wide eyes, they both turned back to Melissa.

"Bo Biggles? What's he doing back in town? I thought he took off after the big drug bust, never to show his face here again."

"Well," Melissa leaned closer to them, oblivious to the treats in the display case, "I guess *never* is a lot shorter when you're a drug dealer trying to establish a business in a new town."

"What did Terry arrest him for?" Erin asked. "Is everything okay? Did he…" She trailed off, afraid to put her concerns into words. She knew that Bo Biggles carried a weapon in his car, if not on his person. "Is everyone okay?"

"Terry and K9 took him down. Just like an episode of Cops on TV," Melissa told them eagerly. "We're not used to such dramatic take-downs in Bald Eagle Falls."

"But Terry's okay?" Erin wondered how he felt about having to arrest someone like Bo Biggles on his first day back from vacation. Nothing like jumping right into the deep end.

"He's just fine. I'm sure he'll have some sore muscles, but he didn't sustain any injuries." Melissa gave a loud laugh. "Which is more than I can say for Biggles."

"He was hurt? What happened?" Erin wanted the whole story all at once without having to tease all of the details out of Melissa. Just get it all out, like ripping off a bandage.

"He didn't go quietly, let's just say that. Nothing serious, it isn't like Terry gave him a broken nose. But he was selling drugs near the school, and the PD does not look kindly on that kind of thing!"

"No," Erin agreed faintly.

"At the school?" Mary Lou repeated. She looked out the door of Auntie Clem's Bakery in the direction of the school, though it was impossible to see the school grounds from there. "Were there… any students involved? Do you know who he's been selling to?"

"I don't know anything about that yet," Melissa admitted. "I guess they'll investigate. But he's not going to be selling to anyone else in the near future, so you can stop worrying about that."

"A mother never stops worrying," Mary Lou said curtly. She clutched her shopping bag close to her, in danger of squashing all of the baked goods. She turned and walked out the door. Erin kept an eye on her as Vic and Melissa talked, watching her put her bag into the car and then immediately pull out her cell phone to call the school or her son to get more details.

It took a while to determine that they'd gotten all of the details out of Melissa that she knew, and then to get her to pick out the treat she wanted to use as her excuse for having come by the bakery and get on her way. Ramped up by all of the excitement, Melissa seemed inclined to stay there all afternoon, endlessly repeating the tidbits she knew.

When she was finally out the door, Erin looked at the time on her phone, wondering whether Terry would be off duty. If he'd had to bring in a felon, he probably had paperwork and interviews to do even though his shift was officially over. The sheriff could conduct the interviews, but Terry would want to do the follow up himself. Erin had a few hours left before she would be finished at the bakery. Hopefully, he would be off at the same time and could fill her in on some of the details that Melissa could not.

"I wonder if that's what Terry and Beaver were talking about yesterday," Vic said.

Erin turned to Vic, focusing on her words. "What's that? Oh, when they took K9 for a walk?" She considered. It was a possibility. If Beaver knew something of Bo Biggles's return to Bald Eagles Falls, then she would want to make sure the locals knew about it. She could have called the sheriff, of course, but she knew she was going to see Terry, so she had chosen just to tell him. "That makes sense, actually. I wondered what was going on at the time."

Vic nodded. "I think that must be it."

Erin looked back out to the street where Mary Lou had been parked, but she had since moved on.

"Mary Lou seemed pretty worried about it," Vic commented, noticing her glance.

"Of course. I would be too if I had a kid in that school. Especially since… Josh has been having problems since… you know."

"You don't think he's doing drugs?"

"I don't know. Mary Lou is worried, and she'd know better than me."

"Yeah. Guess so. Bella said Josh is a pretty nice guy. She went to school with him."

"Being nice doesn't have anything to do with not taking drugs," Erin pointed out. "I knew plenty of kids who were nice and still got messed up by drugs."

Vic nodded. "Yeah. I guess so."

They were both quiet, getting a few jobs done prior to the after-school rush. Erin started on some muffin mixes in the kitchen for the next day. Everything seemed to have been left in good order in the kitchen while they were gone. Erin had been worried about finding everything in a mess. Or worse yet, that there would be equipment missing. The last time she had lost her rolling pin…

She tried to focus on the job at hand and not on what had happened in the past. There was nothing to worry about.

Except Bo Biggles being back in town. What had possessed the drug dealer to show up again after he had run the first time? Why come back to a town that had just been through a huge drug bust? He had to know that people would notice him in such a small community. Especially after the public display he had previously made when Beaver had rear-ended him on Main Street.

Erin couldn't help grinning at the memory. She hadn't known who Beaver was at that point, but she had still admired the woman's pluck in standing up to the thuggish drug dealer. She had just stood there, chewing her gum and looking either bored or amused by his threats and imprecations. Beaver was always cool and unflappable, the kind of person Erin wished she herself was.

Erin glanced out the door to the front of the bakery to see that it was getting busy. She left the muffin batters to soak and went back out to assist Vic.

Terry hadn't stopped by the bakery during the day as he usually did, so Erin knew that he'd been busy and not able to keep to his regular foot patrol. The Bo Biggles case probably involved several other agencies and arrangements to be made. While closing up the bakery, Erin gave him a call to see what his expectations for the evening were.

"Erin," Terry greeted, sounding tired. "Sorry I haven't called or stopped by today. Things have been a little crazy today."

"I heard. Melissa was by to pick up a muffin."

He sighed in exasperation. "Some departments have leaks. This one has a fire hose. And I know the sheriff talked to her about it already. She's going to get herself fired if she keeps it up."

"I don't think she said anything confidential," Erin hurried to tell him. "It was all very general. Nothing more than someone who had seen it go down would know."

"She still shouldn't be sharing what she knows with anyone. She should be more careful than a witness."

"Please don't bring it up because of me. I didn't mean to get her in trouble."

"I won't say anything to the sheriff, but I should at least warn her she's going to get herself in trouble."

"Just… don't tell her that I said something to you. I really didn't mean to cause her any trouble. I don't want her to think that I'm causing her trouble."

Terry grunted. "I'll try to be tactful about it. But I think you could hit that one over the head with a hammer and she wouldn't notice. She's not exactly overly sensitive."

"Well… she is about some things. She may act like she doesn't care what other people think of her, but she does."

"Fine. I'm hoping to be out of here in a couple of hours. Do you want to do a late supper? Or will that make it too hard to get to bed in time?"

"I'd like to see you… if it's just a couple of hours, that should be okay."

"I'll do my best. You go ahead and do what you want to this evening, and I'll call you when I'm getting off. I don't want you to sit around waiting for me to get back to you."

"Okay. If I don't hear from you, I'll call you before bed."

"Good," he agreed, and she could hear the warmth in his voice. Tired and frustrated though he may be, she could still sense how he cared for her and wanted to be with her, even if it didn't always work out the way he hoped.

Erin hung up and realized that Vic was watching her, listening in on her half of the conversation. Vic raised her brows.

"He's not going to make it off?"

"Not yet. Maybe in a couple of hours."

"Willie and I are going out for supper. You want to join us?"

"No, you guys need some alone time. I have a few other things to do tonight, and if Terry gets off in a couple of hours, we'll eat then."

"We don't need to be alone all the time," Vic reminded, rolling her eyes a little. "In fact, I think we might need a little more time with other people."

Erin frowned. "What do you mean? Seeing other people?"

"No, I don't mean like that… just that… I don't know. Willie's been acting a little funny. Like… he doesn't know what to do with himself when we're alone together. Maybe it was too early in our relationship to go on a cruise together, but I thought it would be good."

Erin had wondered the same thing about her and Terry when they were on the ship, Erin feeling like she needed some space and separate rooms. They were used to living in different houses and only sleeping together on occasion. Being right on top of each other in the tiny staterooms had been a bit much for her. Vic and Willie had been together longer than Erin and Terry, but it was still a relatively new relationship, with lots of potential pitfalls.

"He'll be fine now that he's back to his mines and other work," she told Vic, hoping it was true. "He's not someone who likes to be tied down and have to operate on someone else's schedule. He just needs his space."

"I hope that's all it is. Okay, well, if you guys are going out for dinner later, then I guess it's just Willie and me. We're going to celebrate getting our casts off."

"That will make you happy. You guys have been so good about putting up with it, but I know Willie's about ready to take a saw to his himself."

"Well, you know him, he's used to being able to get around and do everything. Having a cast on his leg has put a cramp in his style. Climbing and caving and all of the other stuff he does are a little harder when you can't get around easily."

"I'm glad you both have healed quickly."

Erin studied Vic's face. It was hard to forget the horror she had felt when she realized that the mine had collapsed, blocking her friends' way out and possibly burying them. The hours of waiting for the rescue, not knowing even if they were dead or alive. She wasn't sure how she had gotten through it. But the scrapes and scratches had healed quickly, and now the bones had mended, and Willie and Vic and Jeremy could go on just as if nothing had happened. Erin found it hard to believe that anyone would want to go back into a mine or cave after something like that, but Willie seemed eager to get back to his work.

Erin, on the other hand, would never consider crawling into a cave again.

*A*fter convincing Vic that Erin didn't need to join her and Willie for supper, Erin made her way home. She ate a small sandwich to hold her over until she knew whether Terry could get off or not, and sat down with one of Clementine's thick family history books to browse through it for new stories of interest. Marshmallow joined her, lying down on her feet, but Orange Blossom remained aloof. Erin eyed him for a moment, then decided to ignore him. If he didn't want to be sociable, she wasn't going to force him. Sooner or later, he'd come around.

She had been reading through the fading pages for an hour or more when there was a light knock on the door. Erin looked up but didn't see a vehicle parked in front of the house. Her heart pounding far harder than was warranted, she went to the door and looked out the peephole to see who it was. It was still light enough to make out the tall woman on the step, and she opened the door with a smile.

"Adele! Come on in! Would you like a cup of tea?"

Adele stepped in through the door and took a brief look around before answering. "Are you by yourself? I'm not interrupting anything?"

"No, just me. Come visit for a bit."

"Victoria isn't here?"

"She and Willie are out for supper. I imagine when they get back, they'll just head over to the loft. I don't expect to see them tonight."

Adele nodded and finally entered. "Okay."

"You don't need to avoid Vic, you know. She doesn't hold you responsible for what happened."

"Perhaps not… but it doesn't make for a very comfortable visit. I'd rather… not get in her way."

Erin shook her head. She didn't like to see fissures in her friends' relationships. She wanted them all to get along with each other and to be happy together. But that wasn't the way that life worked. She remembered what it had been like as a young girl in school to have friends that were always arguing with each other, breaking up, dissolving their friendships, and then making up a few days later. It had been hard for Erin. She was always the peacemaker, trying to get them back together again and keep everyone happy.

Adele looked toward the kitchen. "I'll put the kettle on. You just relax, I'm the one interrupting your night."

"I'm not doing anything, just reading. You shouldn't have to make your own tea when you come to visit."

"I'm happy to do it."

As soon as Adele was in the kitchen, Orange Blossom ran down the hall from the bedroom and skittered across the slick tiles of the kitchen, meowing excitedly. Adele laughed and spoke to him quietly as she moved around the kitchen, familiar with where everything was.

"Can I give him a treat?" Adele asked from the kitchen.

"Sure. Just one or two, though. He's been hard to get along with since I got home and I don't want to reward him for bad behavior."

Adele continued to talk to Orange Blossom in the kitchen. She didn't use a baby voice like Vic and some others did, and Erin couldn't make out her words, but it was a soothing, pleasant atmosphere.

In a few minutes, Adele returned from the kitchen, putting a cup of tea down for Erin and sitting down with one herself. Orange Blossom rubbed against Adele's legs and then jumped up beside her on the couch. Adele pushed him back, keeping him away from her cup.

"I don't want cat fur in my tea. Lie down and mind your manners."

In a few minutes, Orange Blossom was settled. He lay curled up against Adele's leg, one eye open to watch Erin.

Erin shook her head at him. "I can't believe he's being so lovey to you. He's been nothing but cold since I came home. Except for last night when I couldn't sleep, he did come in to cuddle after a couple of hours. But then this morning, he's right back to being aloof."

"He's just reacting to the change. He was pretty unhappy the first couple of days you were gone, so he's trying to decide whether you're going to stay or leave him alone again."

"But I made sure he was well taken care of. He didn't lack anything while I was gone. You were there to make sure he had everything he needed."

"Physically, yes, and I gave him all of the attention I could, but that's not the same thing as having his person disappear into thin air and not knowing if you were ever going to come back again."

"Well, I'm back now; it's time for him to start acting like it."

"He will. Give him time."

They both sipped their tea in silence for a few minutes. Orange Blossom closed his other eye and purred quietly.

"It's been very nice to have his companionship while you were gone," Adele commented. "I think I might have to get a cat of my own."

"Really? I thought you didn't believe in owning pets."

"Well... even though I don't quite cotton to the idea of

owning another being… it is awfully nice having another creature around the house. There is Skye, of course, but he's a crow. He doesn't come into the house and doesn't always want to be around when I am outside. He does his own thing. Having a cat in the house… would be nice company."

"Well, if Orange Blossom doesn't shape up pretty soon, maybe I'll let you take him back to the summerhouse with you."

Hearing his name, Orange Blossom lifted his head and looked at Erin for a moment before deciding she wasn't addressing him and putting his head back down to sleep.

~

Adele was on her way out when Terry called to say he was finished work and could come over. Erin grabbed Orange Blossom before Adele opened the door. She didn't need him bolting for the open door and then having to chase him all over creation. With the way he had been behaving, he might decide he wasn't coming back again.

Blossom squirmed and yowled angrily, but Erin kept him under control until the door was closed, then let him go again. The cat jumped up onto the couch and watched out the window until Adele was out of sight. He gave Erin a kitty scowl and stalked back to the bedroom.

Erin was glad that he was no longer near the door. When Terry rolled up in his squad car, she didn't wait for him to come to the door, but immediately headed out to meet him, arming the burglar alarm before closing the door.

Terry opened the car door for her and was leaning his head back against the headrest when she got in, eyes closed.

"You look beat," Erin said. "You haven't slept in the past twenty-four hours, have you?"

"I got a couple of hours in partway through the day," Terry answered, opening his eyes again and giving her a worn smile. "It's not that bad. I've stayed up longer plenty other times. You take what you can get, and if you need to keep working to keep the town safe… well then, that's what you do."

"You need to get your sleep. I don't understand why they kept you for so long. You had the night shift. Couldn't someone else have taken care of Bo Biggles?"

"I wanted to be the one to arrest Biggles. Sure, Tom or the sheriff could have done it, but I was the one who got the lead on him being back in town and I wanted to be the one to bring him in. If I'd waited, he might have disappeared again. I just wanted to swoop in and arrest him before he knew what was happening."

"I still think it could have waited. If he's dealing drugs to the schoolkids, he's not going to do that today and go home tomorrow. He would have stuck around, once he'd established his business."

"Well, the entrepreneur in you has a point. But hoods like Biggles are unpredictable. Here today, gone tomorrow when someone looks at them the wrong way or spooks him somehow. I wanted to get him before he could do any more harm."

Erin got settled and pulled the car door shut. Terry sat up, blinked hard a few times, and put the car in gear.

"Are you sure you're okay to drive? You're looking pretty sleepy."

"No one else is allowed to drive the squad car."

"I could drive my car. You could leave the squad car here."

"I'm fine. Really. It won't be a problem to go that far. We'll just hit the Chinese buffet, if that's okay with you."

"Yes, of course. Whatever you feel like."

Erin kept a careful eye out for any possible hazards. Terry might say that he was just fine, but that didn't mean he was. People fell asleep at the wheel all the time. Or slipped on rain-slick highways. Or were just distracted when they needed to be focused on driving. She wound herself up so much that her heart was pounding when they got to the restaurant, but there hadn't been any problems. Everything was just fine.

"You can trust me," Terry said quietly, and Erin realized he could read her expression. "I'm not going to do anything that will put you in harm's way."

"I know. It's just... since Mr. Inglethorpe and the fire... things seem a lot more dangerous."

He leaned over and kissed her before getting out of the car. "I'll take care of you. Everything is going to be okay."

~

Erin tried to relax as they sat down together and ate. She had to keep telling herself that there was no reason to be anxious. She was at a restaurant with Terry; what was going to happen to her there? She was with a safe person, a person who would protect her if something bad happened.

K9 was stretched out under the table and kept bumping into their legs and feet. Erin saw him yawn a few times and knew it had been a long day for him too. Or maybe just a boring one, since he hadn't been able to go on the usual foot patrol with Terry, but had instead had to stay at the police department while paperwork and interviews were handled. That couldn't have been very interesting for him.

Erin looked up from her plate of food to smile at Terry, not wanting to be distracted during the couple of hours they would have together. Then she would be off to bed and he would hopefully hit the sheets as well and get the sleep that he needed to. He'd been awake for almost two days straight, and the fatigue lines around his eyes were clear. He needed to get a solid eight hours before he would be fully functional, and even that probably wasn't enough to make up for the sleep that he'd lost.

"I'm fine," Terry said, reading her worried expression. "It was a good day. It's always a good day when you can get a guy like Bo Biggles off the street."

"It's such a silly name for a drug dealer. You'd expect him to have some really serious street name. Mr. X or Ice."

"Biggles isn't a particularly scary name," Terry admitted, "but it is pretty unique, and one that people won't forget. You hear it once, and you remember who he is. That's a good quality for a street dealer."

"So…" Erin picked at her food. Even though she hadn't had anything big before their meal, she wasn't very hungry. Her body was probably still recovering from the menu on the cruise. They had all indulged a little too much on Chef Kirschoff's offerings. "Did you find anything out from him? When you talk to someone like that, you're trying to find out more about the drug network around him, right? Did he turn over anyone else in the business?"

"No, he was pretty closed-mouthed. But give it some time, we might still be able to get something out of him."

"He hasn't been sent to the jail yet?"

"No, PD is holding him for now, which means the sheriff is going to be sleeping in his office. Not exactly comfortable for either one of them. But we're hoping to get something out of him before he is transported, and we can't get him moved until tomorrow anyway."

"Not very often you can arrest someone like him," Erin observed.

"Bald Eagle Falls has its share of problems, but luckily, the drug trade has not been too bad within the town. Other than being used as a storage depot. The actual dealing that we've seen has been pretty low-key."

"There are always drugs."

"Always," Terry agreed, munching on some deep-fried shrimp. "But in Bald Eagle Falls, it has mostly been prescription drugs. Or pot grown in the backwoods. For the hard stuff, people have typically had to go into the city, which makes it a little easier to keep it out of the hands of young kids. Someone like Biggles comes into town, though, and starts handing out free samples and hanging around the school, and that's a big problem."

"I can't believe he would be so bold about it. He must have known that someone would see him and report him."

"He was keeping out of sight." Terry looked like he was going to say something else, but then he stopped.

Erin waited. "What?"

"Nothing." He rubbed his forehead and temples. "Just tired."

"We won't stay out too late. They don't have you starting too early tomorrow, do they?"

"Not first thing. I can sleep."

"Good. You need it."

He put his hand over hers. "And what about you? How did you sleep last night?"

"Restless. But I had Orange Blossom. It was okay."

His eyes lingered on hers and she knew he didn't believe she was being entirely truthful. He knew from sharing a room with her during the cruise that she wasn't just having nightmares every now and then. But he didn't jump in with the suggestion that she needed to get counseling. She appreciated that he didn't bring it up again. She knew he thought she should seek professional help. But Erin had dealt with enough therapists in the past and preferred to deal with it herself. The nightmares would pass eventually.

"So Orange Blossom has forgiven you?"

"No, not exactly. But he was happy to have a warm body to sleep with last night."

Terry let go of Erin's hand to pick up his phone. He looked at the picture on the screen and made a face.

"Sorry. I'll be quick."

He answered the call, turning his body away from her slightly as if that would give him some semblance of privacy.

"Piper."

Erin saw his face turn rapidly ashen.

"Terry, what is it?" She knew it was work and he couldn't tell her what was going on while he was in the middle of a call, but he looked like he might faint dead away at whatever news was being imparted to him.

"What happened?" Terry demanded, his voice flat.

He listened but didn't like what he was hearing. He turned farther away from Erin so that she could no longer see his expression. He held one hand up to shield the phone in case anyone could hear what was being said or read his lips.

"Who is coming?"

Erin tried to puzzle out what was going on with the few clues that she had. It was something to do with the police; it was obviously bad news. They needed someone else to come in to help. Was it something to do with Bo Biggles? He'd made bail or escaped? It couldn't be bail if he hadn't even gone before a judge yet. He was being held until they could get him to the county jail, and then he could be arraigned and have a bail hearing. So it couldn't be that. Could he have escaped?

Terry ended his call and turned back to her. His face was gray, and Officer Terry Piper wasn't easily upset. He looked at her, not saying anything.

Erin didn't want to push him, but there was clearly something wrong and he would need to give her some explanation before he left. "Is it something to do with Bo Biggles?" Erin asked. "He didn't escape, did he? Or hurt someone?"

He shook his head. "Biggles… is dead."

$\mathcal{E}$rin's mouth hung open. She tried to think of the appropriate thing to say, but it didn't come to her. Her first reaction was 'are you kidding?' but she had been in enough horrible situations to know that that was what people always said, for lack of a better response, and that it didn't make any sense. Of course Terry wasn't kidding that Biggles was dead. The police department wouldn't have called him as a prank, and he wouldn't be trying to tell her something that wasn't true. It wasn't a joke. As unbelievable as it was, Biggles was dead.

"I'm going to have to go back," Terry said.

"Yes... okay. Of course." He couldn't very well go home and sleep when someone had just died, someone he had just been talking to. He would have to find out what had happened and investigate the death. "Will you be okay? You haven't had any sleep."

"I'm not tired anymore. Adrenaline will keep me going for a while. I'll... I guess I won't call you tonight, but I'll talk to you tomorrow sometime, let you know I'm alright."

By the time he was done, she would either be in bed or be up preparing for another day at the bakery.

"What happened? Was it... suicide?"

"I don't know what happened yet." His expression was purposefully blank. He knew more than he was letting on. "I need to go in and find out."

"This is crazy. Maybe it was a drug overdose. He could have been… you know… carrying it internally. Or swallowed something when you arrested him."

"I doubt it. He's not a mule. But they'll have to do an autopsy to determine that."

"Okay… well… why don't you go ahead? I'll settle up here."

"You're not paying."

"I think that you're evolved enough to let me pay for meals now and then. I have the money. You need to take care of your job. Just go."

Terry considered her for a minute, then nodded. "Okay. Thanks."

He stood up and leaned over to kiss her before snapping his fingers for K9 and setting off at a brisk pace. K9 grunted as he got to his feet and hurried after his master.

Erin didn't linger at the restaurant after Terry was gone. She paid the bill, ignoring the waitress's questioning and sympathetic look, and headed back home. It wasn't until she got to the curb that she realized Terry had brought her in his car, and now he was gone again, back to the police department, without either of them recognizing that she didn't have a ride home.

Bald Eagle Falls was a pretty small place. It didn't take long to get from one place to the other. It was generally safe, despite Erin's propensity for stumbling across dead bodies. There weren't street gangs or muggers to worry about.

But despite all of that, she still didn't feel comfortable walking home after dark. Nothing would happen to her, of course. But it could.

Vic and Willie would probably already be settled in at the loft, ready for sleep. Erin didn't want to get them out again. She ran through the list of possibilities before settling on the one person she knew was a night owl and would not have any objection to picking her up. She called her half-sister and partner in the bakery.

"Hi, Charley?"

"Erin! Hey, I meant to get over to the bakery today, but I didn't quite make it. How was the first day back? Everything go okay? I made sure that everything was run according to your standards and put away and everything."

"Yes, it was all good," Erin agreed. "It was nice to come back to everything being where it should be."

"Good. I know it stresses you out when people don't follow your procedures."

Was it possible that Charley was actually maturing? She had, in the past, complained about Erin's lists and procedures and all of her rules about the way things should be run. It was Charley's bakery too, and she thought she should have more say in the rules. Even though she had said that she wanted to keep Auntie Clem's Bakery the same and to capitalize on the goodwill that Erin had already built up.

"So… I actually wasn't calling to ask where you were today. I figured you probably put in enough hours in the past couple of weeks that you needed a day off."

"Well, yeah. That's true. I didn't miss a shift, you know. Got there on time every day."

"Good for you." Erin couldn't help smiling a bit in amusement. For anyone else, that would have gone without saying, but for Charley Campbell, well, she liked to play things a little more fast and loose. "Charley… I need a quick ride. Are you in town, or did you decide to go away for your break?"

"I'm still in town. Where are you? Did that old beater break down? I told you it was going to."

"No, I didn't break down. I'm at the Chinese restaurant. I came with Terry, and he ended up having to leave in an emergency, and so he has his car and mine is at home. I could call someone else if you're busy."

"Not at all. I'll be right over."

"Thank you!" Erin didn't like to rely on anyone else for favors, but Charley didn't make her feel like Erin owed her anything for it. Erin had helped Charley out in the past when she had really needed it. But then, Charley had helped her out of some pretty deep holes too.

Erin put her phone back away and sat down on the bench outside the Chinese restaurant. It was well lit and there was still foot traffic down Main Street.

She rummaged around in her purse, looking for a notepad and pen. She really did need to clean out her purse and get rid of the junk that she didn't need. She flipped open her spiral notepad, and that was the first thing she put on her list.

Clean out purse.

Though, she hated cleaning it out. She always just ended up sorting everything, throwing out any used tissues, and putting everything else right back in again. She liked to have her possessions with her, to be able to physically see and hold them and know that she wasn't going to end up with nothing. Too many moves in the past. Too many times when she had lost precious items, no matter how inconsequential they might seem to other people. She wanted to be able to hold things in her hands. But that meant that she kept half the house in her purse and could never keep it all organized.

She added a few more things to the list, thinking about the way things had gone at the bakery, the upcoming Halloween season, and what kinds of treats she wanted to add to their repertoire. She liked to keep things fresh to keep people coming back. If they thought they were always going to get the same thing, they might get bored.

As much as she tried to focus on what she needed to do for the bakery, her mind wandered back to Bo Biggles.

How could he be dead?

Terry had been quick to dismiss the idea of drugs, but they couldn't be sure of that until an autopsy had been done. Biggles *was* a drug dealer, so Erin thought it wise to consider the possibility that it had something to do with drugs. Terry would have searched Biggles when he was arrested, but it was possible that he had missed something. Or that Biggles had swallowed something. Erin admitted that he probably wasn't muling drugs. Drug mules hid their drugs to transport them long distances and get them over borders; they didn't just do it to walk to the corner.

What else? Terry hadn't ruled out suicide. A lot of deaths in custody were suicide. But wouldn't he at least have waited to see whether he could get bail? He was an experienced organized crime member, not just a kid who panicked that his life was over because the police arrested him. Someone like Biggles, who worked with the Jackson clan, would know all of the ropes.

The Jackson clan. Vic's family. Vic didn't want anything to do with them. But her brothers and the rest of her family were still involved. Not Jeremy, happily. Vic at least had someone in her family that she could rely on.

It was possible that someone from the clan had killed Biggles to keep him quiet and keep him from implicating anyone else. Or maybe someone from the Dysons, the rival clan. That was who Willie had worked for when he had been younger, though he had gotten out of the business a long time ago after he had served his initial term for the family.

Charley's honk made Erin startle wildly. She'd shut out everything going on around her and had forgotten she was even on the street, let along waiting for Charley to pick her up. She put her hand over her rapidly beating heart. There was nothing at all to be worried about. Charley was there to take her home, and she could have a nice soothing bath and get ready for bed.

"Sorry," Charley apologized as Erin climbed into the car. "I didn't mean to scare you."

"I was off in my own little world. It wasn't your fault."

Charley waited until Erin was settled and had her seatbelt on, even though she wasn't wearing one herself, then pulled out onto Main Street with a squeal of tires that made everyone close by turn around and look at her.

"Charley!"

Charley giggled. "There's no need for everyone to be so stiff all the time. Why not have a little fun? What does it hurt them if I rev my engine or spin my tires a bit?"

"It doesn't… but you could be drunk or reckless, and you could end up hurting someone. They don't know. They just know that you're doing something that might be dangerous. Even though you were just showing off."

Charley smiled. She kept her eyes on the road and drove to Erin's house at a sedate speed. "So, what was the big emergency for Officer Piper? I can't believe that he just stranded you there."

"We were both pretty tired. Neither of us even thought about it. I got out to the curb before I realized that I didn't have a car. And he's been on duty since we got back to town, so he's a lot more tired than I am."

"If he hasn't had any sleep, then why don't they let someone else in the department take care of this emergency? They did manage to survive while you guys were on vacation."

"I think he wanted to deal with it himself. I'm sure he could have told them he was too tired and needed a break, but he wanted to go back in."

Charley raised her brows and glanced over at Erin. "And exactly what was so exciting that he would want to go back in again after working twenty-four hours?"

"I… really can't say."

"You can't say because you don't know, or because you don't want to?"

"I don't know what they want to share with the public. Best to wait and see…"

"If he told you, then he's not exactly keeping it confidential. Come on. Dish. What's happening?"

"I really can't. I just know because he was with me when he took the call. I was eavesdropping."

That wasn't exactly the truth, but Erin hoped that it would keep Charley off her back.

"If he's talking about it around you, then that's just the same as if he told you himself."

"No. Just wait and see. I'm sure it will be all around town tomorrow and you'll know more about it than I will."

"You are seriously no fun. What's the point in having a sister who is dating a police officer if I can't get the scoop before anyone else?"

Erin shook her head and didn't answer. "You'll find out soon enough," she repeated.

Charley pulled up in front of Erin's house.

"Do you want me to come in and keep you company?" Charley asked. "Are you going to stay up until Officer Handsome gets home?"

Erin's cheeks warmed in embarrassment. "No. Could be hours. I'm going to have a warm bath and head to bed."

"Okay. So you don't need any company?"

"No, that's okay. I didn't sleep very well last night, so I should try to get to sleep in good time."

Charley nodded her understanding. She was bright-eyed and ready to start her evening. She was a night owl. Erin looked out the window at her front door. Everything looked quiet. She knew she had set the burglar alarm, so if there had been any intruders, she would know it. But she was still reluctant to go in by herself.

"Watch me in?"

Charley raised an eyebrow. "What are you, twelve? Sure, I'll watch you in. If there's any trouble, I'm carrying."

Erin swallowed. That made her even more nervous. She didn't need Charley rushing in and shooting things up. She should have thought things through before telling Charley to make sure she got to the door safely. But it would take all of ten seconds. Nothing was going to happen.

"Okay. See you tomorrow. You going to come by the bakery tomorrow?"

"I'm planning on it. Are we going to have a management meeting?"

"Tomorrow will be too busy, and I haven't figured out what our plans for the fall will be yet. Maybe Sunday morning while we get ready for the church ladies' tea?"

"Morning? How about after the tea?"

Erin rolled her eyes and shrugged. "Okay. After the tea."

"And don't make your plans yet. That's what we're supposed to be talking about. We're supposed to be deciding together."

"I mean… I haven't written down my ideas yet. I won't decide without you."

"Okay, good."

Erin opened her door. "Okay. See you tomorrow, then."

Her gait was awkward as she walked to the door. Like it always was when she knew people were watching her, and it suddenly seemed like she had forgotten how to walk properly. She looked around, watching for any shadows, listening for any movement. But there wasn't anything. It was just a clear, crisp night in Bald Eagle Falls, and nothing was going to happen.

She made it to the door and inserted her key. Nothing bad happened. She pushed the door open and bypassed the door open alarm, leaving the system itself armed. She shut the door and leaned against it, breathing hard, her heart pounding.

Her night wasn't much more restful than the one before. She slept for a longer time, but kept waking up, worrying about Terry and about whether he was home yet. He had said that he wouldn't wake her up, he'd just let her know how everything was in the morning, but she wished she had told him to call her anyway. At least then, she would have been able to calm her mind and have a better rest, knowing that he was home safely and getting the sleep that he needed.

Instead, every time she turned over, she woke up, worrying that something awful was going to happen to Terry during the night. He would have an accident on his way home because he was too tired, or more of Bo Biggles's cohorts would be around and would jump him, or something equally tragic. Bad things could happen, even in a small town like Bald Eagle Falls.

Every time she closed her eyes, she was worried about the pictures she was going to see. Her dreams were filled with the images from Mr. Inglethorpe's murder, although the body in the scene was always different, one of her friends instead of the near-stranger. And all too often, the murder weapon was in Erin's hand.

She knew it was a dream, and she kept telling herself that, but that didn't reduce the terror she felt every time she found herself in the dream again.

Orange Blossom hopped up onto the bed and licked her face. Erin pushed him away. "Ugh, Blossom. Yuck. Don't lick me, just come cuddle. Purr for me. I always feel better when you're purring."

It was a soothing, steady sound. She felt safer knowing that he was there with her and that he was happy and calm. He wouldn't be purring if someone were breaking into the house or something else bad were to happen. He would know it, and he would warn her as he had in the past. He didn't like intruders, and he was loud and obnoxious when he was disturbed.

She rested her face on his body, absorbing his purrs. He was warm and soft, and everything felt right in the world. She could understand why people have therapy animals to help soothe anxiety. She always felt better when she was holding Orange Blossom.

And then her alarm was buzzing and it was time to get up.

Erin groaned and rolled over, looking at her phone in confusion to convince herself that it really was time to get up, and it wasn't just a phone call or some random birthday alert that wasn't supposed to be ringing. But it was, indeed, time to get up and tackle her day, so she forced her feet over the side of the bed, rubbed her eyes, and walked blindly to the bathroom.

A shower to wake herself up, and a strong cup of tea, and then Vic would be up and they would be able to keep each other awake until they were fully in the swing of things. She had several employees who worked shifts at the bakery now, but she liked it best when it was her and Vic. That was how they had started out, and Vic was the person she had the best relationship and sense of rhythm with.

The shower took too long to heat up, but the cold on her skin was probably a blessing because, by the time she got out, she was wide awake and ready to take on the day. She went to the kitchen to start the tea, looking around for Orange Blossom to make sure he wasn't going to trip her up. But he wasn't there. Unless he was already in the kitchen waiting for her, he was obviously still pouting.

Who knew a cat could hold a grudge for so long!

He was not in the kitchen. Erin didn't bother to call him. If he was going to pout, he wasn't going to get any special treats. She would top off his kibble and his water dish, but she wasn't even going to call him to tell him it was time to eat.

She put the kettle on and bent down to scratch Marshmallow behind the ears. At least he wasn't holding a grudge for having been away. He always had been much calmer than Orange Blossom.

Vic unlocked the back door and let herself in, disarming the burglar alarm. "Morning, sunshine," she greeted and covered a wide yawn.

"Morning."

"You sleep better last night?"

"Yes."

Vic poured herself a cup of tea and rubbed her eyes. She had pulled her long, blond hair into a ponytail, and would probably have it in a roll by the time she got to the bakery. Then topped off with her baker's hat, not a hair could fall into the muffin batter.

"Still no feline?" Vic observed.

"Nope. Perverse creature."

"Ah, well. In another day or two, he'll be getting underfoot and driving you wild, and you'll be wishing he was pouting again."

"Probably."

"So you and Terry made it out to supper last night?"

"Yes… for a short supper. Then he was called back in again."

"What? Why was he called back in?"

"Well, you know he arrested Bo Biggles…"

"Right. I was at the bakery when Melissa came by."

"And then he was dealing with that all day. And then…"

Vic raised her brows and nodded her head. "And?"

"He got a call back to say that Bo Biggles was dead!"

"No. Really?"

Erin laughed and shrugged. A predictable response. Like she would lie about Bo Biggles being dead. Like there was some big punch line. "Yes. Really."

Vic swore under her breath. "What happened?"

"Terry didn't know last night. I haven't heard anything yet today. No one will be up yet."

"Sheesh. The Bald Eagle Falls curse strikes again."

"There's no curse," Erin said, pressing her lips together.

Erin was happy to lose herself in the routine of the bakery. There were batters to bake so that they would have fresh, hot muffins and other bakery items ready as soon as the doors opened to accommodate the breakfast and pre-school rush. They would need to be arranged and labeled. There was a lot to be done, and even though they had the routine down pat, they couldn't afford to dawdle or forget anything. It all had to be run ship-shape.

Erin didn't want to think about ships, though. Enough about boats. She just wanted to think about her bakery and her customers. And Terry. Hopefully, everything had gone well the night before and he had gotten to bed in good time. No one was going to mourn the loss of Bo Biggles. There would be paperwork to file, and someone would have to investigate what had happened, but no one was going to miss a lowlife drug dealer.

"Are we going to do some pumpkin muffins this week?" Vic asked. "Now that it's October, I think pumpkins are in order."

"Yes, I think so too. We're supposed to have a management meeting Sunday, but I think we can sneak the pumpkins in before that without anyone being too upset about it."

"Has Charley got her panties in a twist over something?"

"No, I just promised her that I wouldn't be making all of the decisions without consulting her first. I have a partner and I need to make sure she's involved."

Vic nodded. "Even if she doesn't know anything about running a bakery."

"She knows more than she did a few months ago. And she ran things just fine while we were gone."

"That's true," Vic conceded. She and Charley did not get along very well. They seemed to feel that they were rivals for Erin's friendship. "But that's not just her; that's because you have everybody well-trained."

"I'm thrilled with the way it ran while we were gone. Maybe we can take other holidays."

"Somewhere warm."

"Yes, somewhere warm," Erin agreed. She had no desire to go to Alaska again. Victoria, British Columbia had been pretty, but Vic had been cold even there. "Somewhere tropical next time. And no murders."

"Exactly."

Erin looked at her phone to check the time, and moved to the front door. It was still a couple of minutes before she was officially open, but she would let people in to have a look and decide what they wanted to order.

Mary Lou wasn't usually there until later in the day, so Erin was surprised to see her with the small group waiting outside the door. She raised her brows and smiled, giving Mary Lou a friendly nod.

"Hey. Good to see you."

It was also unusual for her to be at the bakery two days in a row. Usually, she put in an appearance once and ordered what she would need for the week, only occasionally coming back a few days later to pick up something else for a quick lunch or dinner.

Everyone came in, smiling at the warm bakery smells. There was nothing like fresh bread and baking to put people into a good mood. And they were already carrying their travel cups of coffee, so they had their caffeine.

Erin went back behind the counter and finished putting the last few baked goods in the display case, while Vic stood by with the price tag signs ready.

"Good morning," Erin greeted the group in general. They all responded with various warm morning greetings. Mary Lou was hanging back, and she looked worried. Erin wondered what was wrong. She thought that Mary Lou would be happy to have heard about Bo Biggles's demise. But maybe words had not circulated yet. She would be relieved once she heard. There would be no more drug dealers hanging around the school her son attended.

The customers talked mostly among themselves. Some had heard of Bo Biggles's arrest, but it didn't sound like the word was out about his death.

Mary Lou allowed the other customers to go ahead of her, so it was quiet again when she reached the counter.

"Did you hear?" Erin asked in a low voice. "About Bo Biggles?"

"About him being arrested?"

"About him being dead."

Mary Lou looked back and forth like she might be overhead, then nodded. "I heard. The school sent out an email late last night, saying that there was nothing to worry about, it had all been taken care of and that Biggles wouldn't be coming back because he had died in custody."

Erin couldn't figure out why Mary Lou would be looking so worried if she knew that. Maybe she thought that someone else would come along to replace Biggles? Would the clan send someone else to take up the school sales again?

"You must be happy as two clams to hear that," Vic drawled.

"I sure would be."

"I don't know."

"You don't know?" Vic repeated, frowning. "Why wouldn't you be happy about that?"

"Because it's going to cause a lot of trouble." Mary Lou looked at Erin. "You of all people should know the kind of trouble that comes from someone being killed, even if it was someone unpopular."

"Well…" Erin's heart sank. "Yes, I know that. But I'm not involved in this one, even peripherally, so… I wasn't worried about that."

"It's not going to be good," Mary Lou warned. "You mark my words. This is the beginning of our troubles, not the end."

Mary Lou didn't even pretend that she had come there to get a muffin. She didn't look at the display case once. She just looked impressively at Vic and Erin one more time, then turned and walked back out.

Erin swallowed. She turned to Vic. "Do you think…?"

"I don't know," Vic admitted. "I didn't think that anyone would care about Biggles being killed. Other than being happy about it, I mean. But she has a point. It isn't like the other deaths in Bald Eagle Falls have been uneventful. Even Charley's case in Moose River… the killing of a mob boss… that one came back to bite us too."

Erin nodded uncomfortably, not liking to think about it. Charley had been in jail, and even though everyone had told Erin to stay away from Charley because of her clan involvement, she hadn't listened. And some very nasty people had come after them.

Would the same thing happen with Bo Biggles? She didn't want assassins trying to track down the responsible parties. Even if Bo Biggles had overdosed or committed suicide, that didn't mean that the clan couldn't decide that someone in Bald Eagle Falls was at fault. Someone like Terry.

She had her phone out before she even formed the conscious thought to call him. If he had been up most of the night, he would be in bed and she shouldn't, but Erin's heart was pounding hard. She needed to be sure that Terry was okay. She hit the speed dial for his phone and waited, holding her breath and chewing on her lip. It was a few rings before Terry finally picked up. His voice sounded groggy and rough.

"Erin? Is everything okay?"

"I'm just… you didn't call me, and I wanted to make sure you were alright. I'm sorry I woke you up. I was worried… I thought that if the clan thought that you were responsible because you arrested Bo Biggles, that they could send someone after you… I just wanted to make sure you're okay."

"I'm fine," he assured her. He didn't rebuke her for having woken him up. "We'll talk later, and I'll fill you in on what I can. Things are… going to be tough for a little while. But it will all work out eventually."

"Tough? What things are going to be tough? What's going on?"

"I can't talk about it right now. I'm not awake enough to rub two thoughts together. We'll talk about it later, okay?"

"Okay." Erin just breathed for a moment, glad that she had called him even if it had meant waking him up. "You'll be careful? Don't put K9 in his crate, and keep your gun close by."

There was a long pause from Terry, and she wondered whether he had fallen back asleep mid-conversation. Then he finally spoke.

"I'll be careful, Erin. Don't you worry."

CHAPTER 9

*O*f course, telling Erin not to worry was no good at all. She was going to worry, and Terry couldn't stop her even with his most reassuring tones. It would have helped if he had told her that he'd had a burglar alarm installed, though when Alton Summers had come after her, he had managed to disarm her burglar alarm and just walk into her house. Orange Blossom had warned her then, and had even attacked the intruder. She hoped that K9 would be able to protect Terry if someone came after him.

And she should give Orange Blossom a treat. The memories of what he had done for her had somehow faded and she had forgotten his attack on Summers. Was she going to let Orange Blossom's pouting keep her from showing him how grateful she was to have him around? She should be showing him her appreciation for what he had done, rather than withholding treats and affection because he was a little upset about her having gone away. She would be upset if someone she loved disappeared from her life for weeks without knowing why too. She should be showing him that she had missed him too and still loved him.

"Erin?"

Erin turned to look at Vic. She lowered her phone from her face and put it away.

"Is everything okay?" Vic asked.

"Yes. He said he's fine. We'll talk about it later."

Erin was fully expecting Melissa to show up at some point during the day to give them an update on what had happened with Bo Biggles. She would have lots to talk about, even if she didn't know any facts. Melissa loved having gossip to share, and a little speculation had never stopped her. Everyone in town would be talking about the arrest of Biggles and his subsequent death.

But curiously, Melissa never showed up. Business was quiet. Maybe just because so many people had shown up the first day that Erin was back. They had all wanted to hear about how her cruise had gone and to tell her how happy they were that she was back again. So maybe they had all stopped by the first day and didn't need to come by the next day as well. That had to be why it was unusually quiet.

Even when people came in, they didn't talk about Bo Biggles. They studied the treats in the bakery case seriously and were subdued and didn't bring up the gossip that must have been circulating like wildfire.

When they locked the front door and were closing up, Erin shook her head at Vic. "That was one of the weirdest days we've had. Almost like when everybody was talking about boycotting the bakery because they thought I might be a witch."

"Has it really been a year since that happened?" Vic ran one of the big mixers, thinking about it. "I guess it was, but it sure doesn't seem that long. And it seems like Adele has lived here forever. We should remind her that it's her anniversary in Bald Eagle Falls."

"I'm sure she remembers."

"I guess so. But we should make her a cake or do something nice."

Erin nodded, her thoughts far away.

"Terry should be out of bed now," Vic offered. "The two of you can talk about Biggles and you can get the scoop."

"Yeah, I was hoping he'd be by here already." Erin glanced back toward the back door, expecting him to show up, but the door didn't open.

"He must have been exhausted. He was probably up half the night dealing with Bo Biggles kicking the bucket. There's probably all kinds of paperwork that has to be done when someone dies in police custody. You know how diligent Terry is. He wouldn't want to put it off until the next day. And there were probably investigators in from the city to help out with the case, because something like that is a little big for our little police department."

Erin barely heard a word of what Vic was saying. She continued to prepare the batters and doughs they would need the next day, her hands working from muscle memory while she pictured Terry in his house, unconscious or dead because no one knew he had been attacked. Anything could happen. They'd had enough experience with the clans to know that they didn't operate on logic. They were bold and brash, and why wouldn't they send someone after Terry if they thought he had somehow contributed to the death of one of their own?

She caught Vic looking at her questioningly, but then Vic turned away, leaving Erin to her contemplations.

After they were finished at the bakery, Erin drove Vic home, but made no move to get out of the car herself. Vic turned back to the car and looked in the window.

"You going over to Terry's?"

"Yes. I have to make sure…" Erin choked up. She didn't want to give away how much she had been worrying about him and the possibility that he was in danger. Vic would laugh and say that she was overreacting and that there was nothing to worry about. Erin knew she was blowing the potential threat to Terry out of proportion, but she couldn't help it. As soon as she started to worry about something lately, her brain immediately swirled into thoughts of the worst possible scenario, and she couldn't get out of the rut. Vic didn't need to know how bad it had gotten.

"Of course," Vic agreed. "Go see how your policeman is. And give him my love." She gave Erin a little wave and headed toward the back of the house.

Erin let out her breath, relieved not to have to explain any further. She watched until Vic was out of sight, took one last glance around to make sure that there was no one lurking in the shadows or watching the house, and drove over to Terry's house.

His car was not parked in front of the house. Erin frowned. Had he gone out already, but she had missed him? Maybe he had shown up at the bakery right after they had left. Or perhaps he was back at the police department dealing with more bureaucracy. There had to be a lot of it surrounding a death in custody. Mary Lou was right. It was something that was going to cause them no end of trouble.

Parking in front of Terry's, Erin dug in her purse for her phone, then called Terry.

"Erin? Hi." He sounded much fresher, but there was a forced cheer in his voice. Erin put a smile on her face and tried to match his tone.

"Hi, Terry. I'm off work, and I thought I would stop by and see how you were doing. But it looks like you're not at home."

"I'm home. Come on in."

Erin stared at the empty parking space in front of the house where Terry's squad car usually resided. Maybe he had been too tired to drive himself home, so he'd had someone else drop him off. That had been a sensible thing to do. She was glad that he had decided not to drive, even that short distance, when he was too tired.

She slid out of her car, locked the doors, and went up to the house. Terry was at the door waiting for her by the time she got up the sidewalk. He kissed her and held her tightly for a minute, making her feel warm and safe and protected. They moved out of the doorway into the house, and Terry looked around, trying to decide where they should sit.

"Did you want to eat? I don't think there's a whole lot in the kitchen, but we could throw together some pasta."

"Sure, that sounds good."

Terry nodded, and they moved into the galley kitchen. K9 followed them in and nuzzled Erin's leg, looking for attention. She scratched his ears and petted him.

"You're feeling better now?" she asked. "It's amazing what a good sleep can do for a person."

"Yes. I was getting pretty frayed last night. And I didn't want to risk saying anything that might…"

He didn't finish the sentence. Erin looked at him, trying to figure out where he had been going with the line, but she couldn't match up an ending in her mind. Terry was quiet, pulling out his saucepan and filling it with water for the pasta.

"Was there any indication what Bo Biggles died from? I know you won't know the medical examiner's findings for quite a while, but could you tell by looking at him…?" Erin shifted uncomfortably, thinking of the other bodies that she had found or cases they had worked together. Too much history. Too many deaths. She wanted to know what had happened to Biggles immediately but, on the other hand, she didn't want anything to do with it. It wasn't just a matter to satisfy her curiosity about. It was a human life, even if it was someone who operated on the wrong side of the law.

"There are several theories," Terry said slowly.

Erin nodded, waiting for more. It didn't sound like it was obvious. Probably not a suicide, then. They would certainly not need to theorize if they'd had to cut him down after a hanging.

Terry didn't explain further. He continued to assemble their dinner, pulling a jar of bottled pasta sauce out of the cupboard to heat up, getting out their dishes, looking through the packets of vegetables in his fridge.

That was fine. Maybe he didn't want to talk until they could sit down and relax. Talk it all out at once and move on to nicer dinner conversations. Erin helped with what she could, but there really wasn't a lot to do. She found some rolls from the bakery in the freezer and set them to thaw slowly in the microwave.

They thoroughly discussed the weather forecast. Erin told Terry about Orange Blossom and her change of heart, deciding to pamper him instead of ignoring him. She talked about it being a year since Adele had shown up in the woods behind Erin's house, marveling that she had become such an old friend in such a short time.

"Some people are like that," Terry agreed, "even though they are newcomers, it feels like you've known them forever. They just click."

Erin nodded. She searched for other topics—Halloween, then Christmas. A lot had happened over the previous year. They hadn't even been together a year before, and now they were, as Vic said, thick as thieves.

They finally sat down at the little table, dishing up the spaghetti. Erin raised her eyes to Terry's. He didn't look tired anymore, but there was something else there. Discouragement? A weariness that didn't come from not being caught up on his sleep.

"What's wrong?"

Terry cleared his throat. He poked at his food but didn't eat. "I've been put on administrative leave."

"Leave? Why?"

"Because they need to investigate my involvement in Bo Biggles's death."

$\mathcal{E}$rin's jaw dropped. She looked at him. "Your involvement? What does that mean? They think you might have done something wrong?"

He nodded.

"But... that doesn't make any sense. They don't really think you did anything wrong. They just have to investigate, to show that you didn't. Right? It's just routine? That must be the policy when something like this happens."

"Pretty much," he agreed. "But... I'm afraid it's not all just academic. They really do... think that it could be my fault."

Erin shook her head in disbelief. "Who thinks that? The sheriff? He wouldn't be so stupid. He knows you. Without you, the Bald Eagle Falls police department would be nothing. There's no way they could operate without you."

"Biggles had bruises... there are concerns that there may have been excessive force used during the arrest or interrogation."

"That's ridiculous! They think you beat him?"

Terry nodded. "They're not using those words, but... yes."

Erin couldn't seem to catch her breath. She looked across the table at Officer Terry Piper, a man she knew to be kind and gentle. The idea that he would have used any more force than necessary was laughable. He had training in the use of force. He could take down a criminal when necessary. But he would never beat someone up.

"How long is this administrative leave going to last?"

"Until they have sorted out the cause and manner of death… and decided that I didn't do it."

"That could be a long time." Erin knew that such investigations could take months. Taking Terry off duty for that long would be disastrous. They would have to bring in someone from outside to cover his position while he was on leave. And his administrative leave would be paid, which meant that they would end up having to pay for an extra person, which would royally screw up the town's budget.

"It could be a very long time," Terry agreed. "I don't know what I'm going to do with myself. I don't think I can not work for three days, let alone weeks or months."

Erin knew the feeling. She had been so eager to get back to the bakery after a two-week vacation. If she had to stay away for months, she would go crazy.

"Maybe you can find something else to do while you're on leave. There's nothing to prevent you, is there? You're still allowed to work somewhere else even when you're on leave?"

"I'll have to check. They might say that I have quit if I do that."

"Yuck." Erin thought about Mary Lou's comment that Bo Biggles's death was going to cause problems for them. She had certainly called that one. Did she know that Terry would be accused of brutality?

"I'm sure the medical examiner will be able to prove that you didn't do anything wrong," she said hopefully. "The bruises he had were probably old, and he'll be able to tell that."

"Some of them probably *were* sustained during the arrest. Biggles didn't exactly go without a fight."

"But that's justified use of force, then. You can't be blamed for that."

"Just because it's legal, that doesn't mean people will take you at your word."

"But the sheriff and Tom—"

"It isn't just the sheriff and Tom. The sheriff answers to his constituents, and if the voters think that he's not performing his office, they can call for an election. The sheriff has to uphold the law, and if there is evidence that one of his officers has stepped over the line, he has to investigate it seriously. No matter what his opinion might be."

Erin was stunned. She sat there looking at Terry, then dropped her eyes to her plate of spaghetti. Neither of them was doing anything but poking at their food.

"They're actually going to investigate you for brutality? These people see you every day. They know what kind of a person you are."

"Not everyone is on good terms with the police."

Of course Erin knew that was true. There would always be people who took a stance against the police, even if they'd never been personally harmed or inconvenienced by them. Others had good reasons to be bitter about something that had happened in the past, and painted all officers with the same brush. But she'd thought that Bald Eagle Falls, with its tiny, friendly police department would have escaped that kind of judgment.

But it didn't matter that they saw Terry peacefully patrolling the streets every day. There would always be those who believed that all cops were monsters just waiting for the opportunity to hurt someone.

"Terry..." Erin cut a few strands of spaghetti with the side of her fork, worrying it. "This sucks."

Terry laughed. And it was a real, good-humored laugh with the dimple appearing in his cheek, not a bitter or forced laugh.

"You hit the nail on the head," he agreed. "It really does suck."

They scraped most of the pasta into the garbage and got out the ice cream. If there were any situation which required ice cream rather than complex carbs, it was Terry being put on leave and suspected of police brutality. They each heaped bowls with their favorite ice cream flavors and toppings, and sat down in the living room instead of at the kitchen table, trying to find some solace in sugar and cuddling.

It was a day when, even though it was still too warm to need one, Erin would have liked a fireplace to curl up beside. Staring into the flames and hearing the crackling of a really good fire was mesmerizing, and she could have used something else to pull her out of her growing anxiety.

Terry needed her. He needed her to be calm and collected and upbeat about the situation he was in. He didn't need her pulling him down with her moodiness.

"So he fought back against being arrested. He had bruises. They think that it was some internal injury that did him in?"

"Possibly. You never know when someone could have internal bleeding, or a concussion, or even just a weak heart. He never said that he was hurt and wanted to go to the hospital or to have a doctor check him out. He never said that a thing was wrong."

"Who found him? Was he on the floor, or still sitting in a chair, or what?"

Terry considered the question, likely evaluating how many of these details would be circulating town by the next day.

"We brought a camp cot into that interview room for him. I had gone to the restaurant to join you for supper. He had lain down on the cot to rest or go to sleep. Clara Jones checked in on him before she left. He was on the cot. She thought he was lying in an awkward position and wondered why. She pointed it out to the sheriff, and he opened the door and went in to check on Biggles. That's when he discovered that Biggles wasn't breathing."

"But there weren't any signs of violence. Like... a struggle. And he hadn't... done anything to himself."

"No. So the premise they are working with is that it was the result of something that happened in custody."

"But you hear about these kinds of things… about prisoners dying within hours of being arrested. It's not that rare."

"And what do you think whenever you hear about one of those cases? Do you think 'oh, I guess he just dropped dead'?"

Erin dragged her spoon through a pool of melting ice cream and chocolate sauce and took a bite. "No. I admit, I'm always a little suspicious of the police and how he was treated at the jail. They can say that there was no foul play, even that it was a natural death, but you always wonder."

"And now people are going to wonder that about me. It's always going to be a blot against my name, even if they can't prove anything. People will always remember that I had a detainee die in custody and got away with it."

Erin's heart ached for him. It was unthinkable that he had done anything wrong. He was always very careful about following protocol, and she knew him to be a decent and caring man. But now that he had this blot against his name, there would always be a cloud of suspicion over him.

Unless she could prove that Biggles's death had been caused by something else entirely.

$\mathcal{E}$rin couldn't exactly jump right into investigating Bo Biggles's death. She had her work at Auntie Clem's, after all, and her employees who had covered all of the shifts for Erin and Vic while they were on their cruise now needed a break. But the bakery was a hot gossip spot and they always did their best business when something tragic had happened and people wanted to talk about it. Erin could find out a lot just by listening to what the townspeople had to say about the matter.

But it also meant that she had to grit her teeth and pretend not to hear what people were saying about Terry. If people were afraid to come in and talk about what had happened, she wouldn't find out anything.

She would have thought that with the number of years Terry had worked for the town and the number of people he had helped over those years, that he would have earned the respect of the residents of Bald Eagle Falls. But the townspeople seemed incredibly quick to jump onto the bandwagon and say that they didn't like to say anything unfair about Officer Piper, but it was awfully suspicious the way that Bo Biggles had died.

"They said he was covered with bruises," Erin heard Lottie Sturm say. She was always a troublemaker, and Erin tried to avoid crossing swords with her. So she focused on carefully packing the dozen cookies that Lottie had ordered into a box while she kept her ears pricked and listened for more. "You hear about police brutality in the big cities, but you never think that it could be an issue in a little place like Bald Eagle Falls. We've had such a good record up until now."

Bella Prost's mother was there to pick up some bread and to get Bella's schedule for the next week. "We've never had trouble like that before."

"But then, you remember when Kay Lourde's grandson was arrested?" Lottie mused. "There was a big to-do about brutality over that one."

Cindy Prost shook her head. "Didn't they decide that he'd been in a fight with some other boys a couple of hours before? His parents were threatening all kinds of lawsuits when they saw the condition he was in, and then the boy finally spoke up and admitted that it hadn't been the police at all."

"Still, you have to wonder. He might have been threatened into saying that. He did end up going to the state pen on those charges, and if the police decide you're a troublemaker and pass it up the line to the staties, they can make all kinds of trouble for him on the inside," Lottie said sagely. As if she knew all about the prison and how it worked. Erin was sure she'd probably never even driven past it. She was just repeating what she had seen on TV or read on the internet. There was always a conspiracy. The criminals accused the police of planting evidence or being dirty. The biggest problem in the prison wasn't the CO's; it was the other prisoners. They were the ones who were most likely to stab someone in the yard or the cafeteria.

"None of that had anything to do with Officer Piper."

"But it shows a culture of violence," Lottie insisted. "If one police officer is acting that way, you think the others are going to turn him in? They obviously didn't, and that means that they put up with it. They approve of it. It's a real problem in police departments all over the country. Once you get one bad apple in there, and the blue wall of silence… well, you may as well give up all of your rights there and then."

Erin shook her head, handing Lottie her box of cookies. "There you are, Mrs. Sturm." She told Lottie the total.

Lottie counted out her cash carefully, finding exact change so that Erin couldn't give her the wrong change back. She looked at Erin, her blue eyes glinting. "Are you still going out with Officer Piper?" she asked, as if she didn't know. Everybody knew that Erin and Terry were dating.

"Yes, ma'am, I am."

"Well, I'm just glad it's not you," Lottie said cryptically.

Erin raised her brows, but Lottie left the bakery, having stirred everything up like she wanted to.

"Land sakes," Vic declared, and let out a whistle. "It's a good thing she's not the one leading the lynch mob. I don't think Officer Piper would be making it to dinner tonight."

"It's not funny," Erin pointed out. "People like that… Terry will lose his job or end up in prison if people keep spreading things like that around."

"Everybody knows Lottie likes to cause trouble," Cindy said. Even though she and Lottie were fast friends, Bella practically worshiped the ground Erin walked on, and her mother had gradually changed from being antagonistic toward Erin to trusting Bella's opinion that Erin was a good, honest person, in spite of being an atheist. "No one is going to listen to anything she has to say, especially when she can't even keep her facts straight."

Erin nodded gratefully. She packed the bread and muffins that Cindy pointed out, giving her a couple of extra muffins for good measure.

"No one is going to railroad your sweetie," Cindy promised. "If he's innocent, that will come out."

If he was innocent. Cindy wasn't going to go all the way and say that she believed that Terry was innocent. She might be defending Terry's rights and showing kindness toward Erin, but that didn't mean she thought he was guiltless in Bo Biggles's death.

"Terry didn't do anything to cause Biggles's death," Erin said evenly.

"I believe that you believe that," Cindy said agreeably. She paid with a credit card rather than counting out her pennies as Lottie had. "But you weren't there and you can't know how hard Officer Piper hit that man, or what kind of damage he may have done. He believed he was arresting a dangerous criminal, so of course he did what he had to do to get him under control." Cindy shook her head. "You can just never tell."

"He might have been sick," Erin pointed out. "He might have had a heart condition or might have overdosed on drugs."

"Or it could have been an allergy," Cindy laughed. "If we're going to throw around alternate theories."

That one froze Erin to the spot. She couldn't say anything else until Cindy was gone.

"Ignore her," Vic advised. Her voice was low and soothing, the southern drawl pitched to calm Erin down. "She's just spouting off nonsense. She isn't accusing you of anything."

Erin cleared her throat. Her eyes were hot with tears and she had a hard time holding them back. She took a quick look at the customers who were waiting and decided that Vic could handle that many for a few minutes.

"Need to go check on those cookies," she blurted and went into the kitchen.

It was hot, and they tried not to bake too much in the heat of the day, but sometimes some special orders or events required more time than they could manage in the cool of the morning. Erin checked on the cookies Peter Foster's mother had ordered for his pre-Halloween costume-designing party, though she knew very well that they wouldn't be done. She slipped into the small office and turned on the desk fan while she sorted through the papers in her inbox.

When there was a lull, Vic left the front of the bakery and appeared in the doorway of the office.

"Are you okay?"

"I didn't give Angela Plaint anything that she was allergic to," Erin insisted, her voice cracking and tears spilling out of her eyes. She was so furious that Cindy would bring up allergic reactions like that, throwing it in her face as if it were a joke. "And I didn't give Trenton those muffins, either. That was Joelle. She planned it out. She wanted to get him out of the way. Neither of those things was my fault."

"No," Vic agreed. Her face was smooth and expressionless. "I know that. And everybody in town knows that. Cindy just doesn't like to be challenged. Everybody has their own opinions about what happened to Bo Biggles, but the fact is that no one knows what happened to him. Nobody is going to know until after the autopsy, and those things can take forever." Vic paused, looking away and pressing her lips together for a moment. "And chances are, they're going to come back and say that he died of unknown causes. Because this isn't TV. They can't always tell what killed somebody."

Erin wiped at the angry tears and set her face. She hated crying, and there was nothing worse than crying when she was angry, which people would take as a sign of weakness, as a sign that she was sad or hurt rather than that she was furious. "Do you think that someone might have killed him intentionally? It *was* just a freak thing, wasn't it?"

"Who could kill him when he was in police custody? No way it could have been murder," Vic dismissed.

CHAPTER 12

*E*rin turned her thoughts to the possibility that Bo Biggles *hadn't* died by accident. What if it had been the result of a deliberate act? Or what if the cause was something that could be proven, thereby clearing Terry of any wrongdoing? He might always have that shadow on his reputation, but if she could prove what had happened, they could at least refute any accusations. That was something.

During their early lunch break, Erin called the police department, not sure whether she would get Melissa or Clara Jones, and not sure which one of them she wanted to talk to. It was Clara who answered the phone.

"Oh, hi, Clara. It's Erin Price."

There was an awkward pause. Clara knew that Erin had Terry's phone number and that even if Terry had been on duty, Erin could have just called him directly.

"Miss Price. What can I do for you?" she asked finally.

"I was just wondering… how you were doing?"

"How *I'm* doing?" Clara's tone was one of confusion. She and Erin were not friends. They knew each other, but that was it.

"I know you were the one who discovered Bo Biggles's body. That must have been horrible."

"Oh!" Clara's voice took on a bit of warmth. In all of the confusion and bureaucracy at the police department with such an unexpected death, no one had probably paid any attention at all to Clara and how she might be feeling or might have been affected by someone dying on the premises. "Well, yes," she drawled out the words, thinking it through. "It was pretty awful. I've never had such a thing happen here before. I'm sure you know we aren't accustomed to people dying in custody. This was a first for me, and it was shocking!"

"I'm sure it was," Erin agreed. "I've had… more experience than I would like in that department. I'm surprised that you're working today. I'm not sure I could."

"It's been difficult. But who else is going to keep things running around here? The sheriff may think that he's in charge and keeps everything running smoothly in the office, but without me… things would go downhill pretty quickly."

Erin laughed. "They always think they're in charge, don't they? But not even taking a single personal day… you're superwoman, Clara."

Clara made approving noises, happy to have the attention and accolades. "It wasn't easy to get up this morning and get in, I'll tell you. Knowing what I would be facing when I came in today… But you simply have to go on. There's a lot to be done. More than usual."

"Are there folks coming in from the city? The FBI or anything like that?"

"Some state boys. So far no FBI, and I hope it doesn't go that far. It's bad enough that the staties are coming in to have a look at things. It's really not their jurisdiction, but we have such a small department here…"

"I'll bet everyone is really happy about that."

"Oh, you know it. Tensions are running pretty high. And we still have the body here!"

"You do?" Erin was shocked. She had assumed that someone would have picked it up. An ambulance from the city, maybe. She didn't know who was responsible for picking up bodies in such a situation, but she would have thought that they would be there within an hour or two to get the body into cold storage and preserve any evidence from the scene.

"I know! Someone was supposed to be by this morning to pick it up. But no one actually wants to do that, so there are excuses about flat tires and a murder scene in the city they had to deal with and anything else that they can come up with. We're just the poor cousins; they don't want to have to pick up our garbage too."

"That's terrible. Does it… stink?"

"It's warm weather, dearie. It's going to be bloated and buzzing by the end of the day. If they don't get it into cold storage soon… I don't know what they're going to be able to tell from the state of the body."

"Ugh. I'm so sorry. I hope your desk isn't too close to the interview room."

"You know how small our office is. Everything is too close to the interview room."

Erin shook her head and let a few seconds of silence pass before inquiring further. "What was it like? I mean, when you realized something was wrong…? What exactly happened?"

Clara cleared her throat. She didn't answer immediately, and Erin pictured her taking off her glasses and letting them hang on the chain around her neck, looking around to make sure that there wasn't anyone nearby who was going to overhear her comments and get her in trouble for speaking out of school.

"I was getting ready to go home at the end of the day. It had been a really long day here, as I'm sure you know. We're not used to big arrests like this—a drug dealer, someone with outstanding warrants, known to be involved in organized crime. We're used to speeding tickets. Kids breaking curfew. Maybe some vandalism. When we make a drug bust, it's usually kids with a roach or two in their pockets. Nothing like that big drug bust the night your bakery burned down. We weren't even involved in that, just told to stay out of the way and let the feds do their thing."

"Right," Erin agreed. It had been chaotic that night, and she didn't know how many agencies had been involved in the cleanup, but it had been way too big for the Bald Eagle Falls police department.

"So we were busy getting all of the forms filled out and making arrangements to have Biggles transported in the morning. That meant someone had to stay here overnight to keep an eye on things, but that's not my job, luckily. In Tennessee, the sheriff is in charge of the jail. And even if we don't have a proper jail cell here, he's the jailer. That's his responsibility."

"And no one could come to transport him to another facility that night?"

"No... and to tell the truth, we didn't really want them to. Terry—Officer Piper—wanted to let him sit and stew, to give him a chance to think about what his options were and what was going to happen to him. Then Terry could talk to him again in the morning, and maybe he would have changed his mind and could provide some details about who else was involved with drug dealing around here. Terry wanted to do more than just arrest one person. He wanted to send the message not to mess with Bald Eagle Falls. We thought we scared the clans away with the big drug bust and that they would steer clear of here for a few years. Having Biggles show up again so soon... well, none of us were happy about it."

"Of course not," Erin agreed. She tried to move the story along more quickly. "So you were just getting ready to go home at the end of the day..."

"Right. The sheriff was going to have to stay and keep an eye on the prisoner, and I looked in on him to make sure that his dishes had been cleared away and that he was settled for the night."

"You went into the room?"

"No, I just looked in the window. I could have gone in; it only locks on the inside, you don't need a key to get in. But I wouldn't put myself in the room with a guy like that."

"He wasn't restrained?"

"No. You can't keep someone in handcuffs all night. There are guidelines, you know, to prevent..." Clara trailed off uncertainly. She didn't finish the thought.

"To prevent what?" Erin prompted. "I would think that if you don't have a proper jail cell, you would need to keep him in handcuffs, just for security. He could attack someone coming in the door. Or he could... I don't know... try to find a way out, or to harm himself."

"I know it seems like that. But there are rules because of... stuff like positional asphyxiation."

Erin blinked. She frowned at her phone, trying to figure out what Clara was talking about. Did she mean that someone could come in and smother Biggles while he was in handcuffs? Did he need his hands free to protect himself? That didn't make any sense. "What exactly is positional asphyxiation?"

"Normally, when you are sitting or lying down, you can breathe freely, right? But if someone does something to restrict your breathing, even just a little bit, it can eventually cause... well... asphyxiation. You can smother, just because you couldn't get your body in the right position to breathe freely. It's more common in men who are big and heavy, and Biggles wasn't any featherweight. If you lay someone face down, for example, then their weight can eventually restrict their breathing enough that they die. And the same thing with pulling their hands back behind their back, especially with someone who's pretty wide, because putting their shoulders back like that hinders their breathing."

"So you're not allowed to keep someone in handcuffs all night, because they could stop breathing."

"Yes. It's one of those things that we're supposed to do to help prevent... what happened."

Erin thought about that. "Huh. Things that you never know if you don't work for the police department."

"We have to be careful," Clara said sagely. "We're supposed to take good care of people who are in custody. You don't know how much trouble we could get into if someone starts making accusations… Because even if it never happened, people will believe it and be suspicious. It can throw a black cloud over the whole department, even if they never did anything. So we have to make sure that everything is documented, and you don't treat them… like the lowlifes they are."

Erin snorted. Vic looked over at her. She had been pretending not to be listening in on Erin's conversation, and she couldn't hear what Clara had to say, but it was apparent that she was paying attention.

"So what did you see when you looked in the window? Did… did he look dead?"

Clara hemmed and hawed. "Well, it's hard to explain. He didn't look dead, like he wasn't lying there with his eyes rolled back in his head and his tongue hanging out or anything like that. But he just… didn't look quite right. So I told the sheriff, and he went and had a look. Neither of us really thought that there was anything wrong, but he went in just to make sure."

"And that's when he found out Biggles was dead."

"Yes. After he checked him out to make sure that he was really dead, he had me call Terry. So that's when Terry came back in, and we have to inform all of the proper authorities…"

Clara had been the one to call Terry. Erin remembered how Terry had looked, his face drained of blood. He had been so tired and fatigued, and yet he'd had to go back in to deal with it.

"What did the sheriff think he died from? Did he have any ideas?"

Clara clicked her tongue. She didn't answer right away. But Erin wasn't ready to let her off the hook. Erin needed to find out what had happened if she were going to help Terry.

"Did he look like he'd smothered or choked on something?" she persisted. "Or maybe like he'd had an overdose?"

"How would we know? He looked… dead. That's all I can say.

He was lying in sort of an awkward position, with his arm kind of thrown to the side and his face turned against the cot..." Clara cleared her throat and covered the phone receiver to speak to someone else in the office. Erin thought for a moment that Clara was going to hang up on her to cover up the fact that she'd been talking about the case. But there was silence for a few minutes, and then Clara was back, speaking in a lower, confidential voice.

"I know you want me to tell you that it wasn't Officer Piper. But I can't tell you that. He was the last one in there with Biggles. And Biggles had bruises. They weren't there earlier when he was brought in. I'm sorry, but... everything points toward Terry."

"No," Erin protested, the word escaping her lips before she had a chance to check it.

"What else could have happened? Somebody beat Biggles up. I don't know what he died of, but the medical examiner will determine whether he had internal bleeding or a head injury, or whether the swelling in his throat cut off his breathing. Officer Piper left here and thought he got away with it; he didn't know that Biggles would die and we would discover what had happened."

"Why would he do something like that?" Erin demanded. "It's not like he could think he was going to get away with it. There aren't that many people in the police department. It isn't like in a big city where they can all point their fingers at each other. If Terry did something like that, he would know that he would get caught. So why would he want to go to prison over someone like Biggles? He wanted him off the street, that's all. He didn't want him dead."

"Maybe he lost his temper. Terry wanted to get everyone who was working with Biggles. He wanted it bad. And what happened in that room... I don't know. But Terry was the one questioning him."

"Terry's the only one who talked to him?"

"Well... no. He wasn't the only one to talk to him. But he was the one who arrested Biggles, and he was the one who was in charge of the questioning. He took control of it. This was his case, not anyone else's. He was determined to keep dealers like Biggles out of Bald Eagle Falls."

CHAPTER 13

$\mathcal{E}$rin hung up the phone slowly and looked at her sandwich. She wasn't hungry. But ice cream for dinner the night before and tea for breakfast probably wasn't going to get her through her day. She didn't want to be fainting from low blood sugar during the afternoon rush.

"Are you okay?" Vic asked.

"I don't know. I guess so. I'm okay. It's Terry I'm worried about."

"You know he didn't kill that guy."

"I know he didn't… but I feel like you and I are the only ones who believe that. Clara works with him every day; how can she think that he would do something like that? She's acting like he's some vigilante and went after Biggles with… whatever you torture someone with… a rubber hose? She's acting like he's the villain, and he's not. He's just a cop that arrested a drug dealer."

"Clara's just overexcited."

"But she's doing real damage to his reputation."

"Depends on who she's repeating it to. Right now, it was just to you. You don't know that she's spreading it to other people. She knows she's supposed to keep the investigation confidential."

"If she talked to me about it, she'll talk to other people about it too."

Vic sighed. "Probably. But people know Terry. After they get over the initial shock, they'll remember that he's just the same cop who has been protecting them all along."

"Clara said Biggles had bruises. Bruises that weren't there when Terry brought him in. And she talked about his throat swelling. So… maybe some of the bruises were on his neck."

Vic considered this, carefully cleaning up the crumbs from her sandwich. "Well… that's not good news for Terry."

Erin felt like crying. They had to go back on duty soon. People would be waiting for her to flip the sign back to 'open,' and instead of finding something that would exonerate Terry, she had found the opposite.

"He could have been hurt before Terry arrested him," Vic said slowly. "Bruises don't always show up right away. Then they show up after a few hours… people think that means he sustained them while he was in custody, but that isn't necessarily what happened."

"Who would have beaten him up? He was selling drugs when Terry arrested him. If you were beaten up, wouldn't you go home? Take a hot bath or put some ice on your injuries, and worry about selling the next day?"

"Maybe he had to fight for the real estate. It was another drug dealer's corner, and he had to fight him to get it."

"There aren't that many drug dealers staking out claims around Bald Eagle Falls."

"No," Vic admitted. "It isn't like you see them staked out on street corners. But somebody else *could* have hit him or choked him before Terry arrested him."

"Right."

"Or… it could have been someone else in the police department."

"That's what I said to Clara. She said that it was mostly Terry's collar, but the others did have contact with him too. Something could have happened behind closed doors… that no one saw."

"Sure." Vic nodded. "But do you really want to accuse Tom or the sheriff? Do you see either of them doing anything like this?"

Erin liked Tom and Sheriff Wilmot. They had both been kind and respectful toward her and had helped her out in the past. Despite Erin previously falling under suspicion, neither of them had ever mistreated her. She had to admit that she couldn't see either one of them smacking Bo Biggles around.

Yet someone had.

Erin was exhausted after work. Not so much because of the early schedule and long hours that she kept as a baker; she was pretty used to those. But the emotional stress about Terry and worrying about what was going to happen to him was taking a toll. She called him as soon as she got home, not wanting to wait another minute.

"Hey, Erin," he greeted casually, as if it were just a typical day and not one of the most stressful in his life.

"Hi, I'm home. You want to come over?"

"Sure. About time I looked at that leaky washer in your bathroom."

Erin was startled by the offer. But she supposed he was probably looking for things to keep him busy and keep his mind off of the recent events. And events in the near future.

"Uh—okay. Sure."

"Great. Be there soon. You don't mind if K9 tags along?"

"When have you ever gone anywhere without K9?"

"I know… but that's because he's my partner, and since I'm not on active duty, I don't have to bring him, and I was just wondering…"

"Of course. I don't think I'd let you come without him. He could come without you, but not vice versa."

Terry chuckled. "Good. We'll be there in two shakes."

And he was. Erin had a sneaking suspicion that he had already been in his truck when she had called, just waiting for her to get finished at the bakery. He knew what time she closed up and often popped in to help her to tidy up and make sure everything was secure. When he was on duty, of course. Now that he wasn't, she wasn't sure what to expect.

Erin stood at the door to let them in, greeting Terry with a hug and quick kiss. "I was worrying about you all day."

"I'm fine," he brushed it off. "What's a few days of vacation?"

Erin was slightly hurt by his dismissal. She had expressed her feelings and he had simply ignored them. That wasn't something he usually did.

"Glad you called," Terry said as he looked around the living room, maybe sensing that he had responded too quickly. "I've been a little stir-crazy at home. After finishing most of the little jobs that I've been putting off for the last few months… I didn't know what to do. Do I like to read? Watch movies? I'm told there's this thing about binge watching on Netflix. I could do that, I suppose."

Erin shuddered at the thought of him sitting in front of the TV or tablet in his underwear, a side table full of empty beer bottles beside him. She didn't want him to go to seed. He needed to stay sharp and feel like he was needed. There were only so many home repairs he could do around Erin's house too. A few days, and he would run out of things to fix.

"We can actually have an uninterrupted dinner tonight," she suggested. "I don't know when the last time was that we could do that without worry that you might get interrupted and called back on duty or to take care of some emergency call. Maybe never."

"Yeah, sure. Of course. Where would you like to go? We could go into the city if you like, that would kill a couple more hours…"

"I don't think I have enough time for that. It's still a 'school day' for me tomorrow."

"Oh, right. Of course."

K9 nosed at Erin, whining very quietly. "And I suppose you

want a treat. Come on. Let's get you something. I guess he knows we're talking about food."

"Yeah, and he's wondering what I'm doing staying home all day. I don't know when the last time was that I didn't have to pop in to the police department for one thing or another, even if it was just to sign timesheets or some other report."

K9 followed Erin into the kitchen and waited politely while she got him a biscuit.

"And where's my kitty?" Erin called. "Orange Blossom! Come and get a treat!"

There was silence. After a few seconds, she heard Marshmallow's approach and got a stick of celery out for him. She scratched his head and told him how much she had missed him when she had been on the cruise, then called Orange Blossom again. This time, she heard him jump off of the bed, but when she poked her head out the kitchen door, he was not in the hallway.

Trying to decide just how much she needed to be punished by his cold shoulder, she supposed.

"Blossom…"

She walked down the hall to the bedroom, where he was sitting just inside the doorway. His ears flicked a few times when she saw him and he looked around like he'd heard a flying insect.

"I know you can hear me. Now come on. You want treats too, don't you?" She bent over and picked him up. This time, Blossom didn't kick at her or try to escape. He just looked into her eyes quizzically. Erin kissed the top of his head, scratched his ears, and took him into the kitchen.

He squirmed away when he saw K9, and stalked over to the corner, turning his back on the room while he washed. Erin went into the pantry to fetch his can of treats and started skidding them across the floor. Orange Blossom quickly forgot his aloofness and was running after them and jumping on top of them before tossing them in the air with both paws and then gobbling them up. Erin laughed.

"Yeah, that's more like it!"

She gave him a few more than she normally would to make up for the time she had been withholding them. And for the time that she had been on vacation, though she was sure that Adele had probably given him plenty of treats while she was gone. That wasn't the point.

Terry leaned his shoulder against the doorway and watched her. "So you two have made up?"

"I just had to make the first move. I decided there isn't any point in me holding back waiting for him to change his mind. Just who is the adult in this relationship?"

The dimple appeared in his cheek. "I'm not sure."

"Me!" Erin flicked him with the dishtowel she had just dried her hands on. "The adult is me!"

CHAPTER 14

They decided on dinner at the family restaurant, which Erin thought was a good choice as it wouldn't remind them of their dinner at the Chinese restaurant being interrupted by the call about Bo Biggles. But she didn't think about the fact that to get to the family restaurant, they would have to drive behind Town Hall, where the police department was located, right past the parking lot where Terry's squad car was parked while he was off the job. His truck was not as comfortable, but Erin hadn't said anything about that. She didn't want to do or say anything that would make Terry feel worse about his situation than he already did. He might be pretending that it wasn't bothering him, but Erin didn't believe it.

Terry slowed as they got closer to the parking lot, his eyes going to the van that was backed into the parking space the sheriff usually used. Erin looked at it.

"Who is it?"

"I don't recognize the van." Terry's eyes were sharp. The truck barely crawled forward.

"We probably shouldn't be interfering," Erin said anxiously.

"Interfering? What am I interfering with? I want to see whose van that is. I know all of the vehicles that are normally in this lot. I want to make sure that nothing is going on that shouldn't be."

"You're not on duty."

"That doesn't make me blind."

Erin chewed on a fingernail. She knew there would be no talking Terry out of it. And what was the problem with him looking to see what was going on at the police department while he was away? Were the state investigators going to come bursting out to demand to know why he was impeding their investigation?

While the truck was creeping forward, a man came out the back door of the Town Hall. Erin didn't recognize him at first. He had dark hair and a heavy build. It wasn't the sheriff or Tom or anyone she knew from the town council. But Terry sat up straighter.

"Do you know him?" Erin asked.

"Yes, and you do too. Or at least, you've met."

"We have? When?"

"When you were in Moose River."

Erin started to shake her head, and then she remembered. Jack Ward. Detective Jack Ward from the Moose River police department. She let out a breath.

"What does that mean? Is he here about Bo Biggles? What does he have to do with this?"

"I talked to him Monday. Someone from his department was supposed to be coming to transport Biggles."

"Does that mean that no one told him Biggles was dead? He thought he was coming today to transport him?"

"No… I don't think so. The sheriff would have let him know yesterday what had happened. Unless there was a miscommunication. More likely, he's here to transport the body now."

"Oh." Erin felt nauseated. She stared at Jack Ward, who turned around as if he felt her gaze and stared at the truck. Erin looked over at Terry. They looked suspicious just sitting there watching to see what was going on. But it would look even more suspicious if they peeled off. It would attract even more attention.

Terry pulled over to the curb and parked the truck. Erin put her hand on his leg. "Terry? What...?"

"Just wait here," he advised. He climbed down from the truck and walked partway across the parking lot. He didn't walk right up to Ward or attempt to get by him into the police department. He stood well back of the van and nodded to Ward. Ward approached him and they met in the middle of the parking lot. Erin rolled down the truck window, but couldn't hear what they were saying.

She waited, watching their faces and their body language, trying to tell what they were saying and thinking. Discussing what had happened to Biggles. Where Jack Ward was transporting the body to. Terry's administrative leave. Ward would be very interested in everything that had happened.

Eventually, Terry nodded, shook hands with Ward, and headed back toward the truck. Erin watched as he got back into the truck and put it back into gear. He did not comment on the window being open, though Erin was ready with a comment about how warm it was and that she needed the fresh air.

"Yeah, he'll transport the body to the medical examiner," Terry acknowledged. "Probably not the kind of thing we want to talk about before dinner."

"No... I guess not..." Erin took a deep breath and let it back out again. "You saw him after? When he was dead?"

Terry looked at her for a minute and then nodded. They drove the rest of the way to the family restaurant in silence.

"I heard he had bruises."

"Gossip isn't always accurate."

Erin wasn't sure it could be classified as gossip when she had talked to someone who was actually there. It wasn't just idle chatter that had been repeated from one person to the next. Clara was a witness. She knew. She might be exaggerating or trying to get more attention than she deserved, but she had been there.

"Yes, he had bruises," Terry admitted.

He climbed down out of the truck again and went around the vehicle to Erin's side to give her a hand down. She didn't need it, but it felt good to have Terry looking after her, taking her hand, steadying her as she hopped down from the cab. Terry stopped, looking down into her face, his eyes intense.

"Do you really want to know the details?" he asked. "I don't think this is something you want to hear about. You have enough nightmares without adding new elements."

He might have something there. That was all true. But it would be worse to lose Terry. Jack Ward was already taking his measure. Wondering, as he stood there talking to Terry, whether he would be transporting Terry Piper to jail next. Erin had seen it in his eyes and the way he stood and held himself separate from Terry as they spoke.

If they put Terry in jail, they would have to put him in segregation so that he wouldn't be hurt. Criminals didn't like cops. It would be a lonely, miserable existence for him.

Sitting at the table, waiting for their 'meat plus three,' Erin answered Terry's question. "I want to know. About Biggles. I want to know what happened to him."

He looked across at her and took a sip of his drink. "Is that because you're planning on investigating it? Because I think we both know that's not a good idea."

"So it's true that he had bruises?"

Terry nodded. "He did."

"But he didn't have them when you arrested him?"

"Bruises can take a while to show up. It's conceivable that he had a fight before I arrested him."

"Will the medical examiner be able to tell that?"

"They might be able to tell how long it was before he died that he got them… but it won't be exact. And that's assuming that the body is still in good shape when they get it. It shouldn't have taken until now for it to be picked up. And I don't know whether Ward is going straight to the morgue. I assume so. You wouldn't want to be dragging a ripe corpse around for long. Kind of ruins the ambiance."

Erin wrinkled her nose. She did not need to be imagining the state of Biggles's body by the time it arrived at the medical examiner's office. "Why did it take so long for them to pick it up? Don't we have anywhere to store a body properly…?"

"Bald Eagle Falls is a small town. And bodies are not easy to move around. You don't just drag a man the size of Biggles from place to place without planning and at least a couple of men working together."

Erin nodded. "He couldn't have been easy for you to subdue, either. What do you do when you have someone that big who resists arrest?"

"I've got K9, a taser, pepper spray, a baton, and a gun. I'm well-prepared to take care of someone who resists."

"Did you have to use any of those things?"

"I used the taser," Terry admitted. "And the baton and considerable force. He wasn't going quietly."

"Wow. He must have really given you a fight."

Terry nodded grimly. "So there's no telling how many of those bruises might have been from the arrest. It took quite a bit of work to get him into handcuffs and the car."

"Were there bruises on his throat? I heard… that there were."

"I didn't choke him."

Erin nodded, accepting this. "But did he have bruises on his throat? If he did, then that means he did have a fight with someone other than you."

Terry considered his RC Cola. Erin suspected by the way Terry was looking at it that he wished he had ordered something a little stronger this time. He didn't usually have alcohol when they ate together. He felt that he needed to be prepared to be on duty at any time, and therefore, he did not drink regularly. But he wasn't going to get called in this time.

"Right. It would mean that he fought with someone other

than me. Because I never put my hands or my arm around his neck. Chokeholds of any kind are expressly forbidden."

"So he did have bruising on his neck?"

"Yes."

Erin ran her finger around the rim of her glass, thinking about that. So Biggles had been in an altercation with someone else. Who? And had it been before he had been arrested, or while he had been in custody? "Could it have been someone else in the police department? You weren't the only one who questioned him?"

"I wasn't with him the whole time he was in custody. But I'm not going to accuse someone else in the department of having brutalized him."

"No… but at least you have some defense… an alternate explanation. And if we can find out who it was that hurt him, we might be able to prove that you weren't the cause of Bo Biggles's death."

Terry grunted. He took a sip of his drink. They were quiet for a while, holding hands across the table, just thinking about the situation. Sandy, a perky waitress who was always telling dumb jokes to the children who ate at the restaurant, bustled over with their orders.

"Here you go. Y'all enjoy your meals!"

They both thanked her. Erin took a couple of bites of fried chicken. "What about the taser? Could it have… caused heart problems?"

"So we're back to me causing his death?"

"No… if he's resisting arrest and is a threat, then you have the right to use your taser. They're supposed to be safe. I'm just… wondering if that might have had something to do with it."

"It's possible," Terry conceded. "There have been several cases where deaths in custody have occurred after a taser was used, particularly on someone who is very young, elderly, or has a preexisting condition. But Biggles wasn't any of those things. He was a big, strong guy. In the peak of health, by all appearances."

"Just because he looked strong, that doesn't mean he was. I mean… he did die. He might have been a drug user, not just a dealer. Right?"

"Could be. A lot of these guys use recreationally."

"So he could have damaged his heart with drug use, and then the taser, and the stress of being arrested… it could all just be 'natural causes' couldn't it?"

"It was natural causes. Because I didn't do anything to cause his death."

"Right. That's what I mean. It wasn't your fault. Either it was from these other injuries that he sustained, or it was natural causes resulting from his arrest. It wasn't because you beat him up."

"No."

Terry concentrated on his steak. Erin looked away from the bloody meat.

Erin heard familiar voices and was diverted by the Fosters traipsing into the restaurant. The Fosters, and young Peter, in particular, were Erin's favorite customers. She smiled at the busy little family. At first, they were only concerned with their seating arrangements but, in a few minutes, the children were bored and looking around, and spotted Erin sitting with Terry.

"Cookie! Cookie!" Traci insisted, pointing at Erin excitedly. She knew who gave them the delicious cookies when she was out shopping with her mother.

Erin laughed. "I'm going to have to start carrying emergency cookies with me. I feel bad about not having something to give to her!"

She excused herself from the table and went over to greet the family, being sure to say hello to each child. She left Peter for last, and he chattered excitedly when she reached him.

"Thank you for making cookies for my party! Well, it wasn't actually a party, it was an important meeting…"

Mrs. Foster gave a little eye roll at that.

"You guys were designing your Halloween costumes?" Erin asked.

Peter nodded vigorously. "We want to have really good costumes this year. Not just something bought from the store."

"Yeah? What did you decide on?"

"Before I was thinking a superhero costume. I've been a superhero almost every year since I was born. But Monday I saw this guy in an ape mask, and it was really cool. Like it looked real."

Erin nodded, smiling.

"No masks," Mrs. Foster said flatly.

"Mom! I need a mask. I need a really real mask like that ape mask I saw," he told her seriously.

"The school won't let you wear masks, only face paint. And you can't wear a mask when you're going trick or treating, because you won't be able to see properly. So no masks."

"It was so cool! It looked just like a real ape!"

"I'm sure it was very cool," Mrs. Foster agreed. "But you need a costume without a mask."

Peter sat back, rolling his eyes and looking just like a teenager dealing with an unreasonable parent. Erin wondered how many times she had given her foster parents such looks. She had tried to be 'good,' but not showing her exasperation was not high on her list of things to worry about. It was no wonder they had gotten so irritated with her.

"Well, I'm sure you'll work something out," Erin assured Peter, staying out of the argument between mother and son. She had observed negotiations between Peter and his mother, and Peter usually managed to get his own way. Maybe he'd be able to wear a monkey mask at his own party and face paint at school and for trick or treating.

She smiled and tousled his hair and gave a little wave to the children. "I have to go back to my dinner before it gets cold. You guys enjoy yours!"

Erin returned to Terry, still smiling.

"You've appeased your adoring public?"

"Yes, even without cookies."

As they got into the truck, Erin caught sight of a familiar station wagon. Despite the weeks that had passed, Beaver hadn't repaired the damage to her front end. She had rear-ended Bo Biggles the last time he had been in town, resulting in a loud argument right in the middle of Main Street. Beaver had, Erin suspected, been trying to goad Bo Biggles into doing something he could be arrested for.

Terry started the engine. Erin put her hand on his arm to stop him. "Just wait for a minute."

He followed her gaze and saw Beaver's car. "You think something is going on?"

Erin shrugged. "Maybe. Let's wait and see."

Behind the seat, K9 let out a loud, exasperated sigh. Terry looked over the seat at him, the dimple appearing in his cheek. "Sorry, pardner. Stakeout for a few minutes."

K9 grumbled.

"You have to wonder how much they understand sometimes," Erin commented. She turned her attention back to Beaver's truck. "She's sitting waiting for someone, I think."

"Maybe. Maybe she's watching us, wondering why we're sitting here."

Erin pictured them both sitting watching each other and laughed. "Well, we'll see who breaks first."

But it didn't appear that Beaver had eyes on them after all. In a few minutes, another figure approached the dented vehicle: a slim figure, either a woman or a teenager.

"Who is it? Can you tell?"

Terry hesitated. He waited for a few seconds, then reached behind the seat, pushing things around until he came up with a pair of binoculars. Erin raised her brows. "You have surveillance equipment in your private vehicle?"

"What do you think I drive when I want to be unobtrusive? Besides, I didn't want to leave anything of mine in the squad car, in case..." He trailed off, not finishing the thought. He didn't need to. He didn't want to leave anything in his car in case he never got back to active duty again.

Terry raised the binoculars to his face and looked through them, focusing on the person Beaver was meeting with. He was still for a few minutes. Then he finally lowered them. He looked at Erin, frowning.

"Who is it?" Erin asked, reaching to take the binoculars from him and to have a look herself.

"Looks like one of the Cox boys. Campbell or Josh."

"Cam's been working with Beaver, so it must be him."

"Why would they be meeting here? I thought Campbell was out of town. Didn't he go into the city?"

"Yeah, but he could be here to see Beaver, or to visit Mary Lou. Who knows. There could be something going on at the school or something else that he wanted to be here for."

"Or there might be something else going on that he wanted to get the scoop on."

"Like what?" Erin took a couple of beats to connect it up. "You mean Bo Biggles's death? What would Cam have to do with that?"

"Nothing. At least, nothing that I can think of. But obviously there is something going on that we're not aware of."

He finally handed the binoculars to Erin and she took a look for herself. "Is that Campbell? Or is it Josh? They look so much alike, and I'm not sure I can tell them apart."

"I'm not sure either."

Erin watched him talking animatedly to Beaver. They were too far away for her to read their lips.

"Campbell is working with Beaver as some kind of informant. Maybe Josh is too. He could tell her what was going on at the high school better than Campbell. Cam's dropped out, at least temporarily."

"At the school where Biggles was dealing drugs."

"Yeah."

"What would his involvement be? A customer? A middleman? Or just someone who was keeping his ear to the ground?"

"I don't know. Mary Lou said that he's been having a hard time in school. I don't know who or what he might be involved with."

"I don't imagine things are too easy for a kid when his father has been incarcerated."

"No, I think they're having a pretty hard time. Even Mary Lou has been having problems with people she thought were friends, judging Roger and judging Mary Lou for what Roger did."

Terry shook his head. "The man is ill. That's not his fault or Mary Lou's."

"And especially not Campbell's or Josh's, but kids are cruel. And having to deal with something like that can be pretty distracting from schoolwork."

"Yeah."

They watched Beaver in her car for a few minutes, then Terry shrugged. "Not really anything else for us to see."

"I suppose not. I was hoping it would be something significant. Beaver does know some things about Bo Biggles. I don't know how much she shares about what she knows."

"She can be pretty closed-mouthed."

Terry put the truck into gear, and they headed to Erin's house.

Erin tried to concentrate on Clementine's family history files, but her mind kept wandering and she couldn't keep focused on what she was doing. Terry was watching TV, something he normally did very little of. He looked over at her when she sighed and pushed the file away from her.

"Too tired?"

"Tired… and antsy… anxious and exhausted… I feel like a caged animal." Erin looked at their animal companions. "No offense."

"I would suggest getting some exercise or getting out to do something, but if you do that you won't be able to get to sleep tonight. A warm bath? Or… maybe a massage…?" He raised his eyebrows, giving her a mischievous look.

Erin shrugged, trying to suppress a smile. "Maybe."

"Maybe?" He shifted closer to her. "What would I have to do to get you to a yes?"

"I don't know. Probably not too much."

"Good." Terry got to his feet. Erin stood up but, in a second, he had swept her off of her feet and was carrying her toward the bedroom.

"Hey!" Erin swatted at his arm. "I didn't say yes yet!"

"You will."

"I'm too heavy for you to carry!"

"You're as light as a feather." He took a deep breath, stopping to look her in the eye. "A very heavy feather."

"Hey!"

In a moment, he had carried her into the bedroom, and he pushed the door shut behind him to keep unwanted visitors out.

Terry dropped her to the mattress from a little higher than was strictly necessary, and Erin giggled as she bounced. One knee on the bed, Terry bent down and embraced her, brushing her cheek with a kiss.

"So, is it a yes?"

Erin nodded.

~

Terry's massage and the subsequent extracurricular activities relaxed Erin and cleared her mind so that she was able to fall asleep quickly. She awoke a couple of hours later and lay still, listening to Terry putting K9 into his crate and taking care of the other animals and the burglar alarm. He didn't usually go to sleep as early as she did, so it wasn't strange that he was still up. She lay there relaxed and drowsy, listening to his movements and, eventually, he returned to the bed and settled in for sleep. Erin cuddled up to him and, feeling warm and safe, dropped off to sleep again.

In the middle of the night, there was a loud yowl. Erin sat bolt upright in bed, heart pounding, trying to figure out what was going on. Terry moved beside her, not panicky like she was, but with stealthy, furtive movements.

"What was that?" Erin demanded, grabbing onto his arm. "Is it a burglar?"

"I armed the system. I don't think you need to be worried. Probably, Blossom just had a nightmare or saw a neighbor's cat in his yard. I'll go see."

Erin listened for any clues. "Be careful."

"I will."

She heard the soft clink of his belt buckle as he picked up his pants and pulled them on. He reached for something on the side table and then crept silently out of the room.

There was no noise of breaking glass or a car engine and tires as a vehicle made a quick departure. Everything remained quiet, the wind sighing outside, and the house creaking its usual old-house noises.

She heard Terry's low voice. "What are you making such a racket for, Blossom? You know you woke Erin up?"

And then she could hear Orange Blossom's loud, rumbling purrs. Erin relaxed, lying back down on her pillow and smoothing out her blanket. As long as Blossom was purring, she didn't need to worry that there was an intruder in the house. He did not take kindly to strangers being there in the night. He'd been her alarm more than once when something was not as it should be.

Terry returned to the bedroom. He was holding Orange Blossom and dumped him onto the bed on top of Erin.

"Maybe you can explain to him that yowling at things in the yard at two o'clock in the morning is not very polite. We need our beauty sleep."

Erin pulled the cat close and cuddled him. "It was probably just another cat, like you said. Or a possum. He doesn't like other critters in his territory."

"I didn't see or hear anyone nearby."

"Okay. Thanks for checking."

She heard him put his gun down on the bedside table and then the mattress sank down as he sat and removed his pants again. "Always happy to be at your service, Miss Price."

"Mmm. Then come cuddle up and help me go back to sleep."

He obeyed, putting his arms around her, and she let his warmth and Orange Blossom's purrs lull her back to sleep again.

She couldn't breathe.

There were hands around her throat, squeezing, cutting off her breath and the oxygenated blood to her brain.

Erin pried at the hands, trying to pull them away and get precious oxygen. She tried to protest, but couldn't make a sound, her vocal cords paralyzed by the pressure.

She reached out for Terry, feeling for him, trying to call for help.

The room was dark, but bright spots of light started to pop before her eyes like flashbulbs as consciousness began to fade.

"Erin."

She couldn't move. She thought she might be dead as he shook her and tried to get some response out of her. It was too late. The murderer had come and gone, and Erin was his latest victim.

Then she took a deep gasp of air, and full consciousness rushed back to her. Terry was shaking her, worriedly calling her name.

Released from her paralysis, Erin threw her arms around Terry and squeezed herself to him.

"Are you okay?" Terry demanded. "You scared me. Is everything okay?"

"I couldn't breathe."

"You're breathing now. Everything is going to be alright."

"I couldn't move. I couldn't call you. Everything was frozen."

He rubbed her back soothingly. "It's okay. Just another nightmare."

"It was just a dream?"

"Yes. Must have been a pretty bad one, huh?"

"Someone was choking me. Killing me."

"Oh, I'm sorry." He kissed her hair. "It's okay now."

Erin took a couple of shuddering breaths. "How did you know? I couldn't wake up and I couldn't move."

"I just woke up and couldn't hear you breathing. You were rigid. I thought you were having a seizure."

"Do you think that's what it was? I haven't had a dream like that before. Maybe something is wrong with my brain."

"I think it was just another nightmare. Are you worried? Do you want to see a doctor?"

Seeing a doctor would mean a drive into the city, then sitting in the emergency room waiting area for hours on end, only for the doctor to tell her that he wasn't sure what she had experienced, but there was nothing to indicate that she'd had a seizure or had anything wrong with her brain. And then she'd be stuck with a big medical bill for nothing at all. Better to stay home and go back to sleep. Or she could get up and start her day a few minutes early.

"No. It's okay. I don't need to see anyone. It was... just a dream."

"Maybe you have sleep apnea. You could get a sleep study done. Maybe there's a physical reason for all of the nightmares."

Erin already knew the reason for all of the nightmares. The dream of someone trying to strangle her was a new one, but they had predicted that.

"Someone choked Biggles," she said to Terry.

"Yes. I know."

"But it wasn't you."

"No."

"And he wasn't choked to death."

"Um… I don't know, Erin. We won't know until we hear back from the medical examiner."

"But if he was, that would mean it was someone who was at the police department. Someone you work with."

"Yes. But we can't rule that out just because we don't like it. Sometimes… people we know and trust can do terrible things. Things that we don't understand."

"If he was choked to death, he wouldn't already have a bruised throat when the sheriff found him, would he?"

"Hard to tell. I don't know how long it would have taken for them to develop. We took pictures. The medical examiner will have to tell us how old the bruises were and if that was the cause of death."

"What if it wasn't?"

"Well then… something else killed him."

"Maybe the taser."

"Maybe. But again… it wasn't until later. If it was the taser, wouldn't it have killed him right away?"

"I don't know."

"You should go back to sleep."

"I can't right now. Not when I can still feel those hands on my throat."

He rubbed her back and then stroked her hair back from her face, tucking it behind her ears. "You didn't think that it was me, did you?"

"That killed Biggles?"

"No. That was choking you. You didn't think I was choking you, did you?"

"Oh. No. I was trying to get to you… but I was paralyzed. I couldn't move."

"I've heard about sleep paralysis before. They don't know what causes it."

"Not a seizure?"

"No, I don't think so. We can ask someone tomorrow. Look it up on the internet."

"What if he was poisoned?"

Terry propped himself on one elbow to look down at her. "What?"

"Biggles. You had to feed him, right? Clara said something about picking up the dishes. So if you had to feed him, someone could have put something he was allergic to in the food. Or poison. Or he could have choked on something."

"Uh… I suppose. I couldn't see any sign that it was poisoning. And he didn't get welts like Angela did."

"But Trenton didn't either. Or the captain. Not everyone does. With some people, you can't tell."

"Go back to sleep. We can talk about it in the morning."

He wouldn't get up with her in the morning. He would still be sleeping when she had her tea and went to work.

"We won't be able to talk then. I won't be able to talk to you about it until after work, and then you won't want to."

"After work, we can make a list," he tempted, knowing how she liked to have everything written down in some kind of order. "If you go to sleep now, I'll help you to make a list tomorrow."

"Of everything?"

"Of everything. Whatever is on your mind. Anything that's bothering you."

"Okay." Erin yawned. "We should have made a list tonight."

"I think I enjoyed the way we spent the evening better than I would have writing a list." He chuckled into her neck, his breath giving her goosebumps. Erin squirmed.

"You're naughty. You're going to try to distract me from making a list tonight too, aren't you?"

"Maybe."

She rested in his arms, her body molded against his. The dream was drifting away from her, the terror disappearing.

But for Biggles, it hadn't disappeared. For him, the choking feeling hadn't stopped until he was dead.

*E*rin held Terry to his word the next evening, forcing him to sit down with pen and paper so that they could make lists and work through what they knew about Bo Biggles's death and what they needed to know to prove Terry innocent.

"I really just meant that if you wrote down everything that's been on your mind, it would help lighten the load," Terry said with chagrin, looking down at his pad of lined paper. "It's supposed to help to give you closure and get things off your mind."

"You said we could work on whatever was bothering me. I want to get this down. You said you would."

He grumbled, but he didn't go back on his word.

"Who was at the police department that day?" Erin demanded. "Working or coming in to file a complaint or anything. Everyone who was in and out of there."

"Well, me, of course. Sheriff Wilmot. Tom. Clara Jones. Melissa was in for a while, but not for a long time. I don't remember if Biggles was in custody when she was there or not... I think so."

"And who else? Anyone?"

"We had food brought over by Mr. Cooper, so that we didn't have to go out to get anything."

"Did he have access to Biggles?"

"No… I don't think so."

"Someone else took the food in to him? Who?"

"The sheriff. I'm pretty sure." Terry was still while he replayed the events of the day in his mind. "Yes, it must have been Sheriff Wilmot."

"Who made the food? Mr. Cooper?"

"I don't know. Maybe. Or maybe someone else at the store. They have a little catering department. I don't know who was working there that day."

"Write them all down," Erin insisted, noticing that he hadn't started making a list of the names. "Everyone who had access to the police department that day could be a suspect. And anyone who touched the food. We don't know if Biggles had an allergy or was poisoned. You don't know. Don't forget Roger Cox."

Terry nodded seriously. He started a list, putting down each of the names. "At least you hadn't sent over any cookies that day. And Melissa hadn't picked anything up from the bakery."

Erin nodded. "I don't need anyone adding me to the suspect list. I was far from the police department and have plenty of witnesses to prove it."

"Well, you and Vicky. But it isn't like you were far away. And you don't have customers there all the time. You could run an errand if you wanted to. Taking a tray over to The Book Nook or going out to the grocery or general store to pick up an ingredient that you needed while it was quiet."

"But I didn't. And Vic was there to confirm it."

He nodded, but didn't look convinced.

"I didn't have anything to do with this," Erin insisted, anger rising. She didn't know if he was serious or making a joke of it, but she didn't like to be accused of something she had nothing to do with. She had not been the one to take Biggles his food. And she hadn't provided any of the food that the man had eaten. She hadn't left the bakery, and she had someone to confirm that.

"I know you didn't," Terry agreed. "I'm just saying… when you're looking at alibis, you have to look at more than just what the person says. Of course they're going to say that they were never anywhere near the scene of the crime and that they have someone to provide them with an alibi for the entire time. But it isn't always the truth. People cover up or even forget. You might not remember from one day to the next when you had to take a tray over to The Book Nook or stop by the store to pick something up. People have faulty memories."

"Let's stick to who was at the police department. Because they are the only people who could have had anything to do with Biggles's death."

"Biggles's death was an accident. A freak thing. I know last night you had a nightmare about someone choking you, but that doesn't mean Bo Biggles was strangled. He appeared to be in perfectly good health when I arrested him. But a few hours later he was dead. But that doesn't mean that something I did when I arrested him killed him. And it doesn't mean that it was murder. Sometimes these things happen. People get panicked when they get arrested. They get stressed about it. They think that they don't have anything to look forward to in life."

"They can't talk themselves into dying."

"Well… I think they can. When people think that they have no reason left to live… they can die without any apparent cause."

Erin thought about that. She wasn't quite sure she agreed, but he had a good point. Sometimes people died of a broken heart, or stress, or died mysteriously after they told someone they were going to die. People were told that they had been cursed, and subsequently died just because they thought they were going to. Maybe Terry had a point.

But Biggles was part of an organization. He had experience. He would have known that a simple arrest wasn't a reason to give up. He knew that the clan would get him a good lawyer, that he could negotiate a sentence, that he would be protected on the inside by his gang affiliations and would be able to get out again and go right back to dealing and bringing in buckets of money. Or he could retire from crime and start something new. Second chances were a thing.

"Okay. Maybe he talked himself into it, but I don't think so. And I don't think he was hypnotized to kill himself or to stop breathing."

Terry smiled and shrugged. "No. It was probably something a lot more ordinary."

"He had bruises. Someone choked him either before or after you arrested him. Maybe it had something to do with his death and maybe not, but we have to find out who that was."

There was a tap at the door. Erin looked up from the table to see who it was and motioned for Jeremy to enter. He walked in, smiling and nodding at her, and Beaver entered behind him. She chewed on a thick wad of gum and looked them over.

"Hard at work, I see."

Terry shrugged and Erin caught an eye roll. He looked down at the pad of paper and slid his arm over the list, casually blocking it from view.

"We were just making some lists," Erin said, not sure why Terry would be concerned about keeping the information from Beaver, another law enforcement officer. She was afraid he was embarrassed to be seen making lists with Erin. Maybe he didn't think that it was a good use of their time.

"Have you solved Bo Biggles's murder yet?" Jeremy asked with a laugh.

"Biggles's death hasn't been determined to be a murder," Terry replied evenly. "It might have been accidental or suicide. We don't know yet. We have to wait and see what the medical examiner decides."

"If they decide anything," Beaver said. "It could just as easily end up undetermined. Deaths in custody can be tricky." Her eyes moved over Terry. "If he was killed, then the person who killed him may have been careful to leave no evidence."

"We don't know that anyone *did* kill him," Terry reiterated.

"That's what I said."

"Beaver, it wasn't me. I had nothing to do with his death."

"Well…" Beaver stretched the word out, "I don't know that you can say that you had *nothing* to do with it, when you were the one who arrested and interrogated him. You had at least peripheral involvement. That doesn't mean you were the cause of his death, but you were there. You are the person who had the most contact with him before he died."

"Which is why I am on administrative leave while they investigate it," Terry growled. "I'm well aware of that."

"I'm not accusing you of doing anything wrong."

He glared at her. "It certainly isn't coming off that way."

Jeremy hugged Beaver around the shoulders, pulling her toward him protectively. As if he needed to defend her. It was laughable. Beaver was both older than Jeremy and, as far as Erin could tell, had far more training and experience with physical threats than he did. She wasn't a defenseless little woman who needed his protection. Beaver leaned into Jeremy rather than pulling away. Her eyes were animated as she looked Terry over.

"I sometimes come across as provoking people when I mean nothing of the sort," she drawled. "Don't take me the wrong way."

"I don't think I am."

She just smiled and chewed her gum.

Erin's heart was pounding. She didn't like any conflict and especially didn't want to see it between her friends. She liked and admired Beaver, but the woman was an irritant, and intentionally so. Terry was Erin's partner, and she didn't want to see Beaver trying to get a rise out of him.

"Beaver doesn't mean anything," she told Terry, putting her hand on his arm. "It's just like you said; we won't know anything until the medical examiner comes back with a cause of death. It could be that his heart just failed."

Beaver chewed and nodded. "After he was choked."

"I didn't choke him," Terry said.

"And tased."

"I..." Terry's brows drew down. He looked at her. "How would you know that? That hasn't been released."

"It doesn't need to be released. It's part of your statement."

"And why would you have access to my statements? How are you involved in the investigation?"

Beaver just smiled and raised an eyebrow. Erin had never been able to decide which federal agency Beaver worked for. She was definitely involved in drug enforcement around Bald Eagle Falls so, even if she wasn't involved in the internal affairs investigation of Terry's actions, she might have still had access to his statement under her drug investigation.

"Everything I did was within the bounds of our policies," Terry said. "You know that."

"I did warn you that you might need assistance in bringing him in."

"I managed just fine without any help. K9 and I managed."

K9, stretched out at Terry's feet, raised his head to look at his master. Then he put his head back down again.

Erin looked at Beaver. "*You* told Terry about Biggles? Why didn't you arrest him yourself?"

"I didn't catch him dealing. I just saw him... in town."

There was a look exchanged between Beaver and Terry. Erin tried to interpret it. There was more that Beaver wasn't saying. She had told Terry that he might have trouble arresting Biggles. She knew he had used his taser. What else did she know that she wasn't saying?

"Did you see Biggles when he was in custody?" she asked thoughtfully. "Did you question him too?" She looked over at Terry's list, which was still covered. He hadn't mentioned Beaver being there. But would he have? He'd kept her name out of it otherwise, even though she was apparently the one who had tipped him off to Biggles being in town.

"I might have looked in on him."

"So you could be a suspect in his death just as much as Terry."

"I didn't have any reason to kill Biggles. It was more beneficial to me if he was alive to testify against his co-conspirators."

"But he might not have been intentionally killed. You might have just…"

"Given him a little hug?" Beaver suggested dryly.

Erin had a momentary vision of Beaver choking Biggles. He was a big man and, although Beaver was tall and lanky, Erin wasn't sure she could have put him in a chokehold while he was standing. He would have had to be sitting, kneeling, or lying down. And Terry had said that chokeholds were forbidden. Beaver wouldn't have any excuse for choking him. No one did. No one professional, anyway. Someone with training would not have done that. Someone who was trying to defend themselves or attacking Biggles in a rage, however, that would be different. Where had he gotten the bruises on his throat?

"Nobody killed Biggles on purpose," Jeremy said dismissively. He gave Beaver another squeeze, then let her go. "It was just one of those crazy things. It wasn't anything anyone did wrong."

Erin sighed. She didn't want any of her friends to have had anything to do with his death. She'd had to deal with that before, and she didn't want to find out that someone else she knew had been pushed into killing someone. Even if there was good reason to permanently remove someone like Biggles from Bald Eagle Falls, she didn't want Terry or Beaver or the sheriff or anyone else at the police department to have caused his death. She wanted it to be an outsider. Someone she didn't know or care about.

"Maybe it was a clan thing," she suggested. "Could it have been someone from the Jackson or Dyson clan?"

They all looked at each other, weighing the possibilities. Eventually, everyone was looking at Jeremy for his opinion.

"He's Jackson clan," Jeremy said. "So it wouldn't be Jacksons.

Could it be Dysons? Sure… but why would they kill him when he was in custody? And they'd have to know about the arrest pretty quickly for someone to get there and deal with him. And then… how would they get into the police department? That's a restricted area."

"But he might have had a fight with one of them before Terry arrested him," Erin pointed out. "He could have gotten the bruises earlier, not while he was in custody."

"And if he was in a fight with a Dyson, what happened?" Terry asked. "Why didn't anyone report it? Was he on his own or did he have Jacksons there to watch his back? And why a hand-to-hand fight instead of weapons?"

"I don't know. You're supposed to be helping me come up with explanations."

Terry gave a brief smile. "Yeah. Sorry about that. Forgot myself for a minute."

"If it was while he was in custody, it could have been the Jacksons." Erin pursed her lips and looked at Jeremy. "Maybe they were afraid he was going to talk? Turn in other gang members?"

Jeremy shook his head. "How are they going to get at him? He's locked in a room in the police department. You think they could stroll in there and no one would notice?"

Erin tried to visualize what she knew of the layout of the police department offices. She knew Clara Jones's desk and Terry's office. She'd been in Sheriff Wilmot's office. She wasn't sure of the room where Biggles would have been detained.

"Where exactly was he?" she asked Terry. "Near the back?"

He hesitated, looking at the question from several angles before deciding to answer. "Yes, the room he was in was near the back of the building. You can't walk back there without everybody else in the office seeing you."

"What if someone came in the back door? Like where Jack Ward was parked. Does that lead straight into your offices, or into the Town Hall?"

"There's a shared hallway with some maintenance rooms and a

loading dock area. You'd have to go through a second door to get into the police department through the back."

"But you could do it. There is a way to get in through the back instead of walking past everybody else."

Terry shrugged uncomfortably. "Yes… but no one did. They still would have been seen. It's not that big of a place. And I was with Biggles most of the time. Someone coming in would have been face-to-face with me."

Beaver chomped on her gum, watching Erin's face with disconcerting intensity.

"But if they were watching, you weren't there the whole time. And you guys took a break to eat. Can you take me there? To see where the door is and how it's laid out?"

"No."

"Terry…"

"Erin, I can't even go back there myself. I'm on leave. I have no business going back there."

"Couldn't you find a reason? You need to pick up something personal that you left in your desk. And because you're just stopping in for a minute, and I happened to be along…"

"What are you going to see? Just my office. You've seen that before."

"I want to walk in through the back."

"You're not going to be able to see anything."

"But then I'll stop bugging you."

"Oh, will you?" he challenged.

Erin's face got hot. She shrugged and looked away from him, unable to suppress a smile of embarrassment at Beaver and Jeremy.

"You're not going to find anything," Jeremy chimed in. "It wasn't the Jacksons. You can be sure of that."

"How do you know that?"

He didn't come up with an answer. Erin fixed him with her stare, waiting for him to break. If he didn't have any more contact with the Jacksons, how could he state that they hadn't had any involvement? He couldn't know that.

Beaver tilted her head and looked at her young boyfriend. "Have you talked to someone?" she prodded. "Had any text or email exchanges?"

"No, of course not. I'm just telling you, I know how they work, and they wouldn't break into the police department to beat someone up and kill them while they were in police custody. That would be... like The Godfather or something. Things don't happen like that in real life. Or not with the clans, anyway. Maybe somewhere like New York or Chicago where they have big, powerful organizations. But in Tennessee? Come on."

rin? Earth to Erin!"

Erin blinked and looked up from her mixer to see Vic leaning toward her, trying to get her attention. Erin shook her head, feeling mesmerized by the noise and movement of the mixer. She obviously wasn't getting enough sleep if she could zone out that easily.

"Sorry, what was that?"

"I was asking you about treats for Halloween. Are we going to do some cutout cookies again this year?"

"They were a big hit last year, so probably," Erin agreed. "I'll make sure that everyone is onside Sunday."

"You'll make sure that Charley agrees with you, you mean."

"Well, she is my partner."

"I know, but she can't tell you what to make and not to make. And she doesn't have the experience that you do. You were here for Halloween last year, and you know how things sold."

Erin shook her head. "I can't believe it's been a year. For a few days there, it looked like everything was going to shut down completely. I didn't think the bakery was going to last."

"I know, I remember. It was scary. But this year, no controversy, no one is going to be boycotting us over rumors."

"Seems like there's always some kind of controversy. If it's not one thing, it's another."

"Terry, you mean?" Vic asked, looking sympathetic.

"Yeah. I don't know what he's going to do if he can't get back on active duty. Or if people decide that he's responsible for Biggles's death even though he didn't do anything. What are we going to do?"

"I don't know. I'd hate for you to even think about moving somewhere else. But if he can't work here… I don't know."

"I couldn't ask him to give up police work. It's what he does best. It's what he lives for."

Vic nodded her agreement. "I know."

"Tell Willie thank you for taking Terry with him today. I don't think he could stand another day just hanging around his house. Or mine. He needs to have a mission. Something to do."

"Willie will be around later; you can tell him yourself. He likes Terry. He's happy to help out."

"But there's only so much he can help Willie with too."

"Willie said Terry was going to help him with a security issue today," Vic contributed. "Which probably means stringing wire for a fence. And one day they're going to go fishing. I don't know if they have any plans other than that."

"Yeah. Then I'm going to have to think of ways to keep him busy… but it's going to be more than a couple of days. I'm worried it's going to be weeks… even months. I can't distract him for that long. I don't know what to do."

Vic shrugged, raising her hands up to shoulder height and shaking her head. "I don't know. Maybe he could get another job, temporarily. Security, like Jeremy is doing."

"I thought about that… I'm just worried it will drive him crazy. He's been such a good town cop, he's always got his eye on everything and knows what everyone is up to. It's not just walking a beat, it's actually caring about people and knowing what's going on in town. Just walking around a warehouse, even if he has K9 with him, is a huge step down from what he's been doing. Maybe if he could be a private investigator… but there's not a lot to investigate in Bald Eagle Falls. He'd probably be out of town all the time."

One of the ovens dinged, and Erin moved over to it to take the next couple of trays out to cool. She turned off the timer and looked at the hot, fragrant muffins in front of her.

"I'm going to take these over to the police department."

Vic's eyes widened. "What?"

"It's been a while since they had an order. We have to whet their appetites. Keep them coming back for more."

Vic stood there with her mouth open for a minute. "You're just going over there to snoop."

Erin couldn't help the guilty smile that crept across her face. "I'm just taking some muffins over. Have to keep the boys in blue happy."

"That made sense when Terry was there and you wanted to see him for a minute and do him a favor. Not so much now that he's off."

"And I have to show them that there are no hard feelings. We wouldn't want to lose their business just because Terry isn't there anymore, would we?"

"Well, no ma'am. We wouldn't want that."

"Then I'd better make up a box and take them over while they're still warm."

In a few minutes, Erin was walking down the street with her box of muffins. The days were getting cooler; it didn't feel like stepping out into an oven when she opened the door and went outside. It was pleasant, especially after the chilly days on the cruise ship. She hadn't been bothered by the cold as much as Vic, but it still had been a big change from the warm Tennessee fall to the cold Canadian and Alaskan autumn.

Erin saw Mary Lou through the window at The General Store and decided to stop in for a quick minute.

Mary Lou smiled and patted her hair when Erin entered, making sure that nothing was out of place. She smoothed her pantsuit. "What are you doing out and about today? I thought you were on at Auntie Clem's all week to make up for your vacation."

"I am. But it was quiet, and I decided to run some baking over to the police department."

"Oh." Mary Lou raised both brows, looking surprised at that. "Well, why not? You can take baking wherever you like; it isn't like anyone is going to turn you away." She smiled in good humor.

"I was thinking maybe I'd get one of those little jam and marmalade sets I saw you selling the other day. They're so cute. And then if someone wants something sweet on one of their muffins…"

"Like they're not sweet enough already." Mary Lou shook her head at the idea of putting more sugar on top of the muffins. But she was already moving to pick up one of the sets of little jam jars. She wrapped it in paper to keep anything from getting broken and took it to the till to ring up Erin's order. "Would you like anything else?"

Erin put her box down on the counter and looked around, but couldn't think of anything else that she might conceivably need for the police department or the bakery. She was well-supplied with everything else she needed. "No… I guess that's all. I just wondered… how you're doing."

"Me? I'm about the same as ever." Mary Lou brushed off the inquiry.

"No, really. I want to know how you are. I know it's been tough on you since Roger's… accident. And now with Campbell being out on his own and it just being you and Josh… how's his school going? I worry about how hard it must be, them talking about his dad and teasing him… kids can be so cruel. And even if they're not teasing him, he's probably still distracted... just because of everything that happened. People talk about their teenage years being so ideal, but I remember being a teenager... and it wasn't much fun."

Mary Lou gazed at her for a moment. Her eyes were suddenly shiny, reflecting the light of the room. She turned her face away from Erin, busying herself with putting the jam jars into a bag and punching the price into the till.

"Thank you, Erin. Yes... it's been hard on Josh and I worry about him all day long. I miss the days when he was little and he was at home, and I could look after him. I could make sure that he was safe and keep him happy just by opening the big bin of Lego bricks for him. He was such an active little boy; I didn't know how I was going to last until he was old enough for school. And now... I wish for the simplicity of those days again."

Erin nodded. She wondered whether to mention to Mary Lou that she had seen Campbell or Josh with Beaver the other day, but decided it would probably just make her worry more. But Mary Lou's brain seemed to shift in that direction anyway.

"Josh's marks at school are abysmal. He was always a good student, even after Roger's accident. The boys both worked so hard to keep things normal. But when Roger was arrested... everything changed. Josh has dropped out of all of the sports teams. I have to keep reminding myself that at least he's still going to school. Campbell, on the other hand... I wish I had some clue what he was up to."

"He doesn't tell you anything?"

"Nothing of any substance. He was out with this friend or that friend, at a party or hanging out or doing whatever kids do when they're not out working or doing something constructive. Drinking, I'm sure. Hopefully, nothing worse than that... but he wouldn't tell me if he was. He doesn't want me to have to worry."

"Like you don't worry when you have to imagine it."

Mary Lou nodded her agreement. "Sometimes I think that the things he is really doing couldn't be any worse than what I am imagining… and then I imagine what would be worse than what I was already imagining…"

Erin laughed, nodding. Poor Mary Lou. "But you know he was helping out Beaver, so that must be some reassurance… whatever it is that he's up to, he was at least helping law enforcement. Maybe he'll decide he wants to be a cop."

"He'd have to finish school if he wants a career in law enforcement. But whenever I suggest that he should be going back before it's too late and he's lost too much time… he always tells me that I'm getting too stressed out about it, and he can go back whenever he's ready. And he just isn't ready yet. He's still finding himself. He wants to have some fun while he's still a kid."

When Erin had been Campbell's age, she'd still been going to school but, knowing that she wouldn't be able to get any education past twelfth grade, she had also been trying to build up her work experience so that she would have some chance of supporting herself when she aged out of foster care. Just wanting to have some fun being a kid hadn't been in the cards for her.

"How can he afford to do anything? Is he working?"

Mary Lou shrugged. "Another of the things I can't get pinned down. I think he does some casual labor, maybe some panhandling, whatever he's doing for Beaver… these kids get together in groups to cover the bills, but he doesn't have a place of his own. I wouldn't exactly say he was homeless, but he doesn't have a permanent address."

"Does he come to see you when he comes home to Bald Eagle Falls?" Erin asked, thinking about seeing Cam or Josh talking to Beaver.

"He hasn't been back in town. I don't know if he'll ever come back here. Not to live, for sure. For a visit… I'd like to see him. I assume I will sooner or later."

Mary Lou handed Erin her bag, holding on to it for an instant after Erin took it, both of them connecting in a small way.

Mary Lou's eyes welled with tears again. "When I think about what could have happened if it had been one of my boys that Officer Piper arrested…"

"Oh! Oh, no, don't think like that. Terry didn't do anything wrong. Biggles resisted arrest, and… well, Cam or Josh wouldn't do that. And they're not big guys like Biggles. Terry wouldn't have to… it would be easier for him to control one of them."

Mary Lou just shook her head.

"Terry wouldn't do anything to hurt one of your boys," Erin said urgently. "You can't think that."

"The police will do what they have to… and if they think that someone is a danger…"

"Mary Lou…"

"That could have been one of my boys," Mary Lou said fiercely. "You think it's okay because he was a drug dealer, but it's not. He's someone's son too."

Erin walked the rest of the way to the police department, thinking about Mary Lou's statement. She had thought that Mary Lou would be happy to have Bo Biggles off the street and away from the school; she hadn't thought about how Mary Lou would worry about her boys and how they could end up in trouble like that. Everyone always said what good boys Campbell and Josh were, it was hard for her to adjust her thinking to the fact that they could get into trouble just as easily as any of the other boys Erin had known growing up. Just like Bo Biggles. He'd had to start somewhere. Had he been a nice boy once? Or had he always been a little hood with his fingers in all of the pies?

She felt bad for Mary Lou. Erin was worried about Terry, but she'd never had to worry about kids and about them going off-track. She could remember how she had worried about Carolyn when she was younger. Carolyn was the one who had inspired her to start a gluten-free bakery, a foster sister who just couldn't be different from her friends and go without the nice treats that they could have, even though she had been told it was killing her. She'd needed so much to be the same and to have what everyone else had.

Clara Jones was at her desk at the police department and raised her eyebrows when she saw Erin, doing a doubletake. "What are you doing here? You know Officer Piper is off."

"I know, but I thought you might be pining for some muffins."

Erin put the box down on Clara's desk and opened it up to display the variety of muffins to Clara. "You get first pick. What's your favorite?"

"Oh…" Clara looked at them and inhaled the fragrant steam escaping the box. "They are all so good." Her hand hovered over the box as she decided on first one, and then another. Finally, she went with a blueberry muffin. "You know, I was telling my sister about how none of your baking tastes like it's gluten free. You would swear that it was just normal baking with wheat flour. I would think that you were cheating, only I know people who can't eat wheat or gluten, and they can eat your baking without getting sick."

Erin smiled. It was rare to hear anything positive from Clara, especially something about Erin or Auntie Clem's. "Well, thank you! I'm really glad you enjoy it. I love being able to bake great treats for people who wouldn't normally be able to have them."

"You do a good job," Clara admitted.

"I'll take these to the kitchen for you."

Clara nodded, and Erin removed the box and walked past Clara's desk toward the little kitchen area to put the muffins where everyone could help themselves. She looked at each of the offices quickly as she walked by. Terry's office, empty until they decided he could get back on active duty. Tom didn't qualify for a full office; he shared with Melissa and other part-time workers who were in and out. Erin wasn't sure where the dispatcher worked from. She must have had a dedicated office somewhere else or worked from home or a cell phone. Erin passed Sheriff Wilmot's office last.

Erin stopped at the kitchen counter and put down the muffin box. No one was paying her any attention. It wasn't difficult at all to walk into the police department and have the run of the place without anyone confronting her. As long as she had a good reason to be there. Someone else would have to use a different diversion to get in, but Erin didn't imagine it would be too hard. It was a small town. People trusted each other. Mostly.

She emptied the dregs of the coffee in the carafe and rinsed it out. Then she added grounds to the hopper and started a new batch brewing. It would be nice for everyone to have fresh coffee to go with the muffins. Erin looked around, scoping out the remaining rooms that she was less familiar with. There were three interview rooms. There was another door that might lead to a supply cabinet. There was a small commode so that they didn't have to leave to use the public restrooms in the main part of the Town Hall. Erin took a glance around, then walked toward the interview rooms. No one stopped her or paid any attention.

She looked in the narrow window of the first room. Like the window in a school classroom, it had wires running through the glass to make it stronger and prevent anyone from putting their fist through it. Erin tested the door handle. It turned easily in her hand and she swung the door open. It gave only a small squeak, easily missed with the bustle of a busy office, especially with the coffee maker burbling and a printer spitting out papers on Clara's desk.

Erin took a glance around the room, empty but for a table and chairs. She pulled it shut and went on to the next room. Very similar to the first, but with the chairs upholstered in a dark blue, rather than with plastic seats. The walls were a gross green color that was either supposed to be soothing or to camouflage stains. The third room was smaller, with a camp cot in the corner. It was bare, with no blankets on it. Erin imagined they had all been sent away as evidence. There was a smaller table with just two chairs.

Erin thought at first that it would be dangerous to leave a convict in a cell with chairs that he could throw around and use as a weapon, but when she took a closer look, she saw that they were anchored to the floor. Maybe King Kong could pick them up, but not Erin and not, she didn't suppose, Bo Biggles. The cot was the only thing in the room that was movable.

"Miss Price."

Erin jumped and gave a little squeal. She whirled around to face Sheriff Wilmot. She could feel all of the blood rushing to her face.

CHAPTER 19

"Uh… Sheriff. Hi. Sorry, I was just…"

"Having a look at our crime scene?" He shook his head, brows down. "You don't have any reason to be in here. This is off limits to the public."

"I'm sorry. I brought some muffins, and I just realized as I was putting them out that this must be…"

She didn't know why she couldn't finish her sentences. The look on his face was so forbidding that she just kept trailing off into silence, unable to complete her explanation.

"I can see what you were doing." He waited, looking at her. "Have you seen everything you needed to now?"

Erin looked down at her feet. She knew that she shouldn't have been snooping around. She was supposed to be at the bakery, making and selling her wares, not at the police department poking her nose where it didn't belong. She swallowed. She'd left Vic to take care of all of the customers and had just paraded off to investigate, even though she knew she shouldn't.

"Uh. Sorry. Yeah." Erin looked toward the back door of the suite. "Could I go out this door? I wanted to check on something. I just… I think I can get to…"

Sheriff Wilmot's skepticism was palpable. Erin blushed furiously. She motioned toward the door again. "I'll just be going…"

He didn't make a move to stop her. Erin swallowed hard and walked down the short hall to what looked like an outside door with a crash bar. She pushed it open. No alarms sounded. Erin walked through the doorway and let the door close behind her, taking a glance behind her to see whether the sheriff was following her. He watched her go but did not pursue her.

It led, as Terry had said, to a shared corridor with some pipes, mops, a couple of doorways to utility or storage rooms. Erin didn't open the other doors, worried about opening the door on one of the janitors and having to explain herself again. She'd done such a wonderful job with the sheriff, after all.

Someone could hide in one of those rooms, provided they weren't in use. They could wait there until all was quiet and they could sneak into the police department and access the interview rooms.

Someone would have to be pretty gutsy to do that. Erin felt like throwing up after being caught by Sheriff Wilmot. He'd always been kind to her in the past, even when she was a suspect, and she didn't like to give him a reason to think that she was a nut-job. Or a snoop.

Erin looked around. There was no evidence that anyone had been there and had propped the door or left anything behind. Erin reached back and pulled on the door she had just closed. It was locked.

It could only have been someone who had a key. Or else it had been left unlocked that day, and the fact that it was locked now was just evidence of locking the barn after the horse was gone. Erin pulled on it one more time to make sure that it wasn't just stuck. It was definitely locked.

She walked briskly to the next door, another metal door with a crash bar. She opened it, and there were no alarms. She found herself in the parking lot where she had seen Jack Ward a couple of nights previously.

Was that the first time that Jack Ward had been by? Was there any possibility that he had visited the police department when he heard that Biggles had been arrested? He would know the layout of the police department from previous visits. He'd know that he could probably walk right in without being seen. And if he was seen, he was a law enforcement officer and had good reason to be there. Bo Biggles was from his jurisdiction, and no doubt there were warrants or at least complaints or suspicions that Jack Ward could claim to be following up on. If his department did transport for Bald Eagle Falls regularly, maybe he had a key. He could let himself in the back, into that detention room, and… what? Attack Biggles? If he spent time interrogating Biggles, he would surely have been spotted by the Bald Eagles Falls staff. If he were the one who had choked Biggles, he would have to have been in and out in a couple of minutes, and Erin couldn't think of a scenario where that behavior made much sense.

Erin looked around. There wasn't anything to see in the parking lot.

"Miss Price!"

Erin looked around to see who had called her. It wasn't Sheriff Wilmot's voice this time. Not an adult and not an accusation. Erin spotted a young boy waving. She waved back and, as he got a few steps closer, realized that it was Peter Foster. She strode toward him, happy to leave the police department behind and to see her little friend.

"Peter! How are you?"

"Good! Just going home for lunch!" He made a motion to indicate the crescent behind the Town Hall. Erin wasn't sure which house was his.

"You're nice and close to the school. That's great."

"Yeah. But my mom says that being so close makes me late. People who are farther away are more careful to leave early. I can still run over when I hear the first bell, if I'm really fast, and get to my desk." He smiled, proud of himself and getting pink with embarrassment at the same time.

Erin nodded. "I can see why you wouldn't want to leave until it was time."

"Sometimes I like to go early, so there's time to play with my friends on the playground. But sometimes, I want to see the ending of a show or I don't feel good… and then I'm bad, and I don't go until it's almost too late."

Erin chuckled. "You're not bad, Peter. Just… a little late sometimes."

He smiled and nodded. "Okay, I got to run. I'm not supposed to stop and talk to people on my way home." He rolled his eyes dramatically. "Even if I know them," he said, as if it were a catechism that had been drilled into him.

Erin waved as he hurried away. "See you later!"

Erin served Terry his dessert, some leftover cookies from the bakery, and sat down to help him eat them. The animals were happily munching on their own treats, though Orange Blossom had already gobbled up his and was eyeing K9's biscuit in hopes of getting some of the crumbs.

"So you had a good day working with Willie?"

Terry shrugged. He looked pleasantly fatigued instead of anxious like he had the past few days. At least whatever they had been working on had helped him to forget his troubles for a while. Maybe there was some hope that he could be happy even if he could not get back onto active duty. Maybe he could find something else and be satisfied with it.

"Willie is a good guy," Terry said slowly. "Not always aboveboard as far as the law is concerned… but still good-hearted and always eager to help a friend."

Erin chuckled. "I guess being brought up in one of the clans, you couldn't expect him to always toe the line as far as the law is concerned. But I think he tries."

"He seems determined to only take honest work," Terry said

slowly, pondering it, "but as far as keeping to the letter of the law… he's not so concerned about that."

Erin nibbled at a chocolate chip cookie, hoping to make it last until Terry had cleared the rest off of the serving plate. "As long as he's only taking honest work, why worry about it? Those other little things aren't that much of a concern, are they?"

"Those little things can turn into big things. If you're not going to let the law determine what is right and wrong, and you're not following prescribed religious principles… then what you're doing is deciding for yourself what is right and wrong, setting up your own system of morals… and that can be dangerous. You can justify anything if it benefits you."

"But Willie…" Erin didn't like it when Terry talked about Willie like he was a criminal. He wasn't. He was a good guy like Terry had said, and he took good care of Vic, and he had helped Erin out at times when she had needed it. He wasn't running with the clans or dealing drugs or doing anything else that made him a hazard to Erin or anyone else in Bald Eagle Falls. Terry made it sound like everything he did was shady, and like he was a psychopath who would take out anyone who got in his way. She didn't like to think of Willie that way. "Willie wouldn't do anything to harm any of us. You know that."

Terry polished off another cookie and his hand hovered over the plate for a few seconds before he picked up a ginger snap. "I would trust Willie to take care of you girls and not to do anything to put anyone innocent in physical danger. But who knows what he did while he was a soldier with the Dysons? Trust me; they are not going to allow anyone who has been inducted into their ranks to get away with penny-ante stuff. If you're a soldier with the Dysons, you're all-in."

"But he's out now. He served his term and then he was released. He's not working for them anymore. Or if he does, it's just for things like computer security."

"That's what he says. And I'm not saying that he does anything else for them. But once you have lived that kind of life, I'm not sure I believe you can just turn it off again. Once you've crossed those lines, you're not going to hesitate to do it again just because it's against the law. I'd be a lot happier if I knew exactly what the limits of Willie's personal morality were. But I'm not sure it's a constant. I think he takes every situation as it comes and weighs the personal costs and benefits. And that's a dangerous way to live."

Erin used her finger to wipe up a bit of melted chocolate from the plate and licked off her finger. Orange Blossom was creeping toward K9. He normally stayed as far away from K9 as possible and hissed and puffed up if K9 paid him any attention. But that did not hold true if K9 had a treat and Blossom didn't. Then he would put his usual sensitivities aside and get close enough to lick the crumbs from K9's face. Like Willie, he was flexible in his standards. "You don't think that Willie had anything to do with Biggles's death, do you?"

Terry pressed his lips together. "Willie was with the Dysons. If he's still doing jobs for them, then it is possible he would want to take Biggles out. But why wait until he was in custody? Unless Biggles had information on Willie or could rat the Dysons out for something. It would have made a lot more sense for him to deal with Biggles when he was in town last time, or when he was in Moose River."

"So you don't think Willie had anything to do with it."

"No." He met her gaze. "I don't think *anyone* killed him. I think it was just one of those things. A weird coincidence. Inexplicable. Natural causes. Whatever the medical examiner decides to call it. I don't think anyone intentionally killed him."

Erin nodded. She knew it was a long shot. The only reason she wanted it to be murder was so that they could prove that it hadn't been Terry's fault.

Terry pulled his phone out and put it on the table beside him, tapping the screen. "Sorry. Got a message."

As he looked at the screen, his expression darkened and his mouth turned down.

"What is it?"

He shook his head. "Sheriff wants to see me."

"Why?"

"He says he wants to ask me some questions."

Erin's stomach twisted into a knot. Was the sheriff calling Terry in to talk to him about Erin and her poking around at the police department?

"Did he say what about?"

"There's only one thing he'd be calling me in to talk to him about. And I am not looking forward to being on the other side of the table."

"Couldn't he just talk to you on the phone? You could tell him whatever he needed to know."

"It's not the same as having a face-to-face interview with someone. You miss out on body language; you can't control the environment. The person knows that they can just hang up at any time. It's much more efficient to talk to someone directly."

Erin bit her lip, trying to decide whether to bring up her visit to the police department. Terry misinterpreted her expression. He put a hand over hers and attempted a reassuring smile.

"It will be okay, Erin. I can deal with the sheriff's questions. He's just clearing up loose ends."

"It might be... because of me."

"What?" His frown swiftly returned.

"I took some muffins over to the police department."

The crease between his eyebrows deepened. "The day Biggles died? I don't remember seeing any muffins."

"No. Today."

"Okay...?" He cocked his head.

"It's been a while since I sent anything over, and I thought they might like a treat."

Orange Blossom, sitting just inches in front of K9, looked over at Erin and yowled plaintively. He knew what a treat was, and if someone else was getting one, why wasn't he? Erin laughed, though she was still anxious about explaining to Terry what had happened.

"You thought they might like some muffins," Terry said, deliberately avoiding repeating the word *treat*. "And that you might look around while you were there."

Erin cleared her throat and nodded, looking down at a crumb on the table.

Terry chuckled. "Nothing is going to stop you from investigating this, is it? You are tenacious."

"I just want to show everyone that it wasn't you."

"So you think the sheriff wants to rake me over the coals for sending you over there to snoop around?"

"I guess so."

"So someone must have realized what you were doing there."

"Yeah… he might have happened by when I was checking out the interview rooms."

Despite the stress of the situation, a dimple appeared in Terry's cheek. "I guess that was a little awkward. What excuse did you give for poking around the interview rooms?"

"I didn't… just stammered a little… he knew why I was there."

"I would guess that was pretty obvious. So did you find anything useful? Satisfy your curiosity?"

Erin scratched her ear and looked at him, trying to decide if he really wanted any details.

"I didn't find out anything that you don't already know. But I wanted to see it for myself."

He nodded. "And what did you conclude?"

"It wouldn't be that hard for someone outside the police department to get in through the back and into one of the interview rooms. He wouldn't have to go by anyone's desk. If he was quick and quiet, he could get in and out without being seen."

Terry's brows climbed higher. "Really. How would someone get in through the back?"

"The police department's exit door isn't alarmed. It really should be."

"It's locked, and so is the outside door."

"But anyone who has access to that utility hall could get into the police department. It's just that one door, if someone picked the lock or left it propped open."

Terry shrugged. "But who would do that?"

"Whoever wanted to eliminate Bo Biggles."

"I think you underestimate how easy it is for an amateur to pick a lock. It may look easy on TV, but this is a heavy, well-constructed door. Not something that you could jimmy with a credit card."

"But someone experienced with a pick and a wrench could."

Something else occurred to Erin. She remembered the bump key that Jeremy had used to get into her house not so long ago. He had scared the heck out of her when he had set off the burglar alarm in the middle of the night, and she had been furious with him. He had sworn he would never use it at her house again.

But she hadn't taken it away from him and he hadn't promised never to use it anywhere else. Even if she had confiscated it, that wouldn't stop him from making another one.

She caught Terry looking at her quizzically. "What?"

"Just how much do you know about picking locks?"

"Oh." Erin cleared her throat and took the last cookie from the plate to distract him from her face. "Well... I'm no cat burglar, but I know the basics."

"Could you pick a lock like that?"

Erin inhaled a cookie crumb and started coughing. It wasn't just to cover up her answer; she really couldn't stop the spasming of her muscles as they tried to dislodge the irritant. Terry nudged her glass of milk toward her and, when she kept coughing, got up and patted and rubbed her back until she could stop coughing and take a drink.

"You okay?"

Erin nodded.

"Could you?" Terry asked.

"What?" Erin asked, still coughing weakly.

"Could you pick a lock like that?"

Erin nodded, gulping. "Yes," she admitted. "It wouldn't be that hard."

Erin's assumption that Terry's visit to the police department would be quick was wrong. When he'd been gone for an hour, she started checking the time every few minutes and looking out toward the street, watching for Terry's car. But he didn't come, and as the time dragged on, he still didn't come.

She couldn't stay up late, knowing that she had to be up early in the morning. But even if she went to bed in good time, she wasn't sure how she was going to get a good night's sleep worrying about what had happened to Terry.

She could drink some of her sleepy tea and maybe have a valerian pill, but she knew that if she took anything stronger, she'd be sluggish and dopey in the morning. Too little sleep was a problem, but so was overmedicating, and she knew from experience her body did not like sleeping pills. Vic had no problem taking them and could be off to sleep quickly and still be fresh as a daisy in the morning. Erin envied her that.

Orange Blossom rubbed against Erin's feet, tickling them, and then jumped up into her lap. He nosed at her and purred loudly, clearly wanting to know what was wrong and trying to comfort her. She petted him and cuddled him close.

"Oh, you're a good kitty, aren't you? I'm so glad you're talking to me again."

He purred and chattered and rubbed against her until Erin squashed him down, telling him to be still. He finally settled into a ball on her lap, purring away cozily as she continued to pet him and watch out the window. She knew she should do something productive. Make her lists for the next day, or even just read through some of Clementine's genealogical files. But she wasn't going to be able to focus on anything but Terry and when he would be back.

Time passed slowly. Could she call him? It might be a silly thing to do, but she wanted to know that he was okay. He could growl at her and tell her that he'd be home soon. Or that the sheriff was keeping him later and he didn't know when he'd be back. It wouldn't matter, as long as he told her something to allay her fears.

It was dark outside when she saw a tall, slim figure making its way down the street. She was worried at first, wondering whether it might be someone from out of town. Another drug dealer. Or someone who was friends with or family to Bo Biggles and wanted to get revenge on Terry for what had happened to him. She didn't like the idea of someone lurking out there in the dark, watching her house or getting too close.

She had armed the burglar alarm, as Terry and Willie always drilled her to do. So no one could break in without alerting the neighborhood.

The dark figure turned and made its way up Erin's sidewalk. At first, her stomach clenched, but then she relaxed. If someone was coming to her front door, then she didn't need to worry that they were trying to sneak up or break in. And as the figure got closer, Erin could see that it was Adele.

Erin got up. She shifted Orange Blossom onto the couch, trying not to disturb him, but he opened his eyes and stretched and watched her to see what was going on. Erin opened the door and motioned Adele in.

"Hi, Adele. How are you?"

"You're not usually up this late. Don't you have work tomorrow? I saw your light was still on and thought I'd check in…"

"I'm okay. Just… waiting for Terry. I thought he would be back by now."

"Where is he? I thought he wasn't on duty this week. Because of the… unfortunate incident."

"The unfortunate incident. Yeah. I wish Biggles had never died. Who knew it would cause so much trouble? You would think that when someone like that, a career criminal, happened to pass away, it wouldn't be such a big deal. I mean, yes, he was a person, and you still treat him with respect, but… I didn't think there would be such a fuss."

As soon as she said it, Erin thought about Mary Lou and her anxiety that it could have been one of her sons. What if one of them had gotten himself arrested and Terry had tased him or had hit him to get him under control, or if someone had choked him? Bo Biggles had a mother somewhere, Erin assumed, and maybe brothers and sisters. Maybe a girlfriend. People who cared that he had died. Because he was a person, not just a piece of junk to be disposed of.

Adele sat in one of the easy chairs, her expression pensive. "Much of what happens in the universe is beyond our control, and we'll never know why it happened. We are like little ants here on the earth, scurrying around thinking that we have control over our lives, and it couldn't be further from the truth."

Erin didn't like the sound of that. She was someone who liked to control everything she could. Her practice of making lists and trying to plan everything out had evolved from her lack of control over her life when she was growing up. She couldn't control anything, so she tried to control everything. And she was still trying.

"I guess you're right," she said, not wanting to argue with Adele that she did have some control when she clearly didn't. She couldn't protect Terry from the accusations against him. She couldn't stop people from being killed in Bald Eagle Falls. The best she could do was follow her recipes and hope they came out of the oven looking and tasting good. Even then, things could happen that would sabotage her results. Bad ingredients, cross-contamination, a malfunctioning oven, getting distracted or sick or forgetting to set a timer. She couldn't prevent someone from reacting to it, as Trenton had when Joelle gave him cupcakes she knew he would be allergic to.

All Erin could do was try her best and see how it all came out.

"So is he already working again?" Adele asked. "That seems awfully quick."

"No, he's not working… Sheriff Wilmot called him in to ask him some more questions. I thought he would be back pretty quickly, but it's been hours. I haven't even heard from him."

"It may be that he hasn't been allowed to use the phone."

"But he has his own phone. And why would they stop him from using the phone?"

Adele didn't answer. Orange Blossom jumped off of the couch and went to greet her. After some ear scratches, he jumped up into her lap and settled there.

"You think… that they've arrested him?" Erin asked as Adele's reticence registered. "That's why he hasn't let me know what's going on?"

"I have no way of knowing. I just wondered… why else he wouldn't call to tell you goodnight, that he'd go back to his own house tonight and catch up with you in the morning, so that you could be calm enough to go to sleep."

"He might have just gotten busy. Wrapped up in something and forgot the time."

"Perhaps," Adele agreed.

But Erin had a lump in her stomach. She knew that wasn't why Terry hadn't called her. He'd been concerned about her health and her sleeping patterns since Mr. Inglethorpe's death. He knew that she wouldn't be able to sleep without knowing where he was and that he was okay.

"Do you think I should call him? I was wondering whether I should… just to check in and find out what his plans were for the night. He was going to come back here, but like you say, if he isn't going to be done until late, he'll probably go back to his own house."

"You could call him."

Erin nodded, but she didn't. She looked at her phone again, sitting on the side table, and didn't pick it up.

"This must be a hard time for Officer Piper. And for you."

"Yeah. It is. But… it could be worse. I mean, the sheriff knows that he didn't have anything to do with Bo Biggles's death. He knows Terry didn't do anything wrong."

"How would he know that?"

"Because he knows Terry. He's worked with him forever. He knows that Terry wouldn't hurt someone. He couldn't kill anyone. We were just talking about morality earlier today… I know Terry believes in upholding the law. All of the law, he doesn't pick and choose. And I know that even though he doesn't talk about it very much, he is a Christian and believes all of those commandments, and that includes not killing."

"Accidents still happen. The arrest of that man was… quite violent."

Erin leaned forward, looking at Adele. No one had mentioned having seen what went down that day. Erin had only Terry's sparse description of picking Biggles up near the school, of having to tase him to get him under control. He hadn't wanted to tell her any more than necessary about what had happened.

"Did you see?"

Adele hesitated. "Didn't Officer Piper tell you all of the details?"

"No. Hardly anything."

"I don't think it's my place…"

"As my friend, I think it is absolutely your place. How am I supposed to figure out the truth and to protect him if I don't know what happened?"

"Is it your place to protect him?"

"Yes."

Adele raised her brows and nodded slowly, accepting Erin's assertion. "The school is not far from your woods; the school field abuts your property line. So for Mr. Biggles to stay off of the school property, he was actually on your property."

"Why would he do that?" Erin shook her head, not understanding. "Wasn't the whole point to deal to the school kids?"

"There are more serious charges if he's caught dealing on school grounds."

"Oh. Who knew? Okay. So he was in my woods. How did Terry know where to find him? Did K9 track him? I gather it was Beaver who told him that Biggles was in town and that's why Terry was looking for him."

"It was probably a combination of witness reports and K9's nose. I didn't see the whole process. I was gathering some berries when I saw Mr. Biggles. I kept out of sight because I didn't want to have to deal with him." Adele paused. "I know I'm supposed to keep trespassers off of the property, but there are times when…"

"Of course, you need to take your own safety into account," Erin agreed. "Don't confront some gangland drug dealer. You stay out of the way. Call the police if you think there is something they can do."

Adele nodded. Her shoulders dipped, relieved by Erin's understanding. "I was keeping an eye on him, and I would have called the police if I saw him actually dealing drugs or doing something illegal. But he was very cagey."

"He must have been good at what he did."

"Yes. I think so." Adele shrugged one shoulder. She scratched Orange Blossom's ears, looking like she was concentrating on a difficult problem. "Then Officer Piper showed up. It was just like on TV; telling him to put his hands up, and then going after him when he didn't obey. Biggles threw something away and tried to run. For a big man, he moved very fast. But Piper was faster, especially with K9. K9 brought him down but didn't hurt him. I know they can. Sometimes people get injured when K9 units take them down."

Erin nodded. "They've got teeth, and they dig in when someone struggles."

"Biggles started fighting again when K9 released him and Officer Piper was trying to cuff him. Piper fought with him, then used his taser."

"And when he did that, then Biggles stopped fighting? That's when Terry got him under control and... put the handcuffs on him and took him in."

"No. Even though he had been tased, he was quite combative. He was hitting and kicking, trying to get away, even with the taser claws still in him. Officer Piper was... well, hitting him with his nightstick. You know how they do. Just smacking him and smacking him, trying to get him to stop fighting, or to let go of his weapon... I couldn't see very well. Biggles was on the ground; there was lots of grass and undergrowth so that I couldn't see everything."

Erin nodded. She didn't know what to say. She imagined it all from Adele's perspective, crouched over a patch of berries or hidden behind a tree. Watching in horror, but not wanting to get in the way or to interfere with the arrest. Just wishing that they would finish and she could be alone again and not have to witness any more violence.

Even though Adele was a witch, she wasn't the kind of witch that Erin had grown up seeing on television or hearing about in fairy tales. She was a peaceful person, not someone who wanted anything to do with any type of violence. Not to people, or to animals, or even to plants or anything else on earth. She tried to live in harmony with nature and not to harm any living thing or part of the earth.

Erin sniffled, finding her throat suddenly hot and swollen. "And then... what happened?"

"That was all... he just kept hitting and wrestling with Mr. Biggles until he could get him under control and into a pair of handcuffs. He got him to his feet and took him to his squad car." Adele let out a deep sigh. "That's all I know. That's everything I could see. He sat in the car for what seemed like a long time and then left. To the police department, I assume. I didn't follow him to find out."

"But he didn't choke Biggles."

Adele hesitated.

Erin raised her brows and nodded her head with certainty. "He knows it's against policy, that it's too dangerous."

"I couldn't see very well, Erin. They were both on the ground, Officer Piper trying to wrestle him around and get him under control. I couldn't tell whether he hit or grabbed him by the throat. It wasn't movie violence, where you can see every detail of every punch that's thrown. It's… more like the Tasmanian devil, all a whirl of arms and legs, with both of them grunting and yelling. That's what I saw. I couldn't say whether he ever touched Mr. Biggles's throat or not."

"He didn't."

"You weren't there, Erin. And if you were, you wouldn't be able to say any better than I can."

"I know Terry didn't choke him. I know it one hundred percent."

"Maybe not. I'm not saying he did. I'm just saying; I can't say he didn't."

Erin sat back, feeling exhausted, like she had wrestled with Bo Biggles herself. "I'm going to call Terry."

$\mathscr{A}$dele went on her way to give Erin some privacy. Erin was relieved to find that Terry still had his phone on him and was allowed to answer it when she called. So Adele was wrong. He hadn't been arrested. He hadn't been kept from calling her or communicating with her. He had just been too busy to call her.

"Hi, Erin. I'm so sorry I haven't called you. I keep thinking that I'm going to get out of here, and then… there's more. I'm sure I won't be much longer. But… maybe you should go to bed. I'll head home after I'm done here and we'll touch base tomorrow."

"I'll try. I was hoping you'd be back here tonight."

"You don't want me to wake you up. You might not be able to get back to sleep again."

"I don't know if I'll be able to sleep if you don't come. Are you… is everything okay?"

"I'm still here… I haven't been arrested." Terry gave a long, exhausted sigh. "But things are not looking good, Erin. I'm not sure how much longer I'll be able to stay on this side of the bars. They are… stacking up a lot of evidence against me."

"But you didn't do it. You didn't cause Biggles's death."

"I hope not."

"You didn't, Terry. It wasn't your fault."

"The more they say and the more tired I get, the less certain I am. I might have to… plead to a lesser offense. To avoid having to spend too much time in jail. A police officer in the prison population… it's not a very good thing."

"Don't plead it out," Erin begged. "Don't tell them that you did something wrong when you didn't. I know you didn't cause Biggles's death, and I'm going to prove it. You just have to give me time."

"You can't prove it, Erin. Even when the medical examiner comes back with a cause of death, there's still going to be some question about it. They are going to come after me with everything they have."

"Why?"

He sighed. "I'll talk to you about it tomorrow… when I see you next."

"Will you be home soon?"

"I'll be going home soon. To my house. You go to sleep. Get a good rest. I'll talk to you tomorrow."

"It will look better in the morning," Erin promised him. "Things always look worse when you're tired. So don't plead to anything tonight. Don't let them wear you down. If you're not under arrest, you can leave whenever you want. Just tell them that you're going home."

"Just who is the cop here? I think I know what my rights are."

"But you're thinking about it from a cop's perspective. You need to think like an innocent witness. An innocent witness doesn't have to stay there all night to get it settled. Just come home now. Come here. I need you."

She hoped that appealing to his protective side would help.

Terry clicked his tongue, trying to make a decision. Erin's chest hurt. She had to get him out of there before he did something he would regret later. Her heart was breaking for him, accused of a crime he wasn't guilty of. No matter what had caused Biggles's death, she knew it wasn't Terry's fault.

"Come, please."

"Okay."

Tears sprang to Erin's eyes.

"I'll be there soon," he promised.

Erin put on the tea kettle. She searched the fridge for comfort food that wouldn't be too heavy before bed. They'd already had cookies, so she didn't want to give Terry anything too sugary. She settled on some rolls from the bakery and started to assemble a couple of sandwiches. Complex carbs were good. Dairy. Turkey. They would both be ready to nod off within half an hour of the snack.

She walked into the living room to look out the front window but didn't see his truck. Had the sheriff kept him for longer? Was he still sitting in his truck in the parking lot with his face in his hands having a breakdown? Or had he been too tired and distressed to drive safely?

The kettle began to whistle, so Erin returned to the kitchen to turn it off. She got out mugs and a basket of assorted teas and put them on the table. The rolls were on the table, ready to eat. All she needed was a man to eat them with her.

She walked back out to the living room to look again and saw his truck at the curb. Relieved, Erin hurried to punch her code into the burglar alarm and open the door.

She didn't even let Terry into the house before enfolding him in a tight embrace. "I'm so glad you're home. Are you okay?"

He held her close for a few minutes. She could feel his breathing, tense, shallow breaths. Hopefully, talk, tea, and a bite to eat would help him to relax and decompress.

Terry finally drew back, taking a breath and looking back over his shoulder. It wasn't until then that Erin saw the figure slouching against a beaten-up station wagon. "Beaver? What's she doing here?"

"She's just... making sure everybody's safe."

Erin frowned. "What do you mean? She drove over to make sure you weren't too tired to drive? I *was* a little worried..."

Terry nodded. "That... and to make sure that there's no one suspicious hanging around."

She looked at him, not asking the questions she was sure he was expecting.

"Do you mind if Beaver comes in?"

Erin frowned. She didn't want Beaver there, but she wasn't going to turn her away if Terry thought that she needed to be there for their protection.

"Why would she need to come in? Is there something going on, Terry?"

His eyes slid away from her and he didn't answer.

"Okay, sure," Erin agreed, shaking her head.

Terry turned slightly and made a large motion for Beaver to come in. Beaver straightened and approached the house. She nodded to Erin as she reached the door. She wore a smile, as usual, but her eyes were hooded. Erin wasn't sure why she was there or what she was thinking.

Erin led them into the kitchen and looked at the cups and sandwiches she had prepared. Obviously for only two people. She got another cup out of the cupboard and placed it on the table. "Do you want a sandwich?" she asked Beaver, starting to get a third one prepared before waiting or an answer.

"That would be awfully nice," Beaver agreed. "I've had nothing but junk this week, with everything that's been going on. Switching between sugar and salt isn't exactly what they mean by a balanced diet."

Erin nodded and didn't look at either of them as she prepared the third sandwich. K9 lay down at Terry's feet with a deep sigh.

He sprawled on his side, stretching his feet out, and made a drawn-out groaning noise.

"Doesn't sound like he had much fun today," Erin observed. "Grab him a cookie."

Orange Blossom made himself known, winding around Erin's legs and yowling, and before long, Marshmallow joined them as well so that the whole menagerie was present.

"Terry, do you want to…?" Erin gestured to Orange Blossom in frustration. Normally, she was happy to get them each their treats, but she was tired and at the end of her rope. It was time for bed, and she'd thought she would have some time to unwind with Terry, but now she had a third party to deal with.

Terry obediently got the other animals treats to get them out of the way while Erin finished putting together a sandwich for Beaver. She sat down at the table and made herself some tea. She rubbed her eyes and cupped her palms over them.

"So… what's going on?"

Terry and Beaver were silent at first. Erin peeked at them around her hands before closing her eyes and resting her palms on them again.

"What aren't you telling me?"

Terry shifted restlessly. "Certain facts have come to light that… make me look more guilty."

"What? I don't see how there could be anything else. You just performed an arrest. And then questioned the suspect at the police department. Most of that was right under the sheriff's eyes, so how can they say that you're guilty of anything?"

"For one thing, Davis Plaint."

Erin dropped her hands from her face and stared at him. "Davis Plaint? What does Davis Plaint have to do with anything?"

"Having heard about Biggles's death through the prison grapevine—"

"Or from Melissa."

Terry nodded. "Or from Melissa. He's now decided to claim that I brutalized him after he was arrested."

"What?"

Terry shrugged. "That's what he says."

"And no one else happened to notice this?"

"Well, obviously, everyone else in the department was complicit, so they looked the other way. Davis is only coming out now because there is now evidence to support his story. If I roughed up one person, it probably wasn't the first time. There will probably be convicts coming out of the woodwork for the next three years claiming that I beat them up when I arrested them."

Terry's voice was bitter and defeated. Erin shook her head. "Oh, I'm sorry. But that's ridiculous. And anyone with a head on their shoulders will know that he's just trying to get attention, won't they? It isn't like he filed any complaints about it back then."

"People will believe what they want to. It makes a much better story if there is a suggestion that this isn't the first time I beat up a detainee. That I have a history, but it was covered up."

"No one here is going to believe it."

"Maybe not. But there still has to be an investigation."

"Into whether or not you beat up Davis? It's pretty easy to prove, isn't it? He didn't have any bruises."

"I could have abused him in a way that didn't leave bruises. Of course, the story falls apart there, because if I made a habit of beating people up without leaving bruises, then why was Biggles bruised?"

Erin nodded vigorously. "Exactly! It's obvious that Davis is just making up a story."

"But it doesn't really matter. People like to hear stories, even if they're fanciful."

"It's not like you had any reason to beat Biggles up. You had a lot more reason to beat Davis up, and you never left a bruise on him."

Terry didn't answer. Beaver silently worked her way through her sandwich, the only one of them who was actually eating.

"Terry?" Erin persisted. "Davis was the one who just about

burned my house down with me in it. If you didn't beat him up for that, why would you beat up Bo Biggles?"

Terry didn't answer. He just stirred his tea, looking like he would climb into the mug and disappear if he could.

Beaver wiped her mouth with the back of her hand. "Because of what I told him."

*E*rin looked at Beaver. "What?" She looked from one of them to the other. "What's that supposed to mean? What could you tell Terry that would have any bearing on this?"

Beaver looked at Terry. He didn't look back at her, but kept staring down at his tea. There were fatigue lines around his eyes, dark and sunken. He looked like he hadn't slept or eaten in days. It was shocking how quickly he had gone downhill. A few hours at the police department, and he had been beaten down, almost broken.

"Because I told Officer Piper that I had seen Biggles lurking around your house," Beaver revealed. "The day that you got back from your cruise… I saw him. He was trying to stay out of sight. So, I let your Officer Piper know."

"And I went looking for him the next day," Terry finished.

Everyone went quiet. Erin tried to process what they were telling her. Suddenly Terry had a motive for beating Biggles up, choking him, even killing him. Suddenly he wasn't just an officer pursuing his duty anymore. It was personal. His girlfriend was being threatened. He wanted to make sure that Biggles would never show up at her house again. Whatever it took.

Erin felt like she'd been spinning on a playground merry-go-round. Her head spun and she felt nauseated.

"Excuse me a minute."

She lurched to her feet and headed for the commode. Orange Blossom followed her, meowing inquiringly. It wasn't normal behavior for Erin and he wanted to know what was going on. Erin pushed him back with her foot before shutting the door, shutting him out. She should have known that he wouldn't put up with that. In a minute, he was yowling like she was beating him.

It wasn't like he needed his cat box urgently. He hadn't been trying to get to it; he just wanted to know what Erin was doing. And like any self-respecting two-year-old, he wasn't going to let her shut the door to the bathroom and have a moment of quiet time to herself.

Erin leaned on the counter. She took a few long, steadying breaths to try to get her body under control. Nothing had changed. Everything was as it had been before; she just knew more. How many more secrets were left?

Had Terry gone after Biggles intending to beat him up and run him out of Bald Eagle Falls once and for all in order to protect Erin?

She ran the cold water tap and soaked a washcloth, then used it to sponge her face and the back of her neck. She shouldn't be having such a dramatic reaction to the revelation. So Terry knew that Biggles was in town and went looking for him. Erin had already known that. She had even guessed that it was Beaver who had told him. The only part she hadn't known was that Biggles had been outside the house that day.

She remembered how large and menacing Biggles had looked the day that she saw him on Main Street arguing with Beaver, having fits because Beaver had rear-ended him at the one stoplight on Main Street. He had been lurking outside of her house. He probably carried a gun. Of course he carried a gun. And he knew who Erin was and where she lived.

Beaver had said that the clans would stay out of Bald Eagle

Falls for a long time. They would be scared off by the big drug sting and they wouldn't want to go anywhere near the little town. They no longer had any assets to protect there, so they wouldn't be after Erin or any of her friends.

But she had been wrong. Biggles had come back. He had ignored whatever sage advice the clan leaders had given him about staying out of sight. Or maybe they had sent him back to scope things out and see how easy it would be to target Erin.

So Terry knew that simply warning him off wasn't going to work. He knew that Biggles was too stupid or too cunning to stay away.

What could Terry do?

It was too much for Erin. The nausea swelled up, over-whelming her, and she dropped to her knees in front of the commode to throw up. It was a good thing she hadn't eaten her sandwich. Beaver could have hers too. Beaver could have all of the sandwiches. And go home. Erin didn't want her there any longer.

Beaver was a troublemaker, and she knew it. She loved to stir things up and then see what happened. Was that why she had escorted Terry home? To see what kind of fallout would come from the revelation that Terry had gone after Biggles for revenge?

After a few minutes, there was a tap at the door. Erin could barely hear it over the yowls of the cat.

"Blossom," Terry said in frustration. "Get out of here. Scat!"

There was a scuffle, and then the yowling stopped. Terry tapped the door again.

"Erin? Are you okay? Can I come in?"

"No."

Erin tore off a piece of toilet paper to wipe her nose and mouth, gagging again at the sight and smell of the vomit. She flushed the toilet and leaned against the bathroom counter.

"Erin…?"

"I'll be out in a while. You guys finish visiting and then Beaver can go home."

There was only silence in response, and then a couple of

minutes later, Erin heard Terry walking away, down the hall toward the kitchen again. Clementine's old house creaked and protested, making it easy for Erin to follow Terry's progress away from the bathroom door.

Erin leaned her head in her hand, trying to get past the nausea and worry. Sheriff Wilmot hadn't arrested Terry. That meant that they didn't think they had enough evidence to build a case against him yet. That was good news. Terry was still walking around free and, as an officer that the sheriff was familiar with, he had some level of protection from wrongful prosecution. But who knew how much pressure the sheriff was getting from the public and the other town and state authorities who wanted to make sure that if there was a dirty cop, he was prosecuted to the full extent of the law.

He wouldn't cave.

Not without a lot of evidence.

Erin hoped.

Maybe that was why the sheriff hadn't had anything to say when he had caught Erin snooping around. He was hoping she *would* find something to give him an excuse for not charging Terry with murder, or at least police brutality.

To think that she had been worried that the reason he had called Terry in was to dress him down for allowing Erin to poke her nose in where it wasn't wanted. Sheriff Wilmot didn't care that she'd been getting in the way. He was more concerned about the suggestion Terry had targeted Biggles for personal reasons.

Erin rose unsteadily to her feet and sponged off her face again. She listened at the door. There was a murmur of voices. Then a couple of minutes later, the front door closed and Erin knew that Beaver was gone.

She opened the door as Terry walked down the hall toward her again, his eyes dark and concerned. She pushed him away when he tried to hug her, worried about smelling like puke, and turned toward her bedroom. Terry stopped in the hall, unsure what to do.

"I'm going to lie down," Erin told him. "Come in with me."

He seemed relieved to be told what to do and followed her into the bedroom. "Are you okay?"

"I guess I'll be fine. I was just… surprised."

"I'm sorry I didn't tell you sooner… but I couldn't."

"You could have."

But she knew how hard it must have been for him to admit how much trouble he was really in. He wanted to be her protector, but he might have to go away and leave her to her own devices. It was so bad that he was considering pleading to a lesser charge.

Erin shook her head and closed her eyes as she rested her head on the pillow. They had to get some rest. Neither one of them would be able to think clearly and logically until they were well-rested.

"How does it make any difference?" Erin asked, without turning to him. "You made a good arrest. He was dealing drugs by the school and you arrested him for that. He resisted. There was a witness to that. And once you got him to the police department, you were under supervision. You weren't in the interview room whaling on him. You were asking him questions, and the rest of the department wouldn't look the other way while you beat him."

"The case isn't turning out to be as cut-and-dried as I would like it to."

"But that's the way it happened."

"They need more than just my statement. The fact that I went looking for Biggles because he was hanging around here… that's a big problem. Maybe I should have gotten Tom or the sheriff involved instead of handling it myself. It was an emotional decision. But it was also in the usual line of duty for me… if I'm aware someone is acting inappropriately and breaking the law, it's my duty to go after them. That's my job."

"Yes," Erin agreed. With her eyes closed and Terry lying down behind her, cuddling her close, she felt warm and protected. She could work out all of the details in the morning. If she could just get a good sleep, the pieces would begin to fit together.

She was dozing off when Terry moved away from her and got up. Erin was too tired to even open her eyes. "Come back."

"Need to get out of these sweaty clothes," he whispered. "And I need to check the alarm system. I'll be back."

"Is Beaver still out there?"

He paused by the bedroom door. "Yes," he admitted.

"To make sure that none of Biggles's friends show up?"

"Yes."

Erin breathed out slowly. "Okay."

CHAPTER 23

When she climbed out of bed in the morning, Terry got up as well.

"You need more rest," Erin told him. "You did too much yesterday."

"I didn't do anything yesterday except answer questions. I need to get out and do something active today."

"Maybe see what Willie's up to?"

"I don't know. I want to do something…" He trailed off, not finishing.

"Something to do with Bo Biggles?" Erin suggested.

Terry rubbed his eyes and looked at her, eyes squinted. "Are you reading minds now?"

"No… I just figured… that's what I would want to do. I know you're probably not supposed to have anything to do with it, but I don't know if I could help myself if it was me. I would want to get out there and start turning over stones and figuring out what had happened."

"We both know very well that there is no way you would stay out of it if it were you."

Erin couldn't help smiling. She had really tried to be good at the time and to do what Officer Piper had told her and to stay out of the investigation and let him and the police department do their jobs. But somehow… things kept coming up, and even when she wasn't asking questions and poking around, things tended to *happen*. People told her things or misinterpreted her questions or… things just happened.

"It wasn't really my fault. I wasn't even trying to investigate…"

"Uh-huh." Terry took in a deep breath and let it out. "The alternative is sitting around doing nothing and letting someone else have control over my fate, and I'm getting tired of that. I need to do something. Assemble my defense."

Erin nodded. "I know. I've been hoping that it would all just come together, but I haven't had a lot of luck yet. If we can prove that he died because of something else or because of something that someone else did, then we can prove that you are innocent, and you can get back to work where you belong."

"But only if that's true. If it wasn't someone else or some other cause… If it was the taser or something that happened while I was trying to get him under control and into handcuffs…"

"It wasn't," Erin assured him. They both knew that she couldn't be sure of the fact, but she needed to reassure him. He had to know that she had faith in him and that it would all work out somehow. "Adele said that we really can't control fate and that we have to let the universe sort itself out."

"If I believed that, I wouldn't be a cop."

"I always thought that Christians figured God was in charge of everything and he is the one who will work things out."

Terry grimaced. "Difficult philosophical question," he admitted. "I believe that God is in charge… but I believe that I need to do my part and that I can affect the outcome… sort of."

"If God is in charge, then how can you change that?"

"I can't change it… I can… work within his plan to make things work out the way they are supposed to… in a way that's best for me."

Erin tried to wrap her mind around that. "So you can work against God's plan? Make things go wrong for yourself?"

"Err… I can cause pain and trouble for myself by trying to work against his plan. Things are easier if I work with him than against him."

Erin spread her hands apart. She needed to use the bathroom, so she couldn't very well continue the philosophical discussion. "So what does God want you to do about this case? About your defense?"

Terry looked at her, brows raised, and shook his head slowly.

Erin dashed to the commode. She'd let Terry sort that question out for himself. As an atheist, Erin didn't have to worry about making the choice that God wanted her to make, or even about aligning herself with fate or the universe. She was the one who made choices about her own life and the way it would turn out, and she wanted that life to include Terry.

And not visiting him in prison.

She had a shower and dressed and found Terry in the kitchen ahead of her, preparing toast and tea. After emptying her stomach the night before, Erin found herself much hungrier than she would typically be in the morning and the aroma whet her appetite.

"That smells good."

"My specialty."

"Good choice."

Terry had already let K9 out of his crate and the animals were milling about waiting for their breakfasts. Erin fed them all. She looked toward the front door.

"Is Beaver still out there? Should we offer her something?"

"It would be a nice gesture. Do you want her here, though? You weren't too thrilled with her last night."

"I'm a little less emotional this morning. We can feed her. How long has she been up?"

"I didn't ask. Just accepted her offer to keep an eye out last night. I knew I couldn't be the one to keep watch."

"Did you get enough sleep last night? You don't usually get up this early."

"More than I have the last few nights. I don't usually go to bed as early as I did."

"But you didn't go to sleep when I did; you were up changing, and I heard you in the shower."

"Not long. I was asleep pretty soon after you. I can have a nap this afternoon if I need to... I don't plan on going in for any more police interviews."

"Even if they call you?"

Terry nodded. "Even if they call me. I'm thinking... if they want me back in again today, I might have to get a lawyer."

Erin nodded as she started to butter slices of toast. "I think that would be a good idea. Are there any good criminal lawyers in town? Is there a union lawyer? Or do you have to go into the city to find someone?"

"I've never had to look before. I know some of the guys in town... but I don't know that I would go with any of them. If they've represented criminals in cases that we've investigated... it kind of feels like a conflict of interest. Like they might not put their best efforts into the case."

Erin had to admit he had a point.

She left Terry to the toast and other goodies and walked to the front door. She looked up and down the street. Beaver's car wasn't in sight. But a moment later, Beaver walked around the side of the house and nodded to Erin.

"Hey."

"Hi. You want breakfast?"

"Breakfast would go down real nice about now."

Erin made a gesture inviting her in. Beaver walked across the front of the house, took a good look around, and then joined Erin inside.

"Are you okay?" she asked, chewing on the omnipresent gum. "You were in pretty rough shape last night. And I don't know if… well, you and I. I know we're not best friends or anything, but I hate to have you mad at me because I told Terry about Biggles or because I didn't tell you right at the start that he had been worried you were in danger." Beaver shrugged. "I don't know. It just didn't seem like the right thing to do at the time. I'm used to playing things close to the vest. That can cause relationship problems sometimes."

"We're okay," Erin assured her. She didn't want to get into it any more deeply than that. Beaver had done what she thought was right, and Erin probably would have reacted the same way whether they had told her right away or told her when they did. She couldn't change the past or the choices that any of them had made.

Erin put a few jars of jam on the table, along with butter and honey, plates, glasses, knives, and juice from the fridge. Together with the tea and the toast, the table was pretty full. For someone who usually didn't have any breakfast other than a cup of tea, it was a feast. Beaver sat down, making pleased noises.

"This is gonna be great. Your baking is always the best, Erin."

"How do you know this isn't store-bought bread?"

"First, because it's obviously handmade. And also with the amount of leftovers from the bakery, why would you buy bread at the store? You can't afford to run out of bread at the bakery, so you have to make just a bit too much, and then someone has to eat it."

Erin laughed. "And we've been making plenty of donations to a homeless shelter in the city, too. But there always seems to be more to eat."

"Good thing for me."

They all sat down and began to spread their choices of condiments on the toast.

"So… what other things do you keep close to the vest that causes you relationship problems?" Erin asked. She wasn't usually so nosy about other people's problems, but for once it would be nice not to think about hers or Terry's. She knew that Beaver probably wouldn't answer the question anyway. She was good at deflecting.

"Well… sometimes you find something out that affects someone you know and, being in law enforcement, you can't say anything. When people find out later that you withheld something… they tend not to be too happy about it. Not just surprised and upset, but…" She shrugged with one shoulder. "Breakup mad. Or shoot-you-in-a-fit-of-anger mad."

"Ouch!" Erin stared at Beaver in horror. "You're not serious, are you? You said before that you had been shot, but I thought that was in the line of duty. You're not telling me that you had a boyfriend who shot you because you hadn't told him something in the course of an investigation?"

Beaver took a couple of bites of toast, reflecting on her answer. "Well... that's accurate, but not a complete description of what happened. Sometimes something can be in the line of duty *and* personal at the same time."

Erin frowned, trying to figure that one out.

Terry looked at Beaver; head cocked to the side slightly. "Like when you have a relationship with someone you are investigating?"

"It can happen," Beaver admitted.

Erin thought about how Beaver had taken up with Jeremy after the drug investigation was complete. She *had* waited until after the investigation, hadn't she? She had to be talking about some other case, because Jeremy hadn't shot Beaver. He'd known from the start that she was law enforcement. If Beaver had started a relationship with someone she was investigating, though, Erin could see how that could go very badly very quickly.

"Sheesh, Beaver. You should be more careful."

"I *am* more careful. Now."

They all laughed.

There was a knock at the back door and Vic let herself in. She looked around at the group of them. "Things are as busy in here as a cat with puppies! What's up? Did I miss a memo? Is it a party?"

"No one is partying this early in the morning," Terry asserted. "It's just breakfast. Throw a couple more pieces of bread in the toaster and pull up a chair." Terry eyed Beaver and the stack of toast on her plate. "I think we're going to need a bit more than I had calculated."

Vic nodded and put four more pieces of toast into the toaster. She sat down and picked up a single piece of toast for herself.

"So I get why Terry is here," she drawled, with a wink in his direction. "But why Beaver? What are you doing up so early?"

"Actually, I'm not up early. I'm up late."

"You haven't been to bed? You weren't out with Jeremy, were you? I'll have a talk with that boy about keeping his date up so late."

Beaver shook her head, chewing a large mouthful of toast. She swallowed strenuously. "No, ma'am, don't blame your brother for that one. I was on surveillance."

"Oh." Vic took a dainty bite of her slice of toast, spread thinly with marmalade as she considered this. "Anything I should know about? I didn't think that there was anything for you to investigate in Bald Eagle Falls. Things have been pretty quiet here. Other than..." Vic shrugged, tilting her head toward Terry and looking apologetic, "...you know."

Beaver glanced around the table at Erin and Terry. Terry sighed and nodded.

"There is some concern that there could be retaliation by Biggles's clan. As you can imagine, they are not too happy about his unexpected death."

"Biggles is Jackson clan," Vic said. She fiddled with the handle on her teacup. "You think they're going to send people here to Bald Eagle Falls to get revenge?"

"It's a possibility," Beaver agreed, sitting back in her chair. She was watching the three of them carefully. "There have been some rumblings."

Vic looked sick. Erin thought about her own race to the bathroom the night before and was sympathetic. Vic didn't need to be reminded of her family and their criminal enterprises. She didn't need to be wondering if one of them were going to come to town to deal with Terry. Her brothers had been sent out once before to handle things in Bald Eagle Falls—though the police hadn't been able to prove their involvement in anything that had happened.

Erin reached across the table and touched Vic's arm. "It's okay, Vicky. Nothing is going to happen. It's just... preventative. Being extra careful."

"Nothing is going to happen while I'm on watch," Beaver asserted.

"But you can't be on watch all the time. And you can't be everywhere. It isn't like you can put a tail on Terry twenty-four hours a day. And watch his house, and Erin's, and the bakery, and anywhere else they might attack. Even if you could, how long could you justify it? A few days? A week? They'd just wait for an opening."

"We're not just going to sit back and wait for something to happen. We do have people in place and are managing the situation."

Did the feds have people planted in the clan? High up enough to be able to control some of the decisions being made by the gang? Erin shook her head and let her breath out in a heavy sigh. "Well, it's not like we haven't been here before. We've faced the clan and other criminals before and things have worked out okay." She looked at Terry. "If you believe in God or fate, then you need to have some faith that things will work out the way they are supposed to."

Terry's eyes narrowed. He obviously thought she was mocking his beliefs.

Erin put her hand on his leg under the table, giving it a little squeeze. "Really. I mean it. With Beaver on the case and the universe working for our good, it will all turn out, right?"

His expression relaxed and he nodded, putting his hand over hers briefly, warm and comforting. "Yeah."

Vic looked at them. She nodded, but didn't look reassured. "The whisperings you are hearing about clan activity… you don't know any names, do you?"

"Like whether Joseph and Daniel are involved?" Beaver asked baldly. "No, not that I've heard. But I wouldn't assume anything. If you see either of one of them, don't be too eager for a family reunion."

Vic nodded. She rubbed her palms along her pants. She swallowed. "And Jeremy? He's out, right? He's safely away from the clan and its influence."

Beaver didn't answer.

Beaver had said that she had been involved with people she had been investigating before. Was her relationship with Jeremy merely a front to monitor his involvement with the Jackson clan? Or did she want to help keep him safe from the clan, as she had said before? Erin had never sensed any duplicity about her relationship with him. But Beaver was a professional. She was very good at what she did.

"We'd know if Jeremy had anything to do with the clan," Erin told Vic. "He wouldn't be able to keep that from us for this long. He's not exactly an expert. We knew something was going on before. We'd know if he still had contact with them."

"Maybe." Vic shook her head. Her toast sat on the plate half-eaten. "I thought when I left that I wouldn't have anything else to do with the clan. Leaving home was not exactly in my plans, but it was kind of a relief when I did, and I knew I didn't have to be involved with them. I didn't know how hard it would be, knowing that the boys are still part of that scene. I don't want to believe that Jeremy is still mixed up with the clan. But I'm not sure. He hasn't always been… forthcoming."

"Everybody has secrets," Beaver said around another mouthful of toast. "Even you, Miss Victoria."

Erin blinked at this. Of course she didn't know everything there was to know about Vic. She knew the broad strokes, and she knew Vic's personality and the kind of person she was. Erin would trust Vic with her life and knew that Vic would never do anything to hurt her. But that didn't mean Vic didn't have secrets she'd rather no one knew.

Erin herself had a past and hadn't revealed the details even to Terry. He knew whatever he had turned up when he had investigated her background, and he knew what she had told him about her background and growing up in foster care. He knew everything she did about what had happened to her parents. But everything about her… there were still plenty of things she would rather not talk about, even to him and Vic.

Beaver cut her eyes toward Erin and smiled, clearly guessing where Erin's thoughts had gone. She didn't accuse Erin of having secrets too, but she knew. Beaver probably had a clearer picture of Erin's background than even Terry did. She had more resources at her disposal than a small-town cop.

"But you don't think he's involved with the clan? You don't think he's a danger to any of us?"

"I don't think Jeremy is a danger to you or Erin, no," Beaver agreed.

There wasn't time for a lot of discussion before heading off to the bakery. Normally, Erin just had a quick cup of tea before she and Vic drove over to Auntie Clem's, so she felt a little rushed cleaning up after the breakfast in order to get on her way.

"You go ahead and I'll clean up," Terry ordered, motioning Erin and Vic away from the table. "I'm not going anywhere. I'll make sure it's all ship-shape."

"You don't need to—"

"I'm the one who made breakfast; you wouldn't have eaten before going to work otherwise. Let me clean up my own mess."

Erin nodded and left him to it. She wondered by the sharpness of his answer if he was thinking about more than the dishes when he referred to his 'own mess.' Vic headed out to the car.

"Have a good day today." Terry caught Erin by the arm and tugged her gently to him for a goodbye kiss.

"Okay. You too."

He nodded, holding her for an extra second and then releasing her. He walked her to the door and as she was stepping out, stopped her, frowning. "Erin."

"What is it?"

"Last night, you said there was a witness to Biggles's arrest."

"Yes."

"Who did you mean?"

Erin raised her eyebrows, surprised. "Adele."

"Adele saw it? Where was she?"

"Picking berries. You didn't know?"

"She didn't come forward."

"Oh." Erin considered this, starting down the sidewalk. Terry followed her. "I assumed she had been questioned."

"No. As far as I know, no one has talked to her."

"Then I guess… someone should."

"I'll give the sheriff a call and let him know."

"I guess she won't be very happy about being called in, if she didn't let anyone know she was there. She's pretty reclusive."

"She should have reported it herself, reclusive or no. Once she knew Biggles died, which I assume she did."

"She did." Erin gave Terry a quick peck on the cheek before opening the car door. "Call me if you need me."

"I'll be fine. Have a good day."

"You could come by and bring K9 in for a cookie like you normally would. It's strange not having you stop in."

"I don't know. I'm not exactly welcomed with open arms in Bald Eagle Falls public right now."

"No one would say anything, would they?"

"Not to my face, maybe, but there has been plenty of talk behind my back. And the looks… you would think that I was the one dealing drugs at the school, the way they pull their kids away from me."

"Really?" Erin started to walk away, knowing she had to get to the bakery or she would be late opening. "I was surprised at Mary Lou's reaction… but I guess she's worried about her boys getting arrested… what would happen if one of them got in trouble." Erin waved one last time and pulled out.

It was only a couple of minutes to get to the bakery. When they got there and got started on preparations, Vic spoke.

"I didn't know Mary Lou felt like that about the boys."

Erin nodded. "She was pretty upset. I thought she would be happy, like Terry said, about getting a drug dealer off the street. It wasn't Terry's fault that he died. But she was imagining what would happen if it was one of her boys. How even if they were in trouble, she wouldn't want one of them dead like that." She shrugged. "Gives you a different perspective on criminals, thinking about their moms."

Vic was solemn. "I never really thought… I mean, I know my mom doesn't like my dad and the boys being involved with the clan, but she never really said anything about it. She grew up in a clan family, so to her, that's what's normal. But even though she doesn't say anything about it… she must worry about them when they are out on Jackson business."

Erin and Vic had to boogie to make sure that they could get everything prepared and arranged in the display case by opening time. They didn't discuss Bo Biggles, only the baking in each of the ovens and what still had to be done. By the time they were ready to open, Erin felt like she had spent two hours running through sniper fire, and was ready to go back home and go to sleep. Instead, she pasted a pleasant look on her face and greeted her customers, making sure that everyone felt welcome and cared for. Auntie Clem's was more than just a bakery. People went there for gossip and fellowship and to find out what was going on in town. Erin made it as warm and inviting a place as possible so that people would keep coming, even when they weren't out of bread.

Mrs. Foster and the children traipsed in soon after opening time. Erin marveled over how big the kids were getting, how independent little Traci was. When Erin had moved into town, Traci had still been a baby in a sling. Now she was running everywhere. Mrs. Foster had put on weight around the hips lately that Erin strongly suspected indicated another little Foster was on the way.

"How are you? What can I get you today?"

The kids demanded their little stamp cards from their mother to claim their kid's club cookies, and Erin waited patiently while they looked through the glass and discussed which ones they wanted. She smiled at Peter, presiding over the little group as if he were their guide.

"So, have you settled on your Halloween costume yet?" She was curious as to whether he had succeeded in wearing his mother down with his negotiations yet. While Mrs. Foster had good reasons for not allowing Peter to wear a mask, Erin suspected that Peter would get his way, through one argument or another, before October 31 rolled around.

Peter looked at his mother, then turned back to Erin and rolled his eyes. "I want to be a monster," he said. "A werewolf or something scary like that, with lots of fur and a really scary, realistic face." He looked over his shoulder at his mother again.

"Won't fur be too hot?"

"No. It will be the end of October. The end of October is chilly, so it will be just like wearing a jacket," he told her with authority.

Erin nodded her understanding.

"No mask," Mrs. Foster said. "You can find someone to do realistic makeup for you, but not a mask."

Peter shook his head in despair. The girls distracted him by indicating that they all wanted chocolate chip cookies, which Peter insisted was not practical. They should select different flavors and share. But they all insisted that they had tried all of the flavors and knew what kind they wanted. Peter would have to pick something different if he didn't want chocolate chip.

Erin made a mental note that she would need to add a couple of new flavors to mix things up a little.

She hadn't made turnovers or tarts for quite a while, but wasn't sure she could yet. Not with fruit filling, anyway. Maybe she could make some little quiches and pumpkin pies for the grown-ups. They could do cutout cookies and fancy cupcakes for the children.

"Erin…"

Erin snapped back to attention, realizing that her mind had been drifting into Halloween plans, and she had to wait one more day before making any decisions on those. She handed cookies out to the children and looked at Mrs. Foster to see what else she wanted. Vic was already getting her order together and listed off the items for Erin to ring through the register. Erin smiled at Mrs. Foster as they exchanged money.

"You'll have to come by here when you have your costume on," she told Peter. "We won't be open when you are out trick-or-treating, but maybe you can come by after school. You'll be allowed to wear them to school on Halloween day, right?"

Peter nodded. "Yes. I'll have to check with Mom about coming over. I'm not supposed to go anywhere else or talk to anyone on my way home from school." He looked over at Mrs. Foster, raising his eyebrows in query.

"We'll talk about it and sort it out," Mrs. Foster agreed, moving to break up a squabble between Jody and Traci.

Erin opened her mouth to mention to Mrs. Foster how good Peter had been when she'd seen him behind the Town Hall on his way home for lunch. Then something occurred to her.

"Peter… you said that you saw someone in a mask. A really realistic ape mask."

Peter nodded emphatically. Mrs. Foster looked like she was ready to have a meltdown over Erin bringing up the forbidden topic again. But Erin had to know.

"Where did you see that?"

Peter looked at her for a minute, frowning as if it had been too long ago to remember. Then his face lit up. "Where you were," he said. "Behind the… the place where the police station is. That's where."

"What was he doing? Was there a party? Was he hanging out with friends? Was it a whole ape costume, or just a mask?"

"It was just him," Peter said with a shrug. "I don't know what he was doing. Just a guy with an ape mask."

"Sitting back there in a car…?"

"No. Going in the door. Where you came out."

"What day?"

Erin was sure she knew the answer. Peter would probably not even be able to remember what day it had been, but Erin was sure she knew.

"Monday," Peter said brightly. "The day we came to see you."

The day Bo Biggles had died.

Peter had seen someone going into the police department's back door wearing a mask the afternoon Bo Biggles had died in custody.

At first, Vic wasn't sure what to think about Peter's story of a man in a monkey mask. But after Erin talked it through with her, Vic agreed that it was something they would at least have to pass on to the sheriff and whoever was investigating Bo Biggles's death. It wasn't something they could ignore. Terry's future was on the line, and if it was possible that a masked man had been in the police department and had something to do with Biggles's death, then it could be just the break they had been looking for.

"You'd better let him know," she agreed. "Do you want to call him or go over there? You could go over during lunch if you want to."

They usually took their meal before the official lunch hour, so that they could be available to serve customers during the lunch rush. They got up early so they were ready to eat again earlier than the rest of the town. "If I go during our lunch and I get held up, then you are left with the rush. I'll go over midafternoon before school lets out."

"You're going to run into the same problem with the after-school crowd if you get hung up. You may as well go early. The sooner he knows about it, the sooner he can investigate and prove that Terry didn't do anything wrong."

Erin looked at the time on her phone. "Do you think he'll be questioning Adele right now? I don't want to interrupt her witness statement. If he decides this is more important, then she'll have to wait over there half the day."

Vic shook her head. "I doubt it. She's up late at night. I doubt he could get her over to the police department this early."

"Okay. Yeah, you're probably right. I'll just…" Erin wiped her moist hands on her apron. "I'll just go over there right now. I'm sure it will only take a few minutes, and it should be quiet here until lunch. I'll get back as quickly as I can. I'm not the witness, so he's not going to want to spend time interviewing me."

"But you might need to spend some time convincing him that it's a legitimate lead. He might not think so."

"Yeah." Erin took a breath and prepared herself mentally to go over to the police department once more. She would look even more suspicious this time, going over there when Terry wasn't around. And she wasn't going to take another box of muffins over to smooth her way, or they would start thinking she was guilty of something. She wasn't going there to snoop this time. She was going to give the sheriff a legitimate tip, not to check it out herself. She wasn't doing anything she wasn't supposed to.

Still, when Clara saw Erin's approach, she shook her head, looking forbidding. "He's pretty busy today, Erin, and you know you're not supposed to be poking around here. I got in trouble the other day for letting you past the desk with those muffins. You can't have the run of the place."

"I'm not. I'll stay out here with you until he's free. But I need to see Sheriff Wilmot. I may have found something out. A break in the case."

"What kind of a break?" Clara demanded, her penciled eyebrows drawing down. "What could you know, other than pillow talk?"

Erin's face got hot with a combination of anger and embarrassment. "Just let him know, would you?"

Clara stared at Erin. She wasn't an easy person to get along with at the best of times, and the fact that she'd been reprimanded after Erin's last visit meant that she wasn't about to give Erin anything easily.

Erin went over to a visitor chair and sat down. "I'll just wait here until he's ready."

She sat still and stared straight at Clara, waiting. She didn't get out her phone or her lists or rummage around in her purse for anything. She just sat still, staring, waiting.

It didn't take long before Clara was uncomfortable. She shifted around, pretended not to look at her, tapped furiously on her keyboard, and made several unimportant phone calls to show Erin how low on Clara's list dealing with her was. But she was clearly rattled. Erin kept staring, blinking now and then and remaining focused tightly on Clara.

Eventually, Clara turned away, punching a single button on her office phone and talking into the receiver with her hand over her mouth so that Erin couldn't hear what she was saying or read her lips. She hung up the phone with a crash.

"He'll be out to see you when he has a spare moment."

"Thank you."

It wasn't long before Sheriff Wilmot asked Erin into his office. She sat down on the uncomfortable couch while he sat on a chair close to her. A cozy arrangement that indicated she was a friend rather than a suspect, not relegated to a hard chair in a bare interview room. She wasn't sure what she would have done if he had taken her into one of those rooms. She might have had a panic attack and not been able to handle it.

Maybe the sheriff guessed as much.

He listened to Erin's somewhat meandering story about how

she had found out about the man with the mask from Peter, being sure to tell him that she had only asked Peter a couple of questions and had not suggested the answers. She had let him come up with those on his own, and his recollections put the masked man at the back door of the police department before Biggles's death.

Wilmot rubbed his chin, thinking about it. He pulled a pen out of his pocket and fidgeted with it, not writing any notes, but clicking the top and trying to decide what to do with the information.

"You're sure about all of this?" he asked. "You're sure that it was the day that Biggles died."

"That's what Peter said. You'll have to check the details with him. He said it was Monday after school."

"But this story… it's a bit of a tall tale. He saw a man with a monkey mask? I don't know what to think of that."

"You don't think it's suspicious?"

"You really think that someone broke into the police department, came into one of the interview rooms, killed Biggles, and walked back out of here, and no one saw a thing?"

"Except for Peter. Yes."

"That door isn't flimsy. Someone would have to unlock or pick it. And right in the middle of the day when everybody was here? When he could have been seen at any time? Who would do that?"

"I don't know. That's for you to investigate."

"I just don't know, Erin. It's not a very believable story."

"But Peter wasn't trying to make us believe that he'd seen a murderer. He was just talking about a cool mask he saw. He didn't connect it with Biggles's death or any other criminal activity. He just liked the guy's mask."

"It could have been completely innocent. If it was even the day that he thinks it was."

"Was there a day that there *was* someone here wearing a monkey mask? Was there a pre-Halloween costume party somewhere in the Town Hall? Why would anyone be wearing a mask in the middle of the day, except to avoid being identified?"

"If someone wanted to kill Biggles, it would have made a lot more sense to wait until night, when I would be the only one here, in my office. To do it before everyone had left for the day and might walk in on him? That's too bold. No one would do that."

"If they thought that he was being transported back to Moose River that night, then it was their only chance. They had to get in here and do it before he was moved. This is the weakest part of the chain, security-wise." She grimaced. "Sorry."

"Anyone who had anything to do with the case knew that he was going to be kept here overnight. Even an outsider could have guessed that we'd want him for another day to question him. We can't always get same-day transportation due to the county schedules."

"Then that goes to show that it was an outsider. Or someone who was really desperate. Maybe they wanted to keep him from talking. He could have spilled the beans on other criminal enterprises. Someone might have been desperate to stop him before he could tell you about their part in the drug dealing. A bigger fish for a lighter sentence."

"Biggles wasn't going to talk. He was a professional. He knew to keep his mouth shut. Mob guys know that. They know that no matter what kind of protection we offer or how much lighter the sentence is, they're still going to end up in prison at the mercy of the clan boys who are already on the inside. There isn't anywhere safe in the pen. Not even in isolation."

"If the clan could get him in isolation at the prison, then why couldn't they get to him here in an unguarded room? No armed guards or security cameras. All he needed was a lock pick, stealth, and a bit of luck. And a mask to hide his identity."

The sheriff sat still, gazing off into space, before finally nodding. "Alright," he finally agreed. "I guess I'd better call Mrs. Foster."

Erin filled Terry in on the latest news when she got home. She didn't want to be overheard at the bakery, especially when it involved Peter Foster. She didn't want him or his family being harassed by gossips who wanted to know the details of the investigation. Word of a masked intruder would spread like wild-fire. She had promised the sheriff she would keep it under wraps, but had told him that she was going to talk to Terry about it. Wilmot grimaced, but didn't tell her that she couldn't. He knew she could have lied to him and said she wasn't going to. She was being honest about it, and he didn't have any authority to stop her. She had told him what she knew, and she was free to tell anyone else she wanted to.

And Terry had the right to know.

He nodded and looked thoughtful, but didn't have much to say about it. Vic seemed much more enthusiastic about the news than he did, bouncing on her heels, eyes bright and excited.

"This is good news," she insisted. "It proves that there was foul play; it wasn't just an accident or natural causes. There was someone at the police department who shouldn't have been. It will clear you!"

Terry was cautious. He shook his head. "We'll see. It might

not go anywhere. It might have been someone on their way to a costume party. Someone who worked somewhere else in the Town Hall and just chose to use that hallway and door."

"It wasn't a costume," Vic maintained.

Erin tended to agree, but she understood Terry not wanting to get his hopes up too much. "The sheriff is going to look into it. He thinks it's worth looking at."

"That's good," Terry said without emotion.

Erin sighed and picked up the stack of mail and flyers Terry had put on the coffee table. Mostly junk. A couple of bills. She frowned at one with a handwritten address on the front. "One here for you, Vicky."

Vic snagged it from her hand while Erin was still looking at it. Usually, the mailman managed to sort their mail into the two separate mailboxes, but sometimes one ended up in the wrong box. Erin opened her mouth to ask who the letter was from but, seeing Vic's face, something made her stop. Vic was pink and didn't meet her eyes. She folded the envelope in half and tucked it into her jeans pocket. She turned her wrist to look at her watch.

"I want to shower before Willie gets in, and I'm not sure when that will be, so I guess I'll see you later."

"Sure," Erin agreed. "No shift tomorrow, but don't forget we're having a business meeting after the ladies' tea."

"I won't forget. I'm eager to get started on some cute cookies. It's time for our harvest and Halloween treats to make an appearance."

"Well, once we talk through our strategic plan for the next couple of months, we'll be good to go. After Halloween is over, we need to be thinking about Thanksgiving and Christmas."

"Awesome," Vic agreed. "I can't wait. I love Christmas."

"I'm not sure we'll do quite as much as we did last year for our Christmas dinner..." They had been eating Christmas treats from the freezer for months.

Vic laughed. "No, maybe not quite so much this year."

Erin watched Vic leave through the back door to go to her loft and get ready. She brushed the sweaty hair back from her own face. She needed a shower too. It was hot work, even in the fall. But she wasn't in a hurry.

"What do you make of that?" she asked.

Terry considered for a moment. "She did seem in a bit of a hurry to get out of here."

"And the letter?"

"Who was it from?"

"I don't know. There wasn't a return address. It was handwritten. Looked like a woman's handwriting."

"Could it have been from her mother?"

"It looked like a younger person's writing. Older people, their writing is tighter, sometimes shaky. This looked... more like a school kid."

"Ah." Terry gave a slow nod.

"What does that mean?"

"It means... she's been getting calls and texts from some of those people on the cruise. You know, that LGBT group she was hanging out with."

"Oh. Okay. So maybe it's one of them."

"Probably," Terry agreed.

Erin looked at him sideways. "How do you know she's been getting calls and texts from them?"

"Willie mentioned it when we were working the other day."

"Is he worried about it?"

"Worried... not exactly. But he's... a little uncomfortable. He's not used to her having these other friends. They're outside of Vic and Willie's normal social circle and he doesn't have anything in common with them."

"So he's jealous." Erin nodded, remembering how she had felt on the ship when Vic was spending time with her new friends. Like she had been abandoned. She had been there when Vic hadn't had anyone else, and to suddenly have Vic spending time with a whole different group of friends, laughing like they knew each other and understood each other without the need for a shared history, had been disconcerting and had made her feel uncomfortable and out of sorts. Of course, there was no reason Vic shouldn't have her own friends. And she needed friends who understood her feelings and shared life experiences with her.

But Erin hadn't liked it, and neither had Willie. They had both suddenly felt like outsiders, castoffs, while Vic had forged new relationships.

Terry shrugged. "He's feeling uncomfortable," he repeated.

"Does Vic know that?"

"It's up to the two of them to talk it out. I'm not a relationship counselor."

That sounded like a good policy, though Erin wasn't sure she'd be able to stick to it. She didn't like to get involved in other people's disagreements or problems, but she also didn't want to see problems between her friends. Maybe with just a little nudge, Vic would see how Willie was feeling and reassure him that she wasn't going to leave him in favor of her new friends. She'd helped them see each other's points of view before…

*E*rin was in the shower when Terry knocked and entered. Usually, he waited until she was done, knowing that she wasn't going to be in there for long but just wanted to rinse away the sweat of the workday. It was different when she had a bath before bed and might be soaking in the tub for an hour.

"Hi. What's up?"

"Uh… I was planning to have dinner with you, but I got a call…"

Erin's stomach lurched. "From the sheriff? You know what we talked about. If he's going to keep calling you in for questioning, you need to talk to a lawyer. You don't have to go in."

"No, it wasn't the sheriff."

"Oh." Erin ran her fingers through her short hair and scrubbed her scalp with her fingertips, trying to erase the fatigue of the day with the warm water and light massage. "What was it, then?"

"It was Jack Ward, from Moose River."

"Ward? What did he want?" Erin wasn't sure she wanted Terry to go talk to Jack Ward any more than she wanted him to talk to Sheriff Wilmot.

"He said there have been some things going on in Moose

River. Rumors. He's been talking to friends and business acquaintances of Biggles. He wanted to fill me in and see if we could put our heads together and…"

"I don't know if you should go."

"He's not going to arrest me, Erin. Biggles didn't die in his jurisdiction. The investigation he's doing is a favor for Sheriff Wilmot and the staties."

"Then why is he sharing it with you? Shouldn't he be talking to them? I don't like you going all the way out there to talk to him, just to find out that he's trying to build the case against you."

"He's not going to do that."

"Do you think it's worth the risk, though?"

"It's not a risk." Terry was still and didn't say anything for a minute.

Erin stuck her head around the curtain to look at him.

"I'm not asking you if you think it's a good idea," Terry explained, scratching the back of his head. "I'm just letting you know where I'm going to be. And that I probably won't be home until late. If it's raining hard or I'm tired, then I won't try to drive. I'll stay at the hotel and come back tomorrow. So… you don't need to worry about me."

Erin withdrew and stood once more under the warm spray of water. "Okay."

"It's okay?"

"You said you weren't asking permission."

"Well… I'm not. I just want to make sure that you're not upset. Don't stay up waiting for me. I don't know how long I'll be."

"Tomorrow is a sleep-in day. You and I usually… make time for each other."

"I know." His face was pained. "I wouldn't duck out on you normally. We'll get together tomorrow for sure. I'm sorry. It wasn't planned, but I think I need to go."

"Can't he wait until tomorrow? Surely he has to go to bed sometime too."

"He's making the time for me. I don't want to quibble over schedules."

Erin sighed.

She didn't tell him that it was okay. She just stood there silently in the warm stream of the shower until he decided to go.

Vic was out with Willie, Terry was on his way to Moose River, and Erin didn't want to stay home alone. The animals were good company, but she didn't get the same kind of feedback when she talked to them that she got from her friends of the two-legged variety. Erin considered going to see Mary Lou and taking her over some treats, but she knew that the treats would all just go to Josh and she already knew that Mary Lou was stressed out by Biggles's death and didn't want to have to deal with talk of Terry and if he'd done the right thing.

She decided instead to go out for a drive. Maybe she would go see Adele at the summer house. Or maybe she'd just enjoy the outdoors for a little while and then turn around and go back home. Being out in the fresh air and beautiful autumn leaves was probably just what she needed.

Erin found herself drawn to the place Adele had described when she told Erin about seeing Terry's arrest of Bo Biggles. She parked and walked around the perimeter of the school, sticking to Clementine's woods. Now Erin's woods. She always thought of them as Clementine's or Adele's, finding it hard to believe that she owned all of that land. Circumnavigating the school grounds, she felt like she was doing something wrong and needed to make sure that no one saw her. But she wasn't trespassing. In fact, she was going out of her way to stay off of the school property. Just like Biggles had.

She could see the wild strawberry patch that Adele had probably been picking berries from in a little clearing in the trees. In the shadows of the trees, with her slim figure and dark clothing,

Adele might not be noticeable unless she made a sudden movement or did something else to draw attention to herself. And Biggles had been... where?

Erin mapped it out in her mind. Where Terry would have been able to pull up in his car. Where Adele had been watching from. Where Biggles would have been able to see what was going on in the school grounds and anyone approaching him, and yet still be able to claim that he was not dealing drugs on the school property. She scanned the ground, looking for footprints and torn-up vegetation. They'd had quite a struggle, from what Adele had described and what Terry had been careful not to say. They had both been down on the ground, hitting and wrestling. Biggles was not a small man. And K9 had been there too, employed by Terry to take Biggles down. But then Biggles had tried again to get away. Terry had tased him. Terry had wrestled with him.

She found the trampled vegetation. It was not easy, having been nearly a week since the incident had taken place. The grasses and vegetation had all sprung up again, and any footprints that might have been there initially had been obscured. Had anyone bothered to look at the footprints while they were still fresh? Would they be able to tell anything to either verify or refute Terry's story? Probably not. Prints wouldn't show how hard Terry had hit Biggles, how many times he had tased him, and whether he had employed a chokehold.

Hopefully, Adele had been able to confirm all of those things to the sheriff and the state investigators that afternoon when they had taken her statement. Adele was a good person, an honest person. She didn't like to get mixed up in police matters or other people's business, but she would tell what she had seen straightforwardly and wouldn't try to obfuscate anything.

There was one trampled area where the grass had been scuffed away to the bare earth, and there were cigarette butts scattered around. She imagined it was the place where Biggles had stood, watching the school and peddling his wares.

Erin ran the scenario through her mind. Terry approaching.

Biggles trying to run. Throwing something away. Getting taken down. The ensuing struggle. She played and replayed it, listening to Adele's words.

He'd thrown something away. Drugs, undoubtedly. Get rid of the evidence. Make sure it wasn't found on him. Claim that the cops planted it wherever it was found. And had Terry found it? Or had he been so occupied with getting Biggles under control that he had been distracted from it? He might not have even known that Biggles had thrown something away. She moved her feet slowly through the long grass and underbrush, not about to use her hands and end up finding a snake or spider or even just poison ivy or thistles. It would be very easy for a small item to become lost forever.

She heard cawing overhead and looked up at the crow perched on a branch, watching her while tilting his head this way and that. Very intelligent eyes.

"Skye?"

Erin wasn't sure whether it was Adele's crow or not. He didn't fly away at the sound of her voice, but he didn't get any closer or beg for peanuts either.

"Is this where they were?" she asked aloud. Of course he didn't understand her or answer her, but it was comforting to have an animal to talk to, even away from her house. "This must be where Terry arrested Bo Biggles. And he threw something away. Something incriminating. Were you here with Adele? Did you see?"

It was a large area to search, even if all she did was look a foot or two into the vegetation around the disturbed area. And what exactly did she expect to find? Something that would exonerate Terry? Like what? A handwritten confession?

There was another caw, and the crow flew over Erin's head and landed in the low branches of a tree just outside of the area she'd been searching. He tipped forward, looking down at something on the ground. Erin knew that it was impossible that the bird could have found what she herself was looking for, but she pushed her way carefully through the brush anyway. If she didn't look, she'd never be able to stop thinking about how she could have broken the case if she'd just followed the darn bird.

She couldn't see anything at first. Nothing that she was interested in, and not even anything that would interest a crow, like a termite mound or discarded sweet bun. She moved around the area, trying to put herself at the same viewing angle as the bird, looking down and from the side. There was a glint of light off metal. Erin moved slowly closer, trying to keep her eye on the spot even when the glint disappeared again. She pushed back the yellowing leaves of a rosebush, trying to avoid scratching and pricking herself too much. And then she saw the gun. Shiny silver and lethal-looking. Erin pushed back more vegetation for a better look. It was certainly not a hunting gun or a toy. Nothing that there was an innocent explanation for. As much as she wanted to pick it up for a closer look, she knew better. She mentally mapped the landmarks around it so that she would be able to find it again, and started to work her way out from the gun in a tight spiral, looking for anything else that Biggles might have disposed of. If he knew he was about to be arrested, then getting rid of his gun was a good choice. But he might have had other incriminating items on him as well, things that were equally important to dispose of. He hadn't had much time, so they weren't likely to be scattered far and wide—one toss, and then dealing with Terry.

She was right. There was a billfold with cash inside that had fallen unfolded a few feet away. Anything light had probably blown away. She didn't find any baggies of white powder or pills. Hopefully, that meant that any drugs Biggles had been dealing had been scooped up with him, and had not been found by kids on their way home from school.

Erin figured she had found everything she was going to and, before long, night would start to fall, and she had best get someone out there who could take care of the evidence before it was too dark. She sat in the Y of a stunted tree and pulled out her phone.

She showed Tom Baker and Sheriff Wilmot both the gun and the billfold. After marking the locations with evidence flags and taking pictures, they put on gloves and picked up the gun and the wallet.

"That's a nice gun," the sheriff observed, turning it back and forth to look at every surface. "That's brand-spanking-new. Nickel-plated. A gun you're going to show off. Drug dealers and pimps, they like pretty guns like this."

"We already know Biggles was a drug dealer," Erin agreed.

The sheriff shrugged. "And how about that there wallet, Tom? Anything in there that would indicate who owned it? We're working on the assumption that it was Biggles's, but we want confirmation. There was a struggle out here. If Office Piper happened to drop it while he was making the arrest…"

"That's not Terry's," Erin objected.

The sheriff just looked at her and didn't argue. He knew very well that it wasn't Terry's; he was following procedure. Wearing gloves, Tom opened the billfold pocket gingerly, as if he expected it to be full of rattlesnake eggs. He whistled.

"Nice big wad of cash in here. Someone was making good money."

"I would expect so," Wilmot agreed.

"There's no I.D." He thumbed through the cash to look at the denominations and see if there was anything else folded in with it. "There's a card. A picture or somethin'."

Erin had been trying to stay back out of their way but, at Tom's words, she couldn't help stepping forward to get a look at the picture as Tom tugged it out. Tom looked at it blankly.

It was faded. It had been exposed to the moisture of the grass for almost a week. And maybe it was faded even before that. It looked like an inkjet printing on subpar photographic paper. Better than just printing on copy paper, but it wasn't thick or glossy and didn't hold the ink well.

A boy and a girl. Dressed up for a dance or nice restaurant or even church. Posed stiffly in a position that said, 'this is my boyfriend/girlfriend,' even though they seemed awkward and not quite sure how to hold each other. Erin squinted at it, trying to make out the faces. The boy certainly wasn't Bo Biggles. And Bo wasn't old enough to be a parent to a teen. So maybe a brother or uncle? Why would he be carrying their pictures around unless they were family?

Then Erin gasped as the light shifted and the faces morphed. She knew one of them. While the picture was unclear, she was almost sure she knew the boy.

Wilmot looked at her. He looked down at the picture, studying it thoughtfully. "You know who they are?"

"I'm not sure... the boy... it could be... but I'm not sure..."

"Who?"

"Jeremy. Jeremy Jackson."

Jeremy hadn't been in Bald Eagle Falls for long, so it was understandable that the sheriff and Tom didn't immediately recognize him in the picture. And it was a bad picture, so that even knowing Jeremy as she did, Erin still couldn't be sure it was actually him.

But she directed the sheriff to Jeremy's home, a basement suite not far from Erin's home, which he shared with Rohilda Beaven when she was in town. Since it was a weekend and she didn't have any cases that demanded her attention out of town, Beaver was there when Jeremy answered the door.

Sheriff Wilmot turned to Erin. "You don't need to be here, Erin. Now that you've shown me where Jeremy lives, you can go on home."

Erin shook her head resolutely. "No. I'm staying."

Jeremy looked from the sheriff to Erin and back again. "What's going on? Is it something to do with Terry? Is everything okay?"

"This is not anything to do with Officer Piper. Perhaps tangentially, but not directly. Can I come in, please?" The sheriff angled his body forward so that his arm was already through the door and he was ahead of Erin, preventing her entrance. He didn't want her there, and he couldn't stop her if she was determined, but he was making it obvious that he didn't want her there.

"Uh, yeah. Come in." Jeremy opened the door the rest of the way and the sheriff entered, seeming to expand to fill the room. Erin had usually seen him as a bureaucrat. Someone who was required to do the paperwork and keep the town happy, but who wasn't directly investigating cases and making arrests. He wasn't a cop on the street like Terry, and usually let Terry take the lead on things, even though he was Terry's superior. But without Terry there to take charge, Sheriff Wilmot rose to the occasion. He looked confident and competent.

He nodded to Beaver and selected a kitchen chair, turning it around to straddle it backward to face where Jeremy would be when he sat back down on the couch with Beaver. Jeremy was still at the door, though, looking at Erin as if he didn't know what to do about her. Finally, he motioned for her to enter as well.

"What's this about, Erin? What's going on?"

Erin selected an easy chair and sat down, sitting forward rigidly rather than sinking back into it. She might have identified

Jeremy in that picture, but she wasn't about to turn Jeremy over to the sheriff without at least trying to help him. Jeremy was too young to be left to handle an interview by someone like the sheriff on his own. With Beaver there, Erin probably wasn't needed, but she still worried that Beaver might have motives other than Jeremy's welfare.

Jeremy shut the door and returned to the couch with Beaver, sliding his arm around her and looking curiously at the sheriff. "Now maybe you can tell me what this is all about."

"You come from Moose River."

Jeremy raised an eyebrow. "Yes."

"And you are part of the Jackson family."

"Obviously. My name is Jeremy Jackson."

"And as part of the Jackson family, you were expected to take part in clan activities."

"I'm not in Moose River anymore. And I'm not taking direction from the clan. I left the family and the clan. I came here to be on my own, independent."

Erin knew that Beaver had helped him out significantly, with the bills and getting his apartment, if nothing else. She suspected there had been plenty else. Warnings to the clan to leave Jeremy alone. Finding him a job. Making sure that he was doing all the things he needed to do to keep himself safe and healthy. She was older than he was. Erin didn't have a problem with that. There was a lot more difference in age between Willie and Vic. But she felt it did create an imbalance. Beaver was so much more experienced and mature than Jeremy was and she probably helped him a lot more than was good for him.

"So you haven't had any contact with the Jackson clan."

"No."

"Did you know Mr. Biggles?"

"Did I know him?" People often repeated questions in order to give themselves longer to answer. Erin did it herself when she was stalling for time. "I knew… he was a member of the clan. I knew of him. Were we friends? No, never."

"You didn't do any jobs together?"

"Jobs? No. I didn't do any jobs with Biggles."

"What did you think of him?"

"I didn't think anything of him. He was a guy I knew of. I didn't spend any time thinking about him."

"You and he both came to Bald Eagle Falls at around the same time."

"I've been here a lot longer."

"When you left Moose River, he came here about the same time. Around the time Mr. Inglethorpe died."

Jeremy shrugged. "I wasn't exactly present for that. It was around then, I suppose."

"Which was the same time as Bo Biggles showed up."

"If you say so. I wasn't aware of what anyone else in the clan was doing at the time. That was the whole point in leaving Moose River. To leave all of that behind."

"So you claim you haven't had any interactions with Mr. Biggles."

Jeremy's eyes slid over to Beaver. She chewed on her gum, looking back at him and not giving him any advice on his answer.

"I don't think I said that," Jeremy said slowly.

"What interactions have you had with Biggles?"

"I… we weren't friends. And I wasn't in the clan."

"What interactions have you had?"

"I don't think I should answer that."

Sheriff Wilmot took the evidence bag containing the billfold out of his satchel and placed it on Jeremy's coffee table. "Is that your billfold, Mr. Jackson?"

"Jeremy. I don't like being called Mr. Jackson."

"Is that your billfold?"

"No. I've never seen that before."

"Do you mind showing me your billfold?"

"Well, I don't use one like that." Jeremy worked a wallet out of his back pocket. "There's mine. I don't really carry cash, you know. Just a few cards. I don't need a billfold."

"Your wallet only has cards in it."

Jeremy flipped it open, indicated the cards, opened the money pocket to show that it was empty, and shoved it back into his jeans pocket.

"Have you ever seen this picture before?" The sheriff had put the bad picture into an evidence bag and now placed it in front of Jeremy.

Jeremy peered at it, the color draining from his tanned face. "I don't know. It's pretty blurry."

Sheriff Wilmot was silent for a long few minutes, waiting for Jeremy to volunteer more. Cops were good at using silences. People liked to fill the void. They didn't like to sit in silence, thinking their own thoughts, facing their accusers, and not say anything. Jeremy did well to stay silent.

"Do you want to know what I think, Jeremy?" Sheriff Wilmot leaned forward, resting his arms on the back of the chair. His voice was friendly and nonaccusatory. Personable and inviting. "I think that something happened between you and Bo Biggles. I think that you went to meet with him. To confront him. And I think the two of you fought. A knock-down, drag-out fight. And I think you lost your billfold in that fight. The money is yours, the billfold is yours, and the picture is yours." The sheriff nudged the picture forward a little. "That is you, isn't it? So this was your billfold. And you lost it in that fight with Mr. Biggles."

Jeremy shifted. He squeezed Beaver tightly as if he were afraid she was going to get up and go somewhere else. And then he let her go and moved away from her an inch. He stared at the picture on the coffee table.

"I knew Biggles was here. And I wanted to protect my family. Vic and her friends here. Erin is family. And Terry. And Willie. I didn't want him expanding the drug trade in Bald Eagle Falls. If people want the hard stuff, they can go into the city. There are enough problems here with just alcohol and pot. I didn't want Biggles anywhere near my family. So I confronted him, told him to get out of town or I would make him leave."

"And how did you propose to do that?"

"I didn't have a plan. I mean, I just thought… if I told him I knew he was here and that I didn't want him in town, he'd go. And if he didn't, I'd… encourage him."

"You think he was going to listen to a teenage dropout of the clan? That you were going to be able to force him to leave town? That seems a little naive."

"Well, you ask Vic. I don't claim to always make the best decisions. Sometimes I… overestimate my abilities."

"So did Biggles agree to leave town?"

"Hell, no."

Beaver chuckled. Erin couldn't help smiling herself. Sheriff Wilmot nodded, showing not a crack in his facade.

"And when he said he wasn't going to leave, then what happened?"

"I swung for him. Figured I'd get in the first punch; that would give me a chance of beating him or at least convince him I was serious. But he was… well, he's bigger than me, and stronger, and I didn't exactly make out like a bandit. Before I knew what was happening, he was sitting on my chest laughing at me. I was embarrassed. He'd whipped me like an unweaned kitten. So when he let me up… I booked it out of there. I didn't realize I'd lost the billfold until later. I went back to look for it, but the vegetation is so dense out there…"

Erin nodded. She wouldn't have had much luck if it hadn't been for the crow spotting the shiny gun.

"Why didn't you come forward?" the sheriff asked. "You knew that Terry was being accused of beating Biggles up. And you knew that you'd had an altercation with him. You knew very well that at least some of those bruises might be attributable to your fight with him."

"Terry didn't beat Bo up. I knew he'd be cleared without me ever having to say anything. And my fight with Bo wasn't exactly successful. I didn't land more than a punch or two. So the bruises he had… maybe I gave him a black eye with that first punch, but after that? No."

"And what about the bruises on his throat. You put your hands around his neck? Tried to choke him either during the fight or while he was on top of you, trying to get him off? Or did you get an arm bar on him at some point during the struggle? People don't know how easily those blood vessels in the neck can be damaged."

"I didn't choke him."

"I'm supposed to believe that?"

"Maybe you don't. What's that to me?" Jeremy shrugged indifferently. But his life and liberty were in the balance, so of course he cared.

"What happened later?" Sheriff Wilmot asked.

"Later? Nothing happened later. Like I said, I realized I'd lost my billfold, so I looked for it. But I couldn't find it."

"There's a lot of money in this billfold. You're not making that kind of money acting as a security guard on the farm."

"So I do a few other jobs on the side. And I'm careful with my money." He made a gesture indicating his surroundings. "I don't spend a lot on my comfort."

"Maybe when you couldn't find your billfold, you decided to see whether Mr. Biggles had picked it up. You needed that money back. Maybe you owe someone. So you were desperate."

"I don't owe any leg-breakers."

"So you weren't at all upset about losing the billfold."

"Obviously I was upset. I went and looked for it. But I couldn't find it. And why would I go looking for Bo? If he had it, he wasn't going to give it back, and it wasn't like I could take it from him or convince him to give it to me."

"Maybe you went home to arm yourself. You planned to get the drop on him this time around. Not to rush into things quite so recklessly."

Jeremy shook his head. "He was arrested after our little dust-up. I'd have to wait until he was out of police custody before I could do anything."

"Or you could put on a mask, pick the back door, and confront him right in the police department interview room."

Jeremy raised his eyebrows. "What? Why would I do something like that? That's crazy. What, I'd go in there, start fighting with the guy, somehow get him into a chokehold, and no one would see or hear me? He wouldn't shout and attract attention? He'd just sit there quietly while I offed him?"

The sheriff looked over at Erin, bouncing those questions back to her. How likely was it that someone could have broken into the police department and killed Biggles without anyone having heard?

It made sense if it was a police officer who could do something while Biggles was still in cuffs. Everyone knew Terry was in the interview room with Biggles and would think nothing of it if they heard Biggles shouting. He'd resisted arrest, so a certain amount of combativeness would simply be ignored. Anyone who was concerned could look through the window, and there would be nothing unexpected about Terry questioning him or even manhandling him back into his chair. An outsider, though, would be a different story. They would have to get into the room without being seen. Choke Biggles out—or inject him or whatever it was that had actually killed him—and then get out of there without being seen. With no apparent protest or ruckus from Biggles.

It wasn't the most logical explanation. In fact, it sounded more and more farfetched, even though Erin had been convinced of the story. Peter had seen a man with a mask going into the Town Hall. It had to be someone who was trying to hide his identity. Was it one of the officers or staff? She shook her head, trying to wrap her mind around it.

"Did... the witness... have any description of the person who came out of there, other than the mask?" she asked Wilmot. "Like, size, clothes, that kind of thing."

Wilmot leaned back and stretched, turning his attention to

Erin. He had, Erin suspected, decided that Jeremy was not a viable suspect in the murder of Biggles. It would have been too hard for him to do what Erin had suggested. Too dangerous. "Average height, slim build, blue jeans and t-shirt. Could be almost anyone. He couldn't say for sure whether it had been a man or a woman. He was focused on the mask."

"How soundproof are those rooms?" That, at least, could explain why the police hadn't heard a fight between Biggles and an intruder.

"They're not soundproof. The concrete construction and the door deaden some of the sound, but yelling and screaming; you would still hear something from our desks."

Jeremy looked at Erin. "You know it couldn't have been me, Erin. Why would I do something like that? I'm not that kind of guy. If I lost a stack of money during a fight… you really think I would sneak into police custody and kill the guy for it? Or out of revenge? That's not me."

No, but to protect his sister…?

"I never thought it was you. I never said that. The sheriff is just following up on leads."

He shook his head and leaned back, snuggling closer to Beaver again. "It wasn't me. Yeah, I lost my billfold, but that doesn't make me guilty of whatever conspiracy the police department is cooking up to cover their butts."

CHAPTER 30

*E*rin was glad that the sheriff hadn't had enough evidence to arrest Jeremy. She didn't think Jeremy had any reason to kill Biggles. As much as she sometimes wondered what Jeremy was up to, she didn't think he had it in him to sneak in and out of the police department like that. Something else had happened, and Erin wasn't sure what it was. She was trying to formulate a scenario in her mind that made sense.

She might be able to explain away the others in the police department not hearing any altercation between Biggles and his attacker. The room deadened the sound. Sheriff Wilmot said that they would still be able to hear any shouting at their desks but, with the tapping of computer keys, talking on phones, running the photocopier or printer and the coffee machine, there could definitely be enough noise to cover it up. Someone might have gotten a chokehold on him before he had a chance to shout.

But who would have the nerve to slip in and out of there?

Erin was distracted driving home. It was a good thing there wasn't any traffic to speak of. She arrived home safely and let herself in. She'd only been there for a few minutes when there was a knock on the back door. Erin was used to Vic and Willie using the back at will, and wasn't concerned when she heard a key in the door.

"Erin?" Vic called out. "You home?"

"I'm here." Erin walked down the hall to the kitchen and looked in at her. "What's up?"

"Oh, okay. I thought you were over at Terry's, because both your vehicles were gone earlier. Then when I saw the lights come on…"

"Yeah, it's just me."

"Where did Terry go? Did you have a fight? I thought you'd stay over there the weekend."

"He had to go to Moose River."

Vic frowned. "Moose River? Why?"

Willie came in the door behind her. "Everything okay?" He spotted Erin and nodded a greeting. "I told you she was back."

"Terry had to go to Moose River," Erin explained, catching him up.

Willie put his hand on Vic's waist to draw her closer, but she jerked away from his touch. He stood there looking at her in surprise. Erin stared into Vic's alarmed expression, unable to understand what she was worried about. "Everything is okay. He'll be back tonight or tomorrow. Jack Ward wanted to talk to him."

"About Bo Biggles?"

"I guess, yes. Something about him. He said there was some chatter about what had happened."

Vic looked at Willie. "I think… we should go talk to him."

"To Terry? He'll be back tonight, Erin said."

"To Terry… to Ward… I need to… I think…"

Willie raised an eyebrow. "If you want to, we can," he said agreeably. "But do you want to tell me what's going on? Do you know something that we should know?"

"You might want to stay here tonight," Erin cautioned. "You can always talk to Terry in the morning. Or call Jack Ward. But Jeremy—"

"Jeremy? What does he have to do with anything?"

"The sheriff was over there tonight. To find out what he'd had to do with Biggles. He's not there anymore, and he didn't arrest Jeremy or take him in for questioning. I just think… you might want to stick around just in case anything changes. Or maybe you should call Jeremy first to make sure everything is okay."

"Jeremy didn't have anything to do with Bo Biggles."

"Well, as it turns out, he and Biggles had a fight that day. Jeremy ended up dropping his wallet, with a picture of him with a girl in it, so the sheriff could trace it back to him." Erin didn't explain her involvement in the evening's events.

Vic opened her mouth. She looked at Erin, shaking her head. "What are you talking about? Jeremy had a fight…?"

Erin explained it the best she could, but Vic didn't seem to believe a word of it. Erin focused on the picture, trying to describe it to explain to Vic how everything had happened and how they had figured out that Jeremy had been there with Biggles. Vic sat down on one of the kitchen chairs, as white as a ghost.

"We have to go to Moose River."

Willie tried to calm her, rubbing her shoulders and back. "We can go to Moose River if you want," he assured her. "It's going to be a bit late to talk to Jack Ward, though. By the time we get there, he's going to be home in bed."

"I don't understand," Erin told Vic, trying to read her face. "Why do you think Jeremy is lying about the fight with Biggles? He lost his wallet there."

"It wasn't his wallet. Jeremy doesn't carry cash, especially like that. Where would he get that kind of money?"

"He didn't explain, but he confirmed it was his. And he had a picture of him and a girl in it."

"That wasn't a picture of Jeremy."

Erin and Willie both just stared at Vic, trying to understand how she could know that and why she was so upset.

"I know because it wasn't a picture of Jeremy. It was a picture of me."

CHAPTER 31

*E*rin blinked slowly, comprehension dawning. Not a picture of Jeremy, but of James, Vic's identity before she had transitioned. The boys in the Jackson family all had a strong family resemblance. Erin couldn't yet tell Joseph and Daniel apart.

"That was you," Erin repeated.

Vic nodded her agreement.

"But that wasn't your wallet."

"No. It was his. Biggles's."

Willie's massaging hands stopped moving. "Why would Biggles have a picture of you in his wallet?"

"I don't know why he had it in his wallet. It was Theresa's."

"Who is Theresa?" Erin asked.

"The girl I was with. Bo's cousin. Crazy Theresa Franklin."

"You dated Bo's cousin. But why would he have a picture of the two of you?"

"He had a thing about her. It was Theresa's picture. He must have taken it when she wasn't around. Because you can bet that if she had been there, she would have killed him for even touching it."

They all just looked at each other. None of them put their thoughts into words.

Finally, Vic said, "We need to go to Moose River. I need to talk to her."

"You should call Jack Ward, give him a heads-up," Willie advised.

"I need to talk to her first."

"I don't think that's smart. Tell him first. Even though I can't see how she could have had anything to do with her cousin's death, you don't just go talk to someone you think might have been involved in another person's death. That's like some too-stupid-to-live character on TV."

Vic covered her face with her hands. Erin didn't say anything, waiting for Vic to work it through and make a decision. She understood Vic's wish to confront Theresa, but Willie was right; if Vic thought that Theresa had anything at all to do with Bo's death, they needed to be smart about it.

"Fine," Vic agreed. She pulled out her phone and tapped through several screens. "I don't have his number. And there's nothing on the website but a general number. Their switchboard is going to be closed, and no one is going to agree to wake him up because some girl in Bald Eagle Falls thinks she knows something about Theresa Franklin."

"I think I've still got it." Erin checked her contacts and found Ward's cell number. She handed her phone over to Vic.

Vic tapped the number and waited. It rang and rang and, eventually, Erin heard the tinny sound of Jack Ward's outgoing voicemail message. Vic sighed and shook her head. "Detective Ward, I don't know if you remember me. I work with Erin Price in Bald Eagle Falls. This is her number. I wanted to talk to you about Theresa Franklin; I think she might have had something to do with Bo Biggles's death here… maybe. Or maybe just knows something about it. I don't know. She knows him. I'm going to come out there. Give me a call, and we can meet, or I can give you some more details. Okay."

She hung up and handed the phone back to Erin. Erin decided to see if Terry was still meeting with Ward or could give them any information about where he was. If they were still meeting, then Erin would have expected Ward to answer his phone when he saw her number, but he hadn't. She tried Terry's cell phone, but it rang through to voicemail just as Ward's had.

"Hi, Terry. Listen, Vic needs to talk to Jack Ward, so I'm just wondering whether you are still meeting, or if you have a way to reach him. It's about someone who might have had something to do with Bo Biggles's death... but I'm not sure how. Anyway. Call back. Me or Vicky."

She also hung up. They looked at each other.

"Let's go," Vic said. She put her hand on Willie's arm. "We'll use your truck."

"So..." They were on their way, and it was Willie who broke the silence, eager to find out more details about Bo Biggles and Theresa Franklin and why she needed to talk to Theresa so urgently. "How long since you've seen this Theresa?"

Vic stared out the window into the blackness of the night and the glittering stars overhead. Erin could see Vic's reflection in the glass and saw her biting her lip.

"I haven't seen her since I left home."

Willie nodded. "Heard from her at all?" he asked casually.

"She started sending me letters. A couple of months ago. She's still... she's been through some stuff and is feeling nostalgic about when we were together." Vic shook her head, still not looking at Willie. "We weren't even together for very long, and it was pretty... awkward and innocent. Kids going out to the movies together. Listening to music. Walking to the ice cream store. I was still trying to figure out how to deal with my gender identity. How to live with myself. What kind of relationship I wanted. We were both just experimenting."

"But now, what... she wants to get back together?"

"I don't know what she wants. She wants to see me, yes.

Maybe to see if there are any sparks. But I don't know exactly what. If she's expecting things to be like they were back then." Vic gave a sharp laugh. "I'm not even the same person as I was."

"Does she know about your transition?"

Erin remembered the letter Vic had received earlier in the week. It had been addressed to Victoria, not to James.

"Yeah. She knew before she started writing. I don't know who she talked to; my folks are doing their best to keep it a secret. They just tell people that I ran away. I think Mom is still hoping that one of these days I'll have an epiphany and realize that I want to go back home and live out my life as a boy. And then I'll be able to slide right back into my old place in the community."

"But this Theresa is still interested in you."

Vic turned her head to study Willie. "Is that such a surprise to you? She likes me for myself, not for my gender."

"I didn't mean it that way. Just that... it would be hard for a lot of people to make that shift. Not just about you, but about herself and what attracts her."

"Like you did?"

"Yes. Like I did." He put his hand on her knee. "Sometimes, life surprises us."

Vic turned back away from him, but she put her hand over his. "Yeah, she's still interested. But I'm not interested in a relationship with her. Things weren't good the first time around and I'm already in a committed relationship."

Erin waited a few minutes before breaking the silence. "What went wrong the first time around? I know you were just kids, so it's understandable that it wasn't a long-term relationship. But you make it sound like... maybe Theresa has some issues."

"She wasn't called Crazy Theresa for nothing. She's not exactly stable."

And they were going to meet with her. Not the smartest thing Erin could think of to do. But they would first talk to Ward and Terry.

"Do you think that Theresa had something to do with Biggles's death?" Willie asked.

"I wasn't there, so I can't say. Maybe she had nothing to do with it, and it was just an accident or natural death. But him having her picture… the possibilities just make me cold all over." Vic shuddered. "I don't know Bo. I never met him. But she's mentioned him in her letters, and I remember her talking about her cousin when we were together. How mean he was toward her. I thought at the time… he must have a crush on her. But she didn't like him. She's not one of those girls who's attracted to someone who bullies them."

"Do you think Biggles knew who you were?" Erin asked. Bo had the picture with him for a reason. Had he recognized Vic as the former James Jackson? If he saw Vic as a rival, then showing up in town and especially his hanging around outside of Erin's— and Vic's—property took on an even more sinister meaning. Maybe he wasn't there for revenge against the women who had brought down the clan's drug trade in Bald Eagle Falls or to start up his own business dealing to the high school students. Maybe his whole reason for being there was to get rid of a romantic rival.

"I think so. This guy… I never met him, but I remember Theresa telling me the crap he would pull. If he was twisted enough to think that he had a better chance at Theresa if he got me out of the way… he would."

Erin thought about Jeremy and Terry. Both of them had been involved in an altercation with Bo Biggles, if Jeremy had been telling the truth about his encounter and not just making it up to protect his sister. If one of them had thought that Biggles was a threat to Vic or Erin… the idea that Terry or Jeremy might have had something to do with Bo Biggles's death was suddenly not so far-fetched. They had a solid motive.

Erin found herself hoping against hope that Theresa *had* been the culprit.

~

It seemed like the trip to Moose River took much longer than it should have. But they were finally there. Vic gave Willie directions through the semi-rural area to Theresa's family home. It was not quite a farmhouse, but not quite in town either.

Erin tried several times to reach Ward or Terry, but neither of them would answer their phones. Erin's stomach was getting tighter, forming a heavy, solid ball that ached and pulsed with her heartbeats.

"I don't think this is a good idea," Willie opined again. "We should wait until the morning. After we have a chance to talk to Jack Ward or Terry."

Vic shook her head. "Theresa isn't going to do anything to hurt me," she pointed out. "That would undo everything she's been trying to build up between us. If she wants me to be interested in her, she can't do anything to push me away. That means she can't do anything to either of you. I'm not going to ask her whether she killed her cousin. Or any other questions that are going to get her wound up. Just casual chit chat with an old friend."

Willie shook his head. He left Erin and Vic in the truck, telling them to stay put, and got out to reconnoiter. But as he got closer to the house to peek in the windows, motion-triggered floodlights came on, turning the darkness into midday and making them all cover their eyes.

Vic swore. Erin held her palms over her eyes, waiting for them to stop burning. It was a minute or two before she was able to scrub away the tears and squint around at the others and their surroundings.

Theresa stood in the doorway of the house, looking down at them from three steps above them, with a big weapon cradled in one arm. It looked like something that a soldier would carry. She was a young woman, like Vic, with a generous mouth and mouse-brown hair. She wasn't unattractive, but not a memorable beauty either.

"Identify yourselves," she ordered in a tough, flat voice.

Willie held his hands above his head, still pushing his face into his arm to shade his eyes from the blinding light. "We're friends," he said gruffly. "My name is Willie."

"Well, Willie, since I have no idea who you are, I highly doubt you're my friend. Plan on keeping your hands up nice and high."

Erin looked over at Vic, waiting for her to introduce herself. Theresa wouldn't know Erin from Adam. The only person she was likely to recognize or care about was Vic. It didn't matter who the rest of them were.

Vic was looking directly at Theresa, no longer covering or shading her eyes. She didn't introduce herself, and it dawned on Erin that she was waiting for Theresa to recognize her without prompting.

"What are you doing coming onto my property in the middle of the night? You get lost?" Theresa demanded.

"We're not lost," Vic said. "Why don't you show us some of that famous hospitality, Tess?"

Theresa stared at Vic. "Get out of the car."

Both Vic and Erin got out of the car, moving slowly, keeping their hands visible. There was no sudden exclamation of recognition. Maybe Theresa had known who they were all along. She motioned them into the house with the barrel of her gun. Erin wished Theresa would stop waving it around and just put it down. She didn't like having guns pointed at her.

Willie entered the house first, his hands still up, looking around carefully. Erin knew he would be thinking about means of escape, analyzing all of the ways in and out and what was on hand that they might be able to use. Having Theresa holding the gun on them was not conducive to getting friendly or running away. So much for not being in any danger from the woman.

Crazy Theresa, indeed.

Erin paused, waiting for Vic to enter the house ahead of her. But Theresa motioned Erin forward with the gun, impatient for her to get inside. Erin turned to look at Vic, and Vic nodded that she should go in next. Vic would bring up the rear.

Did Vic have her gun? She was almost always armed, even when she popped over in her pajamas to see Erin. Erin couldn't see a holster, but that didn't mean that Vic wasn't wearing one somewhere. And Willie? Erin didn't think he usually carried a gun, but had he decided to slip one into a hidden pocket or holster before they got on their way? Erin would feel better knowing that they had more guns on their side.

Erin entered the house and, instead of making herself at home in the living room, turned to watch Vic and make sure she was safe. When Vic got to the doorstep, Theresa stepped in front of her, blocking her, the big gun held between the two of them and her body uncomfortably close to Vic's.

"Hello, Victoria," Theresa said softly.

"Long time, no see, Tess."

"What are you doing here?"

"I just wanted to talk. You said you wanted to see me again, didn't you? So… here I am. Are you going to let me in?"

Theresa remained there for several long seconds before finally stepping back far enough for Vic to enter. Theresa kicked the door shut, the slam making them all jump.

Theresa motioned for Erin and Vic to take seats on a worn couch draped with a hand-stitched quilt, which they did. Willie sat in an easy chair. Erin remembered Sheriff Wilmot interviewing Jeremy on his couch not many hours previous. She wished that he was the one standing over them instead of the unstable woman with a big gun.

"To what do I owe the pleasure of your visit?" Theresa demanded.

"Just what I said. You said you wanted to see me again."

"A normal person calls and sets up a time. They don't just show up in the middle of the night."

"There seems to be something wrong with our phones tonight. Maybe the satellites are having some technical problems. Everything seems to go through to voicemail. Did your phone ring?"

Theresa just sneered.

"So..." Vic looked for an appropriate conversation starter. "You mentioned your cousin in your letters. Bo Biggles. Remembering how he used to treat you. I wondered whether..."

"*Used* to treat me? Not used to. Treated me every day of my life." She smiled, showing teeth gritted tightly together. "Until he died."

That answered the question as to whether she knew Bo Biggles was dead. They at least didn't have to break the news to her. Finding out whether she'd had a hand in it was another story. Erin let her shoulder brush against Vic's, trying to show her moral support. But Theresa's eyes picked up on even the very slight contact.

"So this is the new girlfriend I've been hearing all about."

Erin's jaw dropped and she couldn't collect the words to protest Theresa's categorization of their relationship. Vic's eyes got bigger, maybe not as shocked as Erin, but still surprised. She looked automatically over to Willie. Theresa followed her gaze.

"All three of you?" she sneered. "Whatever happened to your good Christian values, Victoria?"

"No." Vic shook her head. "I told you. Willie and I are together. Not Erin. We're just friends. We work together."

"Yeah, I didn't believe you when you told me then, either. You like girls, not boys. I remember. You can't wipe out all the time you and I spent together."

"I was..." Vic swallowed and tried again. "I was trying to do what everyone expected. What everyone said was the right thing. I wasn't... living true to myself yet. I'm sorry... if that hurts you. I didn't want to make you feel bad."

"Bo told me about the two of you keeping time. Laughing and calling me names because you decided to start dressing like a girl. Making all kinds of disgusting comments about you and her, or about me."

Theresa's eyes burned brightly with fury. She didn't seem to be aware of the gun in her hands, handling it as casually as if it were a toy or book. Erin watched every time the gun shifted. Willie too had his eyes fastened on it. Vic wasn't paying any attention to the weapon, caught up in the memories Theresa brought back and the accusations she made. Erin hated the pain that recounting the past always brought to Vic's eyes. But it had been Vic's choice to confront Theresa. Maybe she needed to face her to put that part of her past behind her. Whether Theresa was going to let that happen or not, Erin didn't know.

She had a sneaking suspicion that Theresa didn't have plans to allow any of them to leave the house.

Ever.

"There's nothing wrong with you," Vic told Theresa. "It doesn't matter what Bo said. You know he's been like that since you were a kid. Always saying stupid, hurtful stuff to you, trying to get your attention because he liked you. He's one of those guys who always has to be mean to get a reaction."

"You have a filthy mind, you know that? You think I wanted to get together with my cousin? He was vile. We were like brother and sister. I wouldn't have touched him with a ten-foot pole."

"I didn't mean you wanted to get together. I just meant Bo hurt you with all the stuff he said. But there's nothing wrong with you. None of the stuff he said was true."

Theresa shifted the gun in her hands restlessly. Erin wished she would fidget with something other than the huge weapon.

"And what if I liked you?" Theresa asked. "There's gotta be something wrong with me if I liked you."

Vic dropped her eyes. "You didn't do anything wrong. We were both trying to figure things out. I'm sorry for hurting you."

"You kicked me to the curb. You led me on. Acted like you liked me. And then you didn't want to be with me anymore. Wouldn't return my calls. Wouldn't even look at me when we passed in the halls at school. Why?"

Erin expected Vic to try to explain to her again how she had been trying to sort out her own feelings about herself and her relationships. But Vic chewed on her lip, not answering.

Willie coughed. Everyone jumped and looked at him. Willie covered his mouth. "Sorry. Just came out of nowhere." He cleared his throat and coughed a little more. "You must have a dog," he said to Theresa. "They always get me choked up. Could I help myself to a glass of water? I think I have an antihistamine." He patted his pockets.

Erin and Vic stared at him. Willie was not allergic to dogs. He wasn't allergic to anything and certainly didn't carry antihistamines around with him.

Theresa made an impatient motion toward the kitchen, which flowed into the front room of the little house. It was more of a galley, not a big kitchen like the one in the farmhouse Vic had grown up in, where her mother could do all of the cooking for a big family, as well as canning and putting up preserves.

Willie got to his feet and shuffled into the kitchen. They all watched him as he got a glass out of one of the cupboards. He managed to find the fictitious antihistamine pill in his pants pocket and mimed popping it into his mouth, washing it down with a couple of gulps of water. Theresa decided he wasn't trying to rush her or get away, and her eyes went back to Vic.

Willie made a motion to Erin, commanding her attention. He walked from the kitchen back to his previous seat, dragging one foot a little as he walked. Was he hurt? Had his leg fallen asleep while he sat there or was the recently healed break bothering him? Erin was looking down at his feet, and when he stepped from the tiled area to the rug, she realized that he'd slid something across the floor with his foot. Something small and shiny, like a quarter.

He settled into his chair and didn't look back at it or her. He wiped his forehead like he was sweating excessively. "Dogs will do it to me every time."

Oddly, Theresa didn't confirm or deny whether there was a dog around. Erin looked down at the little silver circle. The size of a dog tag. Like K9's.

$\mathcal{E}$rin didn't gasp aloud, but she was sure it was clear to Willie that she had just made the connection.

Ward had asked Terry to go to Moose River to talk to him about rumors and developments. Neither of them was answering his phone. Theresa had been expecting Vic, ready at the door with her big gun. And there was something that looked like a dog tag on the floor.

Had Terry and Ward ended up going to Theresa's house to talk to her about Bo Biggles? Maybe they thought that she was just a family member, someone good to bounce ideas off of, not realizing that she might be complicit in his death. If she had taken them by surprise, was is possible that she could have subdued Terry, Ward, and K9 all by herself? One woman against two trained cops and a dog?

She had a bigger gun. She probably had the element of surprise. Vic called her Crazy Theresa, suggesting she might just try something as reckless as attacking two police officers without provocation.

Erin tried to look casual and unemotional about the discussion. As if she weren't threatened by Theresa's weapon. She looked around what she could see of Theresa's house for any sign of blood or a violent confrontation. She couldn't see any blood, bullet holes, or overturned or damaged furniture. Just the broken dog tag, which could have belonged to any dog or cat and didn't prove that there was anything out of place.

She sniffed the air, trying to ignore the dust and farm smells. Was there a whiff of dog? Of Terry's cologne? It could have been her imagination, just the power of suggestion. They might have been there to talk to Theresa and then left. Their cars were not parked in the driveway in front of the house. K9 might have lost a tag there innocently, just a loose ring that had snagged on something.

"Why did you come here?" Theresa demanded, casting her eyes around the room in agitation. "I asked you before and you wouldn't come. So why now?"

Vic shifted in her seat, her knee knocking against Erin's. "Bo had your picture in his wallet. Our picture." She rubbed her forehead and looked at Theresa. "You know, the one of you and me."

Theresa swore. She paced across the floor, looking down at the hallway toward the back of the house. "I knew he had something to do with it disappearing. He must have broken into the house while I was out on a job. And of course, the clan wouldn't do anything about it because it's an old boys' network and they protect their own. Who cares about a woman, even if she is an asset to the clan? Some two-bit drug dealer is more important than a woman, even one who—" Theresa cut herself off. "Why did you leave Moose River and the clan? You should have stayed."

"I couldn't stay there. Not the way my parents reacted when I came out."

Theresa shrugged. "Your parents. Big deal. It's not like they're high-ranking. You could still have stayed. The clan would have taken care of you, even with your..." Theresa made a gesture toward Vic, "transformation."

"I wasn't interested in being part of the clan."

"You always talked about it when we were together. How you

were going to be one of the top guys. You were better with a gun than any of the other boys."

"Yeah, but you gotta do a lot more than shoot targets if you're going to be a soldier with the clan." Vic glanced fleetingly at Willie, who had lived to regret signing on with his clan. "I was scared. I was trying to figure things out, find my own place. And the clan… wasn't it."

Theresa snorted. "You should have stayed." She paced back and forth across the living room again. "You should have stayed with me and the clan and not changed who you were."

"I didn't change who I was. I stopped pretending to be someone else."

"You and me could have been together. Bo would have left me alone if you had stuck around. But since I'm not with anyone, he still thought he had a chance." She growled to herself. "Breaking into my house! Stealing that picture! Why would he take it away? It didn't mean anything to him."

Vic shrugged and shook her head. Theresa scowled at Erin and kicked her foot as she paced across the living room again. "What's your problem, milquetoast? Cat got your tongue? If you've got something to say, then say it!"

Erin sat bolt upright, startled and instantly defensive, holding up her hands against a further attack. "I… I thought maybe he had the picture to compare it to Vic… to see if it was really her."

Theresa nodded jerkily. She bared her teeth at Vic in a crazed smile. "Well, now you don't have to worry who he might show that picture to, do you? He can't show it to anybody anymore."

"Uh…" Vic swallowed and nodded. "No."

"We can do whatever we want. It doesn't matter what anyone else has to say."

"Bo was never in control of that. He wasn't the one making the decisions."

"No. That was you, wasn't it?" Theresa's voice was a hard, angry growl. "You were the one making that call!"

She raised the gun up over Vic suddenly, butt down like she

was going to use it to bludgeon Vic in the head. Erin shrieked and dove over Vic, trying to block the falling blow and to knock the gun away or wrench it from Theresa's hands. The stock of the weapon hit her in the shoulder, causing a blast of pain that made her see stars. Erin cried out, but kept her body between Theresa and Vic.

"Leave her be!" she shouted, ripping her throat raw with the force of it. "You don't have any right!"

"I knew you two were lovers!" Theresa accused, as if Erin protecting Vic were proof of their relationship. "Bo said you were, and I denied it, but I knew it was true! It was the only reason you would stay away from me, the only reason you wouldn't come back to me when I *begged* you!"

She raised the gun to hit Erin again, her face red and contorted with rage. Erin flinched, trying to keep her eyes open to avoid the worst of the blow, but bracing for the pain.

Something stopped the descent of the gun, and then it was jerked out of Theresa's hands. Willie held it in both hands and used it to shove Theresa down, so she toppled into a heap with Erin and Vic.

Erin tried to untangle the three of them, to get Theresa sitting between her and Vic. A couple of times, Theresa tried to bounce to her feet, only to be shoved roughly back down again by Willie. She finally stopped and sat there, simmering, staring up at Willie with hate-filled eyes.

"Why don't you get out of here? You're trespassing. Get out of here and don't come back. And you!" Theresa looked at Vic. "I can't believe you'd let him treat me that way! You think that's any way to treat a woman? These clansmen are all the same! Old goats who think they've got the right to trample over women. You were better. At least, one time I thought you were. Now you're…" Theresa's face twisted in a snarl. "Now you're just going to sit there and pretend to be a lady."

Vic's eyes blazed. Erin hadn't ever seen her so angry. "And you're just the same as *you've* always been. So full of violence and hate… I couldn't deal with it. Even while I was struggling to figure out how to live my life, I knew how I didn't want to live it. I didn't want to live it like you! Or with someone like you."

"You loved me! You said so!"

"I was fifteen! That's what I was supposed to say. But it wasn't love. It was just the thrill of having a pretty girl pay attention to me. Just like you never loved me. You wanted the rep of dating one of the Jackson boys. It never worked between us. It never felt right."

"You're lying! You just don't want your new girlfriend and boyfriend to know the truth."

Vic took a deep breath and let it out. She looked at Willie, but didn't turn her head to look at Erin; to do so would mean she had to look at Theresa.

Willie was the one holding the gun so, for the first time, they had the upper hand. He wasn't pointing it at Theresa, but he wasn't relaxed, either. He held it balanced in his arm as if he were intimately familiar with it. Erin closed her eyes and tried not to think about him working for the Dyson clan. That was in the past. He was no longer a soldier for them. And his experience was beneficial to them. If they had all been as inexperienced with guns as Erin was, they would have been in big trouble. Erin would never have dared to grab the weapon from Theresa.

Theresa was breathing hard. She stared up at Willie, seething. "I told you to get out of my house."

"First, you're going to answer a few questions."

"I don't have to answer your questions."

He raised one eyebrow. None of them moved. Theresa looked back and forth at Vic and Erin, sitting on either side of her, like an animal trying to avoid being trapped. But they already had the upper hand. Willie was the one with the gun.

"You don't want to tell us what happened with Bo?" Willie asked. "I thought you would want to brag about pulling that off and getting away with it."

Theresa considered this, eyes glittering. She started to smile again.

"You want to know about Bo?" she repeated. "I can tell you all about Bo. Everything you want to know. First, you put down the gun."

"I don't think so."

"Then I'm not going to tell you."

Willie shrugged. He stood there like a statue. He didn't fidget. He didn't pace as Theresa had done. He was like a rock. Granite. Theresa licked her lips a few times. She looked around the room. She couldn't keep still and keep her mouth shut.

"Bo's been calling me ever since he went back to Bald Eagle Falls. Calling me every day. Ten times a day, sometimes. Telling me all about what he sees in that stupid little town. About all the whispers and rumors about the two of them." Theresa jerked her head in Vic's direction. "Always ragging on me about how James switched teams, and now I'm in love with a girl, calling me all kinds of disgusting names. And of course, telling me how I need a real man in my life again, and how he can show me..."

She made a face and shook her head, looking absolutely revolted. She swore.

"Like I've never been with anyone else." Theresa looked at Vic. "I've been with plenty of other guys. All of them better than you."

"Good."

Theresa jabbed at her with an elbow, angry. Willie touched the muzzle of the gun to her shoulder and pushed her back. Theresa stopped trying to hurt Vic and was still, lapsing back to a simmer.

"So he's been harassing you," Willie summed up. "And you just took it."

"I didn't just take it!"

"I didn't see you in Bald Eagle Falls doing anything about it. You didn't call the police or get a restraining order. You just took it."

Theresa's jaw clenched. "I did not." She leaned forward slightly. "He keeps talking about how he's going to tell everyone about it. He's going to tell everyone in Bald Eagle Falls that *Victoria* is really a boy, and he's going to tell everyone who knows me that I'm crushing on a girl." Theresa was spitting the words out in staccato. "He's going to tell my parents. The clan. He's going to spread it all over Moose River. He's going to tell any guy I want to get together with. He's gonna mess things up so bad for me that I'll have to leave."

She shook her head, throat working and lips quivering. Erin couldn't help feeling sorry for her. She might be crazy, she might even be a killer, but Erin empathized with all that Bo Biggles had put her through.

"He's been after me since I was a little girl! The guy's ten years older than me and when I was little—" A stream of tears leaked from the corner of one eye.

Theresa suddenly jumped to her feet, going straight for Willie, crazed, heedless of the gun. Erin gasped and tried to grab her, worried about what would happen if Willie reacted too quickly. Vic also tried to grab Theresa to pull her back, managing to catch the back of her shirt and to slow her down. Between the three of them, they managed to throw her back to the couch and pin her there. Willie stared down at her. "Do we have to tie you up?"

"You think I care? You're nothing. You think you're a tough clansman? You're just like all of the other men around here; you haven't got a clue what I can do! You haven't got one inkling of what I could do to you!"

Willie shook his head. He jerked his chin at Erin. "Go see what she's got in the kitchen. String, duct tape, wire, whatever. I don't want her going after one of us every thirty seconds."

Erin nodded and went into the kitchen. She looked through the drawers for anything that would be helpful. She couldn't help inventorying Theresa's kitchen as she did so. Theresa didn't do much cooking, and probably no baking at all. It was evident by the paucity of tools and dishes in the kitchen that she mostly got take out or warmed food up in the microwave. The oven had probably never been used since she had moved into the house.

She shook her head at herself for being distracted by kitchen implements—or the lack thereof—and kept looking through the drawers until she found twine from a hardware store. She took it back over to where Theresa was sitting on the couch.

"Do her up tight," Willie warned.

Erin did her best to tie Theresa's wrists and ankles securely, using the entire ball of twine. She got back to her feet and looked around.

"So, what did you do to Bo, Theresa?" Willie prompted again.

Theresa laughed darkly. "The dog calls me after he's been arrested. He needs to get a message to the clan. He needs to make sure they know where he is and what's going on so they can get him out. They can send a lawyer, or they can break him out when he gets transported, or find some other way to get him loose so that he can get out of Bald Eagle Falls. He's decided he doesn't really *like* it there," she said with heavy sarcasm.

"He called you to get him out," Vic said in disbelief.

"Not me, because what am I? I'm just a girl. A little girl he's been messing around with. He wants me to be his messenger and get the big guns on the case. He thinks he's hot stuff and the clan won't want to lose him. He's *nothing*. Nobody cares about him.

His own mother never cared about him. Why was he always staying with us? She didn't want him around, and she took off after some out-of-state slimeball by the time he was fifteen. Didn't care, just left him behind."

Erin did not want to feel sorry for Bo Biggles. No matter what had happened to him in life, he hadn't tried to stay on the straight and narrow. He hadn't tried to make the right choices and to treat people around him with respect. He'd decided to do the opposite, treating everyone else with the same hate and neglect that he'd been treated with.

People could still choose.

There was a noise outside. Everyone froze. Willie lifted the gun and pointed it in the direction the noise had come from. Erin was at the door in an instant, not sure what she was going to see or what she was going to do about it, but how much worse could it be than crazy Theresa Franklin? Unless it was the big guns in the Jackson clan. That might not be such a good thing either.

"Erin!" Willie warned in a whisper.

She looked back at him as she reached for the doorknob.

"Be careful. Stand to the side of the door when you open it." His eyes flicked to the living room window. "The floodlights are still on, so you won't be blind and backlit, but be careful. We don't know who's out there."

"It could be Ward or his men. Or it could be nothing, just an animal."

Willie gave a nod of agreement. Erin turned the handle and gave the door a gentle tug open. Vic was out of the couch as well, ducking below the level of the window and making her way toward Erin.

They all waited. Erin didn't hear anything else, so she took a quick peek around the wall and through the open door to catch a glimpse of the intruder. Maybe it was just the wind. All she saw was Willie's truck, still sitting in the floodlit yard where they had left it. She didn't see any movement. No other vehicle. She stayed pasted against the wall where she was and looked at Willie, who had a better viewing angle but was farther back. He shook his head. Crouching and moving to the side, he approached the door as well.

"I don't see anything."

"Something blew over and made a noise. That's all. We're just all jumpy."

Erin peered around the doorway and took a longer look outside. She shook her head. She looked at Willie. "If Terry was here with K9 and maybe with Ward… where are they now? Did they just leave?"

"If she didn't give away that she knew anything about Bo's death, then maybe they did. Left here, stopped at a diner to eat. Somewhere there isn't good cell reception."

"We should call them again. Now that we know…" Erin looked over at Theresa, sitting tied up on the couch. "We *do* know, don't we? She did it. She's the one who killed Bo."

"We still don't have proof, but I think it's a foregone conclusion."

"She hated Bo," Vic said. "And now he's gone. She was the one who knew where he was. He probably told her all about the layout so the clan would know how to get in and out. He never thought she would come after him."

Erin shuddered. Would Theresa really have been that gutsy? Or that careful? She hadn't shown herself to be someone who had the best judgment or control of her feelings. Erin could see her killing Bo in a fit of anger, filling him full of holes with that big gun of hers, but a cold-blooded, planned attack?

"We should call Terry again," she suggested. The air coming in the door was cool, and she tried to rub away the goosebumps that popped out on her skin. "If they were just out of range for a while, maybe they're back now and we can get them."

"Yeah, try again," Vic agreed.

Erin took out her phone and tapped on the icon for Terry's cell phone. A picture of K9.

Somewhere in the back of the house, a phone started to ring.

*E*rin couldn't breathe. Her throat swelled up so suddenly, with such a hard lump in the middle of it, she was sure she was having an anaphylactic reaction to something and was going to die. She and Willie and Vic all looked at each other in horror.

Erin slammed the front door shut. Even though Willie was closer to the back of the house, she dashed past him toward the bedrooms like he was standing still.

"Erin, no. Someone else could be back there. We don't know if Theresa was alone!"

She ignored Willie, following the tug at her heart. If anything happened to Terry while they were sitting there in the house talking with Crazy Theresa, she would never forgive herself. There was no way that he would have just sat quietly in the back of the house while he knew she was there and wouldn't try to help her. Only if he were incapacitated, hurt, or dead. And she couldn't bear to think of that.

She opened the first door she came to and groped for the light switch. There was nothing out of the ordinary there. Just a bedroom, no Terry and no Frank Ward tied up with the same twine that Erin had found in the kitchen drawer. She moved left to the bedroom at the end of the hall. That would be the larger one, the master bedroom.

It was a mess. Clothes draped over every piece of furniture, even over lampshades, all kind of clutter and junk on every dresser, side table, and dressing table. But no bodies. She turned to double back and check the other rooms, but Willie had turned right, so he was there ahead of her. He stood in the third bedroom door, frozen. Erin hurried after him, bumping into Vic in her rush to get there. She squeezed in beside Willie, afraid of what she was going to see, but she had to see it anyway.

But as with the other two rooms, there was no one there. No Terry, No Ward, no stranger holding them at gunpoint. Erin followed Willie's eyes and the sound of the ringing phone. There were two phones on a messy desk along with keys, wallets, and other pocket litter. Erin swallowed and looked around.

"Where are they?"

Willie shook his head. "I don't know. Not in here. But they were here." Willie turned slightly and grasped Erin's hand, turning it slightly to look at the face of her phone and tap the red button to hang up the call. "Try 9-1-1. I don't know if they have 9-1-1 service out here, but that's the first recourse. Stay here."

He checked the bathroom at the end of the hall, but there were no bloody bodies stowed in the dirty white bathtub. Erin tried to get a connection to 9-1-1 on her phone without any luck. She tried accessing the internet for a police phone number, but couldn't get internet access either.

She could hear Willie moving through the house again, making a more careful search the second time. He murmured a few words to Vic. Erin followed the sounds of their voices as they met up in the front room again.

"There's no basement or cellar," Willie advised. "That means we're going to have to check outside, and it's pitch black beyond the floodlights. You didn't get anything?"

"No."

"Do you know the number for the police department?" Willie asked Vic. They had both grown up there, but apparently, neither one of them had been forced to memorize the number for the police department. Maybe they had 9-1-1 service in the houses they had grown up in. Or maybe they had just had the phone numbers written beside the wired phone for reference.

Erin turned to her contacts. She had Jack Ward's cell number, but did she have a landline? A switchboard number? Something that would be monitored after hours so that units could be dispatched? There were two other numbers. Erin tried the first one as she followed Willie and Vic to the door. Vic flipped on a series of other switches, lighting up the entire perimeter of the house as bright as noonday.

Erin blinked at the bright lights. Grass rustled and eyes reflected in the darkness past the circles of light the floods created as wild animals fled.

"It's like Neyland Stadium," Vic said in wonder, shading her hand against the brightness of the lights. "Talk about security lights."

Erin almost forgot the phone she was holding to her ear until it rang through to voicemail and she heard Jack Ward's gruff voice telling her to leave a message and he would get back to her.

If he could.

If he were still alive.

Erin stepped out the door with Willie and Vic. Willie had the big gun to his shoulder and swiveled around like an army scout on some thriller movie. Back and forth, searching the brightly lit yard for anything that shouldn't be there.

"Where are they?" Erin murmured.

"Shh," Vic cautioned. She had her gun out. Erin hadn't seen her take it from the concealed holster. She thought about sitting so close to Theresa back in the house. They were lucky that Theresa hadn't searched Vic and hadn't pulled Vic's gun when they had been wrestling on the couch. Erin shuddered. She did not like guns.

As if Vic had heard this thought, she looked back at Erin, at her lack of a weapon either to defend herself or to attack someone else. Who knew if there was a nest of clansmen somewhere close by, guarding the prisoners and just waiting for the visitors to leave or for Theresa to signal to them that everyone had been secured.

"Stay in the house," Vic whispered, motioning Erin back.

Erin ignored the instruction. She could see a hundred yards in every direction. There was no movement. No one was going to be able to sneak up on them with so much light shining from the house security lights. Erin tapped the final number she had for Jack Ward and held the phone to her ear, holding her breath as she listened for any sounds in the night while the ring tone repeated over and over.

As they approached a big barn or garage behind the house, there was suddenly a voice in Erin's ear. "Moose River dispatcher," a bored woman announced.

"Moose River! This is… my name is Erin Price. We need police dispatched to this location…" Erin looked around, trying to find something that would identify where they were. A house number? Crossroads? The name of the farmhouse? There wasn't anything that identified where she was. She looked up at the sky, trying to tell which direction Moose River lay from them, but she couldn't see the lights of the town.

"What is the nature of your emergency?" the dispatcher responded.

"There's… a murderer. And we think Jack Ward has been… abducted or hurt, or maybe killed. We're looking for him. There was a noise out here, but I don't know where he is…"

"Ma'am, did you say a murder? Can you tell me what happened, please?"

"There was a murder in Bald Eagle Springs, but the woman

who did it, she's in Moose River, and Jack Ward was investigating, but we found his phone and not him..."

"Jack Ward is there? Would you put him on the phone?"

Erin shook her head in disbelief. She stayed a few paces behind Willie and Vic, not wanting to be separated from them, but also not wanting to be in the line of fire if something happened. She didn't want her voice to alert anyone of their presence, but Willie had told her to call the police, and he wasn't turning around and waving at her to be quiet. So she persisted, trying to stay close but not too close and to explain to the dimwitted dispatcher just what was going on.

"We haven't found Jack Ward yet. She might have done something to him. We're looking for him."

"Ma'am, can you tell me your location?"

"No... I... I don't know where this is. Can't you ping my phone or something? Won't it give you GPS coordinates?"

"We don't have an integrated system yet, ma'am. How did you get where you are? Can you tell me what buildings you see around you?"

"I wasn't driving. I didn't pay any attention when we left the highway. All that's out here is a farmhouse and barn and some other little buildings..."

Willie had found the big doors of the barn padlocked, and hammered away at it with the stock of the gun. Erin didn't know why he didn't just shoot it off like they did on TV.

"Do you know whose farm it is?"

"Uh... Theresa... Theresa...? I can't remember her last name... She's a young woman with the Jackson clan."

"Crazy Theresa?" the dispatcher asked in disbelief. "Theresa Franklin?"

Erin almost burst into tears of relief. "Yes. Yes, Crazy Theresa Franklin."

The dispatcher muttered something that Erin couldn't make out. "And you think Jack Ward was out there?"

"He was. We're just trying to get into the barn," Erin explained. "He might be locked up in there."

"I'll get all the units I can out there," the dispatcher promised. "We're not very big, but we'll be out in force in ten to fifteen minutes."

Willie's hammering with the gun succeeded and the padlock and latch fell to the ground.

$\mathcal{E}$rin hurried after Willie and Vic as they wrenched the doors open and slipped in, sticking close to the walls of the barn. She stayed as far back from them as she dared, not wanting to lose track of them or to be a target. The barn was full of junk. Some of it old stuff that had probably been part of the farm since before electricity was invented. And some of it pallets of neatly boxed goods with the Amazon logo plastered to the sides. Willie and Vic went in opposite directions, forcing Erin to decide which of them she was going to stay with. She elected to stay with Willie, who had better firepower and was, therefore, better equipped to protect two people than Vic was with her handgun.

He turned his head toward her, aware that she was with him, and continued without a word. She tried to step exactly where he had, though her stride was smaller, not wanting to set off any booby traps or to kick a metal dog dish or something else that would give their position away.

Erin startled at every sound, from the wind pushing branches against the outside of the building to birds in the eaves and the pings and creaks of the old structure. She prayed that they would find Terry there safe, not believing that her prayers would reach any mind but her own, yet hoping beyond hope that there was some way to influence fate with her fervency. Terry's words came back to her. *I believe that God is in charge... but I believe that I need to do my part and that I can affect the outcome...* She hoped that she could help control that outcome.

Willie suddenly dropped into a crouch. Erin's knees bent of their own accord, mirroring his movement within a split second. She stayed frozen, watching Willie. He peered through a metal shelf of paint cans, gun barrel resting in the space between them. He watched for a long minute or two and then started moving again.

Erin tiptoed after him. He walked purposefully toward his goal, alert but no longer as cautious as he had been. Erin closed the distance between them and was almost abreast of him. Willie rounded the corner, looked around for any guards or other dangers, and then hurried over to the two men tied up and lying in a pile of junk and rags. Willie went to Jack Ward and Erin hurried to Terry's side. Ward was kicking and struggling. When Willie managed to pull the gag from his mouth, he let out a blue streak of curses and tried to turn to look at both of them at the same time. When his eyes met Erin's, his head fell back, expression relaxing. He swore a couple more times.

"Erin Price. What happened? How did you know where we were?"

"It's going to be okay," Erin said, turning her eyes back to Terry, whose eyes were not open. "Your troops are on the way."

"Good." Jack Ward cleared his throat and spat to the side a couple of times. "Crazy woman! Not you, Erin. Theresa."

"I know."

Willie worked at the bonds immobilizing Ward. "Is Terry okay?"

Erin was touching him, feeling his cheek, watching for the rise and fall of his chest. When she moved his collar to feel for his pulse, she saw bruises across his throat, and her breath caught.

"Oh, no..."

Willie looked over. He abandoned his efforts to free Ward and moved over to Terry. His fingers were quick and competent as he felt Terry's wrist and looked at the bruises Erin had revealed.

"He's alive," Willie confirmed. "It's okay."

"She took him down with a chokehold and smashed his head on the table," Ward said, unable to turn to get a good look at Terry. "He hasn't come to, but I could still hear him breathing."

Willie continued to monitor Terry's vital signs. "Will your department have sent EMS?"

"I'm sure Geraldine would."

Erin took her phone out again, but the service indicator that had previously been there was gone. She slid it back into her pocket. Vic joined them, having completed her circuit around the other side of the barn. "Erin? Are they okay? What did she do to him?"

Erin ran her fingers through Terry's hair, studying his face, willing him to wake up. "They'll be okay," she said, hoping it was true.

Vic walked over to where K9 was tied up and made use of a utility knife laying on a nearby workbench to cut him free of the rope. Once free, K9 dashed over and nosed at Terry, whining, then barking. Terry didn't stir. Erin petted him and murmured to him, trying to reassure herself as much as him. He lay down beside Terry and put down his head, waiting for his master to wake.

Vic approached Ward. She nodded a greeting. "How are you doing? Just hold still, and I'm going to get you free."

"Yeah." Ward was still as Vic worked on his bonds, a combination of ropes and zip ties, with the utility knife. "You must be Victoria."

"That's me," Vic said cautiously. She glanced over at Terry, silent and unmoving. Erin wondered how much Terry had told Ward about Vic. How much Ward knew about who she was and where she had come from. And Ward must have told Terry about Vic's former relationship with Theresa.

Ward suddenly flinched away from Vic. She put one hand on him to hold him still while she cut through a tie.

"You okay?" she asked him again.

"She came at me with a knife," Ward said. "It was out of nowhere. We were talking to her about Biggles, about what had happened in Bald Eagle Falls and who would have had the motive to kill him, and she just grabbed a Ka-Bar knife and came at me."

Erin turned her attention to Ward. Vic's eyes were wide. Her hands froze in position.

"Are you hurt?" Erin asked.

"Durn thing hurts like the dickens," Ward complained.

Vic and Erin looked him over, scanning for any injuries. Erin moved around him and checked his side. Together, she and Vic rolled him toward Vic so Erin could check his back for any injuries. Ward was lying on an uneven pile of junk. When Erin shifted him, she felt something wet. She straightened the folds of Ward's jacket and first saw several puckered holes soaked dark with blood.

Then she saw the knife.

*E*rin fell back, staring in horror at the knife.

Jack Ward wriggled uncomfortably, and Erin pressed her hand down on him. "Stay still. Don't move."

Vic was straining to look over Jack Ward and see what Erin could see. Her mouth dropped open and her face went sheet white. "Willie, you'd better come over here."

"I need to see to Terry. He's in rough shape."

"I'll watch Terry," Erin said, having difficulty speaking with how dry her mouth had gotten. "We need you here."

"Ward is fine," Willie grumbled, leaving his place to walk around them and return to his first patient. He stared down at the Ka-Bar protruding from Jack's back and stopped protesting. "Okay, Erin, go look after Terry. Monitor his pulse and breathing. Talk to him and if he comes to, keep him calm and don't let him move around. Jack," Willie raised his voice slightly and spoke to Jack Ward in a stern voice. "I want you to stay as still as you can."

Jack squirmed slightly. "Is it bad? Hurts like heck. Woman is mad as a hatter!"

"It will be fine if you do what I say," Willie said calmly.

Erin went back over to Terry and immediately checked his breathing. Time was dragging so slowly it seemed to be standing still. The dispatcher had said that the police would be arriving in ten minutes, but it seemed like an hour had already passed. She worried about what would happen if Terry stopped breathing. She could do CPR, but her previous experience with that had not been good. At least then, Terry had been at her side as they took turns.

K9 whined. Erin scratched his ears. "It'll be okay, buddy. Everybody's going to be fine." She split her attention between Terry and Ward. Even though she was only in charge of Terry, she couldn't help being concerned with Ward and how he was doing. Despite his blood-soaked jacket and the knife buried to the haft in his back, he stayed alert and vigorous, talking with Willie and complaining only occasionally about the pain.

At long last, she heard the first thready notes of sirens. She breathed a sigh of relief.

"Why don't you go flag them down, show them where to go," Willie said to Erin. "Vic, you take over on Terry, just keep an eye until Erin gets back."

Erin got quickly to her feet and hurried outside. The barn was much smaller than it had seemed when they were inching their way in, afraid there would be more Jackson clansmen lying in wait. She jogged into the brightly-lit driveway to wait for the emergency vehicles to pull in off the highway. There was a blur of motion from behind Willie's truck, and something solid crashed into Erin, knocking her off her feet. She tried to right herself and figure out what had happened. She realized a split-second before the forearm pinned her to the gravel by her throat that it was Theresa, somehow loose of her bonds. Erin struggled, but it was too late, Theresa squeezing hard to cut off both her breath and the flow of oxygenated blood to her brain. Even before Erin's lungs began to hurt, blackness started to gather around her. Theresa was screaming at her, but Erin couldn't sort out the words.

Then the chokehold was released and Theresa was gone. Erin gasped for breath and tried to get up. The sirens were on top of her, doors were slamming, feet were running in every direction, and someone knelt at her side.

"Are you okay? What happened?"

Erin tried to sit up and nearly passed out. "The barn," she croaked. She motioned in the direction she thought she had come from. "The others are in the barn."

There were orders shouted back and forth, more running feet, more sirens, and eventually, Erin's head stopped whirling in dizzy circles and she was able to sit up with the assistance of one of the Moose River police officers.

"Are you okay? Feeling better?" He cracked a water bottle open and handed it to her, keeping his hand close in case she needed help. Erin took a sip of the soothing cold water.

"Yeah. I'm okay. It was just a few seconds… did you get her?"

He shook his head. He was young, with a round, boyish face that made him look like a teenager. "She ran back there some-where," he waved in the general direction, "had a motorcycle, rode off into the trees. We can't get through in our cars, can't keep up on foot, too dark for any pursuit. She knows all the backroads here, how to get back out to the highway without being spotted. She's long gone."

Erin's head was pounding. She closed her eyes for a moment, leaning back against the boyish officer, trying to get a handle on it all.

"The others? Is everyone okay?" She opened her eyes again.

"Got paramedics taking care of Jack Ward and the other one. Your friends are all fine. Just being debriefed separately before you all get together again."

"I can't believe…" Erin was at a loss for words. It had all happened so fast; she was still trying to process it all.

The young man nodded. "We're not exactly sure what happened here. Someone will talk to you in a few minutes."

Eventually, another policeman knelt beside Erin and let the young man go on to other duties. Erin did the best she could to sit up and focus on what he was saying, distracted by her pounding head, all of the activity around them, and trying to sort out what had happened.

"Is Terry Piper okay?" she asked.

"Everybody is stable. The injured officers are being taken to the hospital where they'll be treated. We have no reason to believe they won't both fully recover."

Erin nodded very slightly, trying not to move her head too much.

"And how about you, ma'am? Have you been checked out by a medical professional?"

"I… don't know. The police, but I don't know if a doctor did…"

"Okay. We'll have someone check you out in a few minutes." He pushed her collar back to look at her throat and nodded. "You're breathing okay? You don't feel like your airway is closing?"

Not until he suggested it.

Erin took a few deeper breaths and nodded. "Yeah. Just sore, I guess."

"You've got a pretty good bruise. Can you tell me what happened here today?"

Erin did her best to relate the evening's events, though she kept getting things out of order and having to go back to explain something.

"You tied Miss Franklin up?"

"Yes… she was dangerous. She was threatening, kept trying to hurt us."

"Don't get me wrong; I'm not criticizing. Just trying to get the whole story."

"Yeah… I found some twine in the kitchen. Heavy-duty stuff. I don't know how she got out of it. I tied the knots pretty tight. I was afraid I was going to cut her circulation off, but I figured for a little while, it would be okay, and it was more important that I didn't let her slip out…"

He nodded his agreement.

"How *did* she get out?" Erin wanted to know.

"Knife. Cut the string."

"Oh." Erin blinked. "I didn't see a knife."

"That girl is pretty cunning. It's not the first time she's slipped through our fingers. She probably had it hidden on her body somewhere."

None of them had checked. They had just assumed that the big gun was her only weapon. They had thought that if she was securely tied, she couldn't get into any mischief.

"Can I get up now? And see my friends?"

He stood up and offered his hand to help Erin to her feet. She took it and leaned on his arm for a moment while waiting for her head to stop spinning. Once she was able to stay upright on her own and walk, he escorted her over to Willie's truck, where Vic and Willie were talking with the other cops. Casual, finished answering questions. K9 was at Vic's side, looking out of place. Willie and Vic turned toward Erin, worried looks in their eyes, and reached out to help her.

"It's okay. I'm fine. I can manage. Can we go to the hospital? See Terry?"

"You bet," Willie agreed, "We were just waiting for you to finish up. Are you sure you're alright?"

"A bit shaken. But I'll be okay."

"She'll be right as rain once she sees her beau," Vic declared.

Erin had to agree. She would feel much better when she saw Terry and knew that he was okay. And even more so when he woke up. She needed to know for herself that nothing was going to change. He would recover and be able to go back to active duty, and everything would return to normal.

"Was he okay? You're sure he's going to be alright?"

"You can never be one hundred percent sure with head injuries," Willie cautioned. "But he was breathing on his own. I'm sure he's probably taken knocks on the head before."

Erin wished he had just said that Terry was going to be perfectly fine. Even if it was a lie, she didn't want any prevarication.

"And how about Jack Ward?" Erin shuddered when she remembered the instant she saw the handle of the knife. "I can't believe… he was still talking and acting just like everything was fine. He had to be the one who caused the noise we heard outside. Trying to get someone's attention."

Willie raised his brows and shook his head. "Never seen anything like it," he admitted. "I've heard about stuff like that but never seen it myself. Best thing is to leave the knife in there, where it's putting internal pressure on the wound. Do whatever else you can to stop bleeding and treat for shock, but… don't mess with it. You never know what damage you're going to do when you pull it out. Leave a surgeon to do that part."

"He shouldn't have survived. Being stabbed that many times. How could he?"

"Today was his lucky day," Vic said with a chuckle. "He had an angel watching over his shoulder. So did Terry. I guess we all did. Theresa could have just opened up on us when we got there."

"Which is why we shouldn't have gone in before the police," Willie reminded her. "You said she wouldn't hurt you."

"Well… she didn't."

"She would have if Erin hadn't gotten in the way and I hadn't taken the gun off of her. That was no love tap."

"Yeah. I guess," Vic admitted, looking sheepish. "I'm sorry about that, Erin. Are you okay? She hit you pretty hard. And then getting attacked out here…"

"Should have searched her properly," Willie grumbled. "I should have stripped her down before hogtying her. No excuse for being so sloppy."

Vic made a shocked face. "Willie, really! I had no idea you had such proclivities."

Willie chuckled. "Let's get on our way. Erin wants to make sure that Terry's okay, and they'll need to check her out at the hospital too."

"I'm fine."

"You still need to be checked out. Theresa wasn't fooling around." Willie looked at Vic as he opened the truck door for the girls. "Just what's the deal with that woman? She thought she could take us all down? That she could get away with killing Bo Biggles? How does a girl that age have the combat skills she does?"

Vic motioned Erin into the truck ahead of her. "You go ahead. I want to make sure you're not going to get dizzy or pass out."

"I'll just sit in the back. You go ahead."

"Not this time. We need to keep an eye on you."

Erin looked for a way to convince Vic otherwise, but neither she nor Willie looked inclined to agree. Erin stepped onto the running board and grasped the inside of the truck to pull herself up. Willie gave her a quick boost with his hands on her hips, practically tossing her into the truck. In a moment, they were all in the cab of the pickup and headed toward the hospital.

"In the Middle East, they train kids to be soldiers," Vic said to Willie, addressing his unanswered question. "It's the same in the clans… if you have an aptitude for violence or some other part of the business, they're happy to teach and train you. Theresa's always been…" Vic searched for words. "A good prospect. Even when we were together, she was… unstable… angry, moody… a bit sadistic."

"I'm glad you got away from her," Erin told her.

Vic stared out the window at the darkened landscape. "I never realized the bullet I dodged there. It was just… a teenage crush, break-up, move on. Not something that stuck with me. Not something that affected the direction of my life—other than that I knew I didn't want to be with someone like that. And that I wasn't attracted to her the same way the boys were." Vic's lips pressed together and she shrugged.

Erin thought that was all she was going to say on the matter. But then Vic went on after a few more minutes had passed in silence.

"When she started writing to me again, I thought it was my chance to still have a friend in Moose River. Someone from my old life who would accept me. In her letters, she seemed okay with my identity. Not like what she said today."

"A little easier to say all the right things in writing," Willie observed. "When you're not actually confronted with reality. She thought that things could go back to the way they used to be."

Vic chewed on her nail, something that she never did. "She killed Bo because of me."

"No," Willie said sharply. "She killed Bo because of Bo. Because he was constantly harassing her. And unless I miss my guess, he had abused her in the past, when she was too young to do anything about it."

"And that's what was eating her up inside. Why she was so angry and violent."

"And the clan trained her to kill," Erin added.

"So it's Bo's fault? And the clan's fault?"

"It was still Theresa's choice," Willie said. "But there were… certain influences."

CHAPTER 38

s much as Erin wished to avoid an examination at the hospital, Willie was adamant and Vic backed him up. It was two against one, and the nurse they talked to in triage nodded solemnly and agreed that Erin needed to be examined.

"Being choked like that, and there's no telling what vascular damage there could be… better safe than sorry. Sometimes it takes a few hours before someone shows negative aftereffects. Why, there was a case in the papers just the other day of a man who died in custody. You hear about it all the time. Someone gets restrained and everything seems fine, and then a few hours later, or when someone goes to wake them up in the morning…" She trailed off delicately.

Erin couldn't believe she'd cited Bo Biggles's death as an example. But it did convince her that she needed to do as everyone was saying and at least have a cursory examination.

After providing all of her information and waiting what seemed like forever in the waiting room, a nurse took Erin to a curtained bed. "Just take off your shirt and put that on," she told Erin, providing her with a hospital johnny. "The doctor will be right with you."

Erin doubted that anyone would be 'right with her.' Hospitals operated on a different timetable from the rest of the world. She unbuttoned her shirt and attempted to pull it off as the nurse finished making notes on the clipboard, so the nurse was still there to hear Erin's gasp as a bolt of pain shot through her shoulder.

"What is it, dear?" The woman was instantly at her side, pushing her to the bed so that she wouldn't fall down. She examined Erin gently. "Good heavens!"

Erin managed to pry her eyes open again. Looking down at her throbbing shoulder, she saw the big, black bruise. Her fingers were tingling and when she touched the injured shoulder with the opposite hand, she found it swollen and puffy.

"You didn't even mention this," the nurse chastised. "You're supposed to tell me everything. Who did this to you? A boyfriend?"

"No! No, there was a woman. She was attacking my friend and I… got in the way," Erin finished lamely, realizing it didn't sound too heroic.

"What did she hit you with?"

"A gun. The butt of a… a big gun."

"Let me get you some ice to put on that. You're going to need an x-ray. First, let's finish getting you changed." She helped Erin to change into the hospital gown and to lie down before going to get an ice pack. Erin sighed. It was going to be a much longer night than she had thought. It was going to take even longer to see Terry and find out how he was doing.

Despite all of the testing and delays, Erin was beside Terry's bed when his eyes finally opened and he looked around to try to figure out where he was. He stared at Erin for a few minutes with vague, clouded eyes before he finally blinked and tried to speak.

Erin offered him a sip of water from the cup beside the bed. The doctor had warned that he would probably have a sore throat, something Erin could attest to. Terry drank the lukewarm water through the straw and cleared his throat.

"What happened?" he asked. "Why am I here? And what happened to you?"

Erin sat with her arm in a sling to help ease the pain of her bruised collarbone, and she imagined he could probably see the darkening bruise across her throat that matched his.

"Theresa Franklin happened."

He stared at her, trying to access his memories and make sense of everything. Erin took his hand and intertwined their fingers. K9 looked up and whined.

"He's okay," Erin told him. "You can come see."

He stood and looked up at Terry's hand and arm, then stood on his hind legs to see Terry lying on the bed. He couldn't jump up onto the bed with the sides up, but thrust his nose as close to Terry's face as he could, and stretched out his long tongue to lick Terry's face.

"Get down," Terry ordered, laughing. "You know better than that! Lie down and behave."

K9 stood there, not lying down immediately as he usually did. He stared up toward his master, his tail waving back and forth slowly.

"He's okay," Erin repeated. "Lie down, now. You don't want to get kicked out of here for being too rambunctious."

K9 lay down again. Erin squeezed Terry's hand.

"We were going out to talk to a witness," Terry remembered. "A young woman in Bo Biggles's family. Jack Ward said that he had lived with her family."

"Theresa. She and Vic were friends. Back… before."

"I can't remember what happened."

"It might be a while before you do," Erin said, repeating what the doctor had told her. "Don't try to force it."

"Do you know what happened?"

"Theresa is the one who killed Biggles. She snuck into the

police department to break him out… only she didn't break him out."

"She killed him? Ward just thought she was a background witness."

"He didn't know about their… personal issues, I guess. You guys went over there, and she attacked you. Ward first, I think; stabbed him with a knife, and then went after you. Choked you, like with Biggles… only she didn't kill you… she hit you on the head to knock you out."

He looked at her, bemused, and she wondered how much of what she was saying he was actually understanding and going to remember later. "What happened to you?"

Erin sighed. She gave his hand a squeeze and tried to summarize it succinctly. "Vic and Willie and I went to see Theresa. We got her tied up and were looking for you and Ward. But she got away. Cut the ropes. So then when I went back outside to flag down the police, she attacked me."

Terry shook his head. "They got her?"

"No… she got away on a motorcycle. They're still looking for her, but the police department here isn't that much bigger than the one in Bald Eagle Falls, and they don't have enough people for roadblocks and that kind of thing. They probably won't find her unless she does something stupid to give herself away."

Jack Ward came through surgery with flying colors. All four of them were not allowed to see him at the same time, and they had to wait until his wife was willing to leave his side to go down to the cafeteria. Then Erin and Vic were allowed in, as long as they promised not to get him excited.

Ward didn't seem like he was going to excite too easily. He had been calm and lucid when they had found him in the barn and, even though he'd only been out of surgery for a couple of hours, he looked like he was ready to get up and go home, rather than to convalesce after being stabbed multiple times.

"Here are a couple of rays of sunshine to brighten my day," he commented, his creased face breaking into a smile.

Erin remembered meeting him when Charley had been arrested. He hadn't seemed like such a friendly person that day.

"Hey. How are you feeling?" Erin asked him.

"Better than I have any right to, by all accounts." His eyes went over the two of them. "Well, you don't look too bad," he told Vic. "But you look like you met our lovely Theresa Franklin." His eyes rested on Erin.

"Yes," she admitted. "We sort of… had words."

"I hope they've got her in a jail cell in shackles by now."

"No." Vic shook her head. "She got away."

He swore. "She's a durn slippery one. You don't know how many times we thought we had her on something, and it's gone away. When her folks disappeared, I was sure we had her dead to rights. But…" He shrugged with one shoulder and shook his head. "No such luck. Couldn't seem to get her on anything."

"Her folks?" Vic repeated.

"Yes. Maybe a year ago now. They just… dropped off the face of the earth. According to her, they're traveling. But of course, there's no sign of them anywhere. But we don't have any proof of foul play. Can't get a warrant for their bank accounts or to take cadaver dogs onto the property. Other people in the clan have confirmed that there's nothing to be concerned about, they've just left town."

"So they're covering for her."

"For some reason… yes. You wouldn't think that anyone would want to cover for someone who was—if you'll excuse my French—so bat-crap crazy. But for some reason, they are."

Vic grimaced. "We were kind of talking about that. How she could be so… skilled. Breaking in and killing Bo while he was in police custody and all. I think they've spent a lot of time training her. So now they're protecting their asset."

Jack nodded his agreement. "They protect their own. We have a backlog of unsolved clan-related killings that I think I'm going to need to take another look at. Never would have thought that they would use a woman. And one so young. They must have had her killing before she was even out of school."

CHAPTER 39

rin was glad to be home, back in Bald Eagle Falls where she belonged—keeping a regular schedule, baking at the bakery with her regular employees. Even taking time off to spend at home with her animals, genealogy, and Terry.

Terry wasn't back on active duty yet, but that was because he was on short-term disability, no longer under investigation. The doctors said it might be a few weeks before he felt like himself again, and that he shouldn't push it to be back at work too quickly.

So he was at home when she got there, eager to spend time with her, help around the house, and occasionally even have dinner on the table—takeout or frozen pizza—when she got home. She felt relaxed and comfortable once more.

But the nightmares were still bothersome, sometimes waking her up several times during the night. It helped when Terry was there, but didn't stop. At some point, she might have to break down and follow his suggestion to see a therapist.

Erin had been in the bakery kitchen to take some bread out of the oven, handling the trays carefully so as not to aggravate her still-sore collarbone. She could hear that there were a number of customers out front and hurried out to help Vic once she had the bread on the cooling racks.

She was carrying a tray of pumpkin-shaped sugar cookies to put into the display case and reached out to set them on the counter for a moment. By the front door, she startled at the sight of a slim figure with a rubber ape mask. Her hand trembled and the cookie sheet hit the top of the display case with a clatter. She tried to brace herself, but her legs were like jelly.

"Erin! Erin!" Vic caught her by the arm and tried to hang on to her. "What's wrong, are you okay?"

"It's…" Erin's vision blurred as she stared at the masked figure.

"Trick or treat!"

Erin recognized the voice as that of Peter Foster. He jumped down from the chair he was standing on.

"Do you like my mask?"

Erin took a couple of deep breaths and forced a smile. "Wow, it's very realistic."

Peter took the mask off and beamed at her. Jody danced and reached for it. "My turn, my turn!"

Peter reluctantly gave it to her and she pulled it on over her head. Jody danced around, making screechy monkey sounds. Erin leaned on the counter, her legs still shaky.

"What a funny little monkey!"

It was good to be back. And hopefully, there would be no more masks or surprises in the near future.

Did you enjoy this book? Reviews and recommendations are vital to making a book successful.

Please leave a review at your favorite book store or review site and share it with your friends.

Don't miss the following bonus material:
Sign up for mailing list to get a free ebook
Read a sneak preview chapter
Other books by P.D. Workman
Learn more about the author

Sign up for my mailing list at pdworkman.com and get Gluten-Free Murder for free!

PREVIEW OF TAI CHI AND CHAI TEA

CHAPTER 1

This time, it was Terry who woke Erin up, rather than the other way around. He was gasping hard like he was running or maybe even having a heart attack. She reached for him beside her and found his body rigid as he fought for breath.

"Terry. Terry!" She shook him, trying to rouse him, her mind jumping to all kinds of possibilities. Maybe he was having a heart attack. Maybe he had suffered some sort of damage in Theresa's attack on him that the doctors hadn't discovered. He had thrown a clot, and it had gone into his lungs or heart. Or something had happened in his brain and it was a seizure.

He'd been hit on the head as well as choked out, and either one could have caused neurological damage. Maybe damage that the doctors hadn't seen or predicted. They had warned that his road to recovery might not be smooth.

"Terry!"

He gasped one last time and sat bolt upright in bed, shoving her away. Erin was hurt even though she knew that he wasn't conscious of what he had done. He was always gentle with her, and being pushed away like that sent her sense of danger into hyperdrive. She was sure, as ridiculous as it was, that she was going to be attacked.

Terry looked around. There was just enough light in the room to see his shape, not the expression on his face.

"Erin? Where are you? Are you okay?"

Erin breathed deeply, trying to slow her racing heart.

"It's okay," she soothed. "You just had a dream. Lie down, and come here."

It took a minute before he reacted, still looking around him as if there might be some danger lurking. He drew in a long breath and let it out slowly.

"It was just a dream?"

"Yes. Come on." She wrapped her arms around him and molded her body against his. She could still feel his rapidly-beating heart as well as her own. "Do you want to talk about it?"

She needed to get up early, so both of them were usually careful to avoid conversation late at night, but she wanted him to know that if he needed a listening ear, she was right there. If it would help him to calm down, then it would help both of them get back to sleep sooner.

"No." He let out a few more quick puffs of breath. "I don't even remember what it was. Not really. I wasn't dreaming something was happening. Just… a feeling."

"Mmm-hm." She cuddled close against him. She'd had plenty of night terrors herself. There wasn't always any narrative to go with the feeling, just that crushing anxiety, that sense of danger. "Do you need anything? A drink? A back rub?"

"No. I'll just go back to sleep."

She knew that he worried about her getting enough to sleep with her early-morning baker's hours. His first instinct would be to protect her rather than to deal with his own needs. She rubbed his shoulders in spite of his answer.

"Are you sure? I can get you something. Milk or tea…?"

"No," he assured her again. "It was just a dream. I'll be able to go back to sleep."

"Okay." She was still again, cuddled up against him, eyes closed, soaking in the warmth of his body and his musky smell.

Despite being woken out of a sound sleep, she felt safe and comfortable with him there, the two of them intertwined. It helped to soothe her own nighttime fears.

"Should I get up and check the burglar alarm?" Terry asked, rousing Erin. "Are you sure that it's armed?"

Usually, he didn't worry about the burglar alarm when he stayed over with her. He was more concerned if she was by herself. If he, an experienced police officer, was there, he didn't think anyone would be stupid enough to break in.

But his squad car wasn't parked in front of the house anymore. Since he had been taken off of active duty, it had been parked in the police department's parking lot. And since Stayner had been contracted to cover Terry's duties, he was the one who had been driving it. He wasn't a full-time hire, so he didn't get to drive it home at the end of his shift as Terry had, but Erin knew that Terry still didn't like the idea of someone else driving 'his' car when he wasn't there.

"I set the alarm," she assured him. "You don't need to check. Besides, if there were a burglar, Orange Blossom would be letting us know. And probably K9 too."

Hearing his name, Orange Blossom gave a soft meow and jumped up on the bed next to Erin. He sniffed her ear, investigating why she wanted him. Erin giggled. K9 was in his crate, but she was sure he would be making noise if he had heard or sensed an intruder in the house. And Orange Blossom, her little attack cat, was very territorial and had raised the alarm in the past when someone had managed to bypass her burglar alarm.

"Blossom, lay down," Erin ordered. She turned away from Terry to deal with him. She scratched his ears and kissed him on top of the head, then pushed him down to lie beside her. It took a few times before he was content to curl up against her, purring loudly in contentment.

"Do you think you could get him to turn the engine down a bit?" Terry asked dryly, putting his arms around Erin from behind her and holding her close again, so that she was sandwiched between the two of them, cozy and warm.

"It doesn't work. The more you ask him to be quiet, the louder he gets."

Terry knew how loud Orange Blossom could be, so he accepted this. They both just lay there, listening to his rumbling purr. It was a comforting sound, and Erin soon found herself drifting off again.

Morning came too soon. It seemed like she had only been asleep for another five minutes when her alarm sounded. Erin reached over to shut it off. She pushed Orange Blossom out of her way and slid her feet out of the bed. She knew better than to hit snooze. If she fell back asleep for even just five more minutes, she would be even more groggy, and she wouldn't have the time she needed to get her engine running before work. She'd be draggy and grumpy all morning.

She would never have considered herself a morning person before starting the bakery. But once she managed to wake herself up, she found the extremely early hours of the morning exhilarating. She loved getting the gluten-free baking into the ovens every morning, working side-by-side with Vic or one of her other employees. The smell of the baking bread and muffins and the quiet of the early morning made her feel calm and peaceful at the beginning of the day, something that she desperately needed with everything that had happened since she had first arrived in Bald Eagle Falls to open Auntie Clem's Bakery.

She used the commode, splashed cold water on her face, and started the kettle heating in the kitchen. Looking across the yard to Vic's loft apartment over the garage, she could see it was still dark. Vic hadn't managed to pry herself out of bed yet. But she would. Despite her youth, Vic was very responsible, and Erin had never had to harass her to get her out of bed in the morning. She loved having Vic just across the back yard from her and hoped that Vic wouldn't move away any time in the near future. The two of them worked well together and were good friends, and it was convenient living so close together. They each had their separate spaces, but even when off work, could often be found in the kitchen together.

It wasn't long before she saw the light go on across the yard. Erin was at the kitchen table drawing up her list of tasks for the day when Vic made her way in the back door, yawning and pulling her long, blond hair into a ponytail behind her head.

"Morning, sunshine," she greeted around the yawn.

Erin laughed. "Good morning. You slept a little late."

"No," Vic yawned again, covering her mouth with the back of her hand. "I think you're mistaken. This is what the rest of the world calls early."

"The rest of the world doesn't run a bakery."

"Good thing, or we'd have too much competition."

Vic went to the kettle and checked the temperature before pouring herself a cup of tea. She sat down to join Erin. Orange Blossom meowed for attention, rubbing against Vic's legs. She bent down to scratch his ears. Marshmallow, seeing that the cat was getting attention, hopped over to Vic to get his long ears scratched too. Vic smiled at the brown and white rabbit and gave him some love as well.

K9 was stretched out on the floor beside Erin and looked up at Vic but didn't bark or go over to her. Orange Blossom didn't like the big shepherd. While K9 would have been perfectly happy to make friends with the ginger cat, Blossom had steadfastly refused to have anything to do with the dog. Unless he was eating a treat. Then the cat was right there to steal whatever crumbs he could snatch or lick off of K9's face.

"Do you know what I found when I was looking for the

Christmas ornaments yesterday?" Erin asked, looking back down at her task list.

"Didn't you know you're not allowed to get out Christmas things until Thanksgiving is past?" Vic teased.

Erin ignored her. She hadn't gotten the ornaments out; she had just been inventorying to see what she would need to add or replace. There was nothing wrong with being prepared.

"I found a huge box of chai spices."

"From Clementine's tea shop?"

Erin nodded. Her aunt Clementine was the one who had left her both the house and the retail space that had been her tea shop, having no other kin after the death of Erin's mother years before. The bakery would never have been anything more than a distant dream if Erin hadn't inherited the little shop on Main Street. She'd barely been able to keep her head above water up until then, working whatever jobs she could find and never able to stick with something for very long. It was hard to believe how fast the months had gone and everything that had happened since she had moved to Bald Eagle Falls. Bald Eagle Falls, Tennessee was now home, even though she had spent most of her growing-up years in Maine.

"So I guess we're going to be drinking chai and nothing else for a while?" Vic suggested.

"I think I'd get tired of it before long," Erin said. She liked variety, and for the brief time that she had known Clementine and "helped" with the tea shop when she was a young child, she had developed a wide-ranging taste for teas. "And I don't think we'd be able to sell that much at the ladies' tea each week. People like their traditional teas. I suspect that's why Clementine ended up with a big box of spices in the attic."

"Strange foreign tea," Vic agreed, sipping her English Breakfast. "What will people think of next?"

"So I was thinking… Thanksgiving is a great time for nice warm, spicy baking. Pumpkin pie, gingerbread, all of those other great spice blends…"

"And how about using chai spices in something?" Vic suggested.

Erin nodded eagerly. "We have them, we might as well use them for something. We can offer chai tea at the ladies Sunday tea as well, but I don't think we'll be able to move more than a cup or two a week."

Vic pursed her lips. "But what can you put it in? People don't really bake with it, do they?"

"Actually, I was looking at some recipes online." Erin looked down at her lists, warming to the topic. "There are a ton of different recipes that you can use chai spices in. Cookies, muffins, apple pie, oatmeal raisin bars… really, anything that you might put cinnamon or pumpkin pie spice in. Just a little twist on some old favorites."

Vic raised her brows. "Well, that might work. Just don't expect everyone to be enamored with the idea. You might not have noticed, but we have a few rednecks around here who are a mite suspicious of anything… different."

Erin laughed. Her gluten-free baking and atheism and Vic's transgender identity had already raised more than a few eyebrows and attracted comments, lectures, and even threats. "Just a mite," she agreed.

Tai Chi and Chai Tea, Book #11 of the *Auntie Clem's Bakery* series by P.D. Workman can be purchased at pdworkman.com

ABOUT THE AUTHOR

Award-winning and USA Today bestselling author P.D. (Pamela) Workman writes riveting mystery/suspense and young adult books dealing with mental illness, addiction, abuse, and other real-life issues. For as long as she can remember, the blank page has held an incredible allure and from a very young age she was trying to write her own books.

Workman wrote her first complete novel at the age of twelve and continued to write as a hobby for many years. She started publishing in 2013. She has won several literary awards from Library Services for Youth in Custody for her young adult fiction. She currently has over 50 published titles and can be found at pdworkman.com.

Born and raised in Alberta, Workman has been married for over 25 years and has one son.

Please visit P.D. Workman at pdworkman.com to see what else she is working on, to join her mailing list, and to link to her social networks.

If you enjoyed this book, please take the time to recommend it to other purchasers with a review or star rating and share it with your friends!

facebook.com/pdworkmanauthor

twitter.com/pdworkmanauthor

instagram.com/pdworkmanauthor

amazon.com/author/pdworkman

bookbub.com/authors/p-d-workman

goodreads.com/pdworkman

linkedin.com/in/pdworkman

pinterest.com/pdworkmanauthor

youtube.com/pdworkman